Dear reader,

Here we go with a new series! I believe that this WW1 alternate story will be appreciated. It was a lot of fun to write and kind of refreshing, as it is not as well-known as WW2.

The historical alterations I have made:

1- Moltke the Younger never removes 180,000 soldiers from his offensive in the West to send them to face the Russian offensive in the East. This makes for a lot closer battle at the Marne and will get things quite interesting.

2- Modern dreadnought battleships Sultân Osmân-1 Evvel (in real history, HMS Azincourt) and Resadiye (in real history, HMS Erin) are delivered to Turkey as agreed by the purchase contract from Istanbul and never requisitioned by Churchill, changing the balance of naval power in the Eastern Mediterranean and giving the edge to the Central Powers in the Black Sea.

   a. The attacks in the Black Sea led by German battlecruiser Goeben happens earlier than in real history, and the Turks join the war earlier, emboldened by the power of their two dreadnoughts against Russia's pre-dreadnought fleet.

3- The German Pacific Fleet is bigger than historically (with battleships), giving a better chance to Admiral von Spee to resist in Tsingtao, which also has more troops. This should make things interesting between the Germans and the Japanese.

4- Just a tad bigger Battle of Heligoland Bight.

   a. The battle for the island in August 1914 happens in September and is a lot more intense (and with a lot more ships) than historically. The winner is to be confirmed, hehe.

5- The Ottomans mobilize sooner in Caucasus, and attack in the fall.

I have threaded the changes as seamlessly as possible in the normal history of the war. It starts much the same as it did historically but then slowly changes as the story progresses forward.

I hope you enjoy the story; this is going to be a very interesting retelling of the First World War. Once book one is over, you will truly see the extent of the new possibilities it opens.

PROLOGUE

Sarajevo, Bosnia Herzegovina, Austro-Hungarian Empire
A twin killing to start it all, June 18th, 1914.

Our story begins in a beautiful Bosnian town called Sarajevo, and under a nice summer sun. The city was located near the center of Bosnia and Herzegovina, in the country of Austria-Hungary. It was a mixture of modern and old buildings, like many European towns in 1914. Looking at the peaceful strolling of the commuters and the nice breeze brushing people's faces, not one person in the entire world could have imagined that something so terrible as the First World War would start here because of one tiny, momentous event.

Gavrilo Princip, a Serbian Nationalist, stormed out of the small store he'd been brooding in for the last hour or so. The man was sad and was in a bad mood at the same time. At least, the few schnapps drinks he'd gulped helped to make him feel somewhat better about his botched assassination attempt a few hours earlier. The annoying feeling of his failure kept poking at his mind and at his morale as he tried to remake the entire scene again and how he should have done differently. He heard an engine noise, a sign that a car was nearby, and then he froze as he looked up to see where the sound came from. Right in front of him was his target, not five feet from him: Archduke Franz Ferdinand, the heir to the throne of Austria-Hungary. The very man he'd tried to kill earlier in the day with a bomb. An extraordinary twist of fate gave him his golden opportunity, and he didn't think twice about seizing it.

The heavily guarded and watched Archduke convoy (they were traveling in a file of six cars) had taken a wrong turn. Supposed to turn on the street called Appel Quay and onto the so-called Franz Joseph Street like the planned route, the driver had been distracted by a few good-looking girls on the sidewalk and just drove along. General Potoirek, the Governor of the Bosnian province and the man responsible for the visit, leaned forward.

"What is this? Where are you going? This is not the right street! We're supposed to take the Appel Quay, you dimwit!" Wide-eyed, the driver put on the brakes and moved the car backward. The Archduke's car stopped right in front of the store where Princip was exiting. No one gave any attention to the young, agape man right beside them as his eyes widened in shock, and surprise, with a smile slowly taking shape on his face. He just couldn't believe his dumb luck.

Gavrilo was part of a growing number of Serb nationalists who wanted to create a greater Serbia and unite all the Balkan Slavs under one banner. He had joined the secret Black Hand Society, a terrorist movement dedicated to the removal of the hated Austro-Hungarians by force.

The organization's main objective was to destroy Austro-Hungarian rule in Bosnia. Princip's mission was to kill the next in line for the Habsburg throne, the Archduke Franz Ferdinand, while the man visited Sarajevo on official business. He'd failed earlier as he and his accomplices had set a bomb that failed to go off, and now fate offered him a second chance.

Bosnia Herzegovina had only recently been included Austro-Hungarian Empire in October 1908, when Vienna simply decided to annex it outright since anyway it had been occupying it since 1878. The move had enraged the Serbs and "Greater Serbia" nationalists and the other Balkan nations while greatly destabilizing the entire region.

Franz Ferdinand was on a visit to Sarajevo to inspect the army maneuvers being held outside town that week. The visit also coincided with his wedding anniversary and was meant to show support to the local governor and reaffirm the province's importance to Austria-Hungary.

Security during the visit was not very good. Franz Ferdinand was a brave man and didn't fancy having too many guards or security people. Nor did he like the idea of a bunch of Austrian soldiers to separate him from the people in the streets. For the most part, Franz Ferdinand was liked by the people. The town was not perceived as hostile territory; it was thus decided that there was no reason to be too hard on the population, even if one of the prominent Habsburgs was in the area.

Thinking quickly on his feet, Gavrilo fished the pistol out of his concealed pocket, moved towards the car, and fired twice. The Archduke and his wife were standing straight, looking ahead. Governor Potoirek, also in the car with the Imperial couple, first believed the shots had missed but still ordered the driver to return to his residence immediately. Princip to kill himself but was jumped by several shocked bystanders around him. The police eventually came around and arrested the roughes Princip from the enraged crowd.

As the car drove full speed away from the shooting scene, a slow spittle of blood shot from Franz Ferdinand's mouth. The man had been hit in the neck. His wife panicked: "*By god! What the problem with you, my dear?*" She sank from her seat, shocked with glazed eyes.

The two, mortally wounded, died minutes later.

Gavrilo Princip was thrown into prison, where he would die four years before dying of tuberculosis, while the world around him descended into the horror of the First World War.

Austria lost its heir to the throne and decided to take advantage of the horrible attack to further advance its agenda of conquest in the Balkans.

Events were in motion.

A chronology of the road to war
End of June to the Guns of August

28th of June 1914
After the killing of Archduke Franz Ferdinand and a quick investigation by imperial authorities, Austro-Hungary identifies Serbia as the sponsor of the massacre.

5-6th of July
Germany issues a *"blank cheque"* to its Austro-Hungarian ally that it will support anything it does to Serbia and, even in the case of a war with Russia.

20-23rd of July
Reacting to spiralling out-of-control events, French and Russia re-affirm their alliance during a French official's visit to St-Petersburg.

26th of July
Austro-Hungarian gives an ultimatum to Belgrade. The ultimatum lists ten unacceptable demands designed to be refused, thus giving Vienna the pretext to declare war.

27th of July
Serbia replies to the ultimatum by agreeing to almost all demands. Nonetheless, Austria-Hungary still decides to break off diplomatic relations with Serbia. War had been decided in Vienna.

28th of July
Austria-Hungary declares war on Serbia.

30th of July
Russian mobilize in support of Serbia, its ally.

1st of August
Germany declares war on Russia because it mobilizes against Austria. France begins general mobilization.

3rd of August

Germany declares war on France.

4th of August
The conflagration soon to engulf the entire world begins with the Germans launching a major offensive in Belgium.

5th of August
England issues an ultimatum to Germany to remove all its troops from Belgium. With no answer from Berlin, London declares war on the German Empire.

The First World War has started.

Town of Semlin on the Sava River
7th Austro-Hungarian Corps, July 28th, 1914

Private soldier Helmut Gottenburg stood near the line of guns about to fire on Belgrade in the afternoon of the 28th of July, 1914. The Austro-Hungarian Army's 7th Corps was deployed on the Sava River, just a few kilometers from the border between Serbia and Austria-Hungary. Helmut could even see the city of Belgrade sprawled large over his field of vision. The Serbian capital was the symbol of defiance against Austro-Hungarian rule, and he felt quite good that they were about to demolish the place and conquer Serbia to teach the small pesky country a lesson it would not soon forget.

Like the rest of his comrades, he was fixated on the line of 8 cm Feldkanone M.5, about to fire in anger at the enemy capital city. Helmut was part of the 21st Landwehr Division. Recruited from a mix of Czech-German civilians in Bohemia, many of them were from the province's main cities. Helmut was from Prague, and his family was German. He spoke both Czech and German since his parents were from Prussia, but they now lived in Prague.

His father was a factory worker, and he would have followed him into the dreary place (an ammunition factory) if not for his volunteering in the Imperial and Royal Army (K.u.K.) at 18 years old to escape a fate he believed worse than death. Helmut had seen his father come back from work late every day. He had seen his back slowly curving from the tough work and the long hours. And he had no intention of repeating the model. The only thing he had not planned was that, as a soldier, he was bound to fight at one point.

The 21st Landwehr Division was made of two brigades, the 41st and the 42nd. In terms of battalions (like most Austro-Hungarian units), it had twelve, each with a machine gun detachment, several artillery units (batteries), some cavalrymen, along with supply and logistic troops.

The 21st Division had four infantry regiments: the 6th, 7th, 8th (the one Helmut belonged to), and the 28th. The 8th Regiment was mainly composed of ethnic Germans, while the 6th was made of Czech. The 7th Regiment was two-thirds Czech and one-third German, while the 28th was almost completely Czech. The arrangement was a complicated one but reflected the multi-national nature of Austria-Hungary. It wasn't very easy to get the four of them to cooperate properly since they didn't all speak the same language.

The division was preparing for the coming offensive by the Sava River. It fielded close to 11,000 riflemen and twenty machine guns(not nearly enough for what was about to be thrown at them), which were about to fire on Belgrade within moments, just like the other units along the border.

On the 25th of July, following the intense diplomatic maneuvering, the general Austro-Hungarian mobilization was ordered by its chief of the general staff, Franz Conrad von Hotzendorf. The units planned for the execution of Case B, the plan of attack against the Serbs and Montenegro: It included a total of nineteen divisions, split along seven corps, a formidable force to deal with the tiny but battle-hardened Serbian Army.

War with Serbia was officially declared an hour before (on 28th July), and their officers had told them to get ready. Then, the mighty line of guns on the Austrian side of the Sava River opened up with intense fury. The division's twenty-four guns fired one at a time and in succession, awing Helmut and his comrades.

He was startled to hear a powerful whistling sound thundering above the Division and was told by a couple of friends nearby that the Army had also set up a battery of 305 mm Skoda mortars just a kilometer back from where they were. These weapons were truly powerful, and Helmut was looking forward to seeing the results on the enemy city. Helmut didn't feel any nervousness since the Division wasn't supposed to enter enemy territory just yet. In its place, he harbored a sort of fascination about what this artillery cannon could do to Belgrade.

The Skoda 305 mm guns were truly powerful weapons compared to the 80 mm Feldkanone M.5 the Division had and was firing at the same time. He watched with glee the landing of the shells on the other side. They started to explode in shattering sounds (the Serbian capital was very close to the border), but Helmut thought it weird that they only seemed to ignite brief balls of light before dying away. After a few minutes, he was relieved to see the guns were having an effect, with smoke columns starting to appear, being obvious signs that fires were burning.

The sound of the cannon shots was deafening, as well as the loud crash their shells made into the city itself. Helmut tried to concentrate on one of them that whistled above his head and followed it to its destination. He knew that Skoda guns were made in a small Czech town called Plzen, about a hundred kilometers from Prague. It wasn't far from where he lived. The Skoda Works Company was a major manufacturer of weapons for the Imperial Army but also for many other countries around Europe. He thought he saw where the shell landed and felt pride as the top of the church it hit exploded to pieces, its debris showering down to the ground.

The bombardment of Belgrade would continue for the next eight days, during which time more and more Austro-Hungarian troops arrived in and around Belgrade for Franz Conrad von Hotzendorff's Case B offensive. In the meantime, soldiers like Helmut Gottenburg just waited for their turn to come. The Division was eventually transferred to the West in preparation for the attack itself; the plan was not to attack Belgrade from the north as he'd thought they would.

Berlin Palace
Kaiser Wilhelm goes to war August 1st, 1914.

In 1871, right after the creation of the German Empire, the Berlin Palace got an upgrade from being a royal to becoming an Imperial Residence. No longer the capital of a mere kingdom, the Berlin Castle became the symbolic heart of an empire that stretched from Königsberg in the east all the way into Alsace-Lorraine in the west. The palace was the official residence of the German Kaiser (Emperor) Wilhelm II.

It was the Imperial Residence when the Kaiser was in town and from where he directed the affairs of the state. Located on the Unter den Linden boulevard in Mitte (the center of the city), it was the heart and soul of the German Empire.

The German Emperor walked the room nervously as the crowd outside was showing impatience at his appearance. It was almost four in the afternoon, and he was scheduled to make an address to his people from the palace balcony. Everyone knew what he would say, but they wanted to hear it from his mouth, nonetheless. The room he was in was richly decorated, just like every room in the building. Expensive and colorful rugs, paintings of Prussia's history and of Frederick the Great adorning the walls, elaborate gildings everywhere. And there was a large and tall double window door leading outside to the balcony, where the crowd cheered and called for him.

And yes, he hesitated. Wilhelm was brash and inconsiderate at times but eventually came back to his senses. It was not his first international crisis, but it was the first time there seemed to be no way out but to go to war. Austria-Hungary had gone too far in its bullying of Serbia, and he'd given Vienna a blank check to act against the Balkan Slavs. This, in turn, forced the hand of the Russian Emperor, Nicolas II, into supporting the Serbs (he had a defensive alliance with them) and ordered his army's mobilization.

Raised to the throne in 1888, Kaiser Wilhelm II was born in 1859. The young Kaiser (Wilhelm acceded to the throne at thirty years old) had one goal. He wanted to make Germany one of the greatest powers in the world, to rival the famed British Empire. He wants to build up a fleet, conquer colonial territories, and confront the rest of Europe with powerful military forces. These wishes went directly against what Chancellor Otto von Bismarck (the architect of the German Empire and a diplomatic genius) had worked to craft in the last thirty years. He thus dismissed him following several arguments with the man.

A long string of bad moves and bad decisions had led to this day, as he was about to address his people about his decision to declare war. He had wanted colonies, a fleet, and everything in between. In the process, he had antagonized most of the great powers in Europe except the Austr-Hungarians and Italy. He shook his head in amazement and inwardly smiled, asking himself if this was the right play. After all, the decision was a momentous one. He was about to declare war on the Russian Empire and the French Republic. Well, he sort of already had, by supporting Austria in its Serbian war and by menacing the Russians and the French by mobilizing. He was too full of himself to accept that it was mostly his fault for his ideas of building a colonial empire and naval fleet, bringing him into direct conflict with the British. For him, Germany had the right to expand and the right to be the most powerful nation on earth. To hell with other countries' susceptibilities.

The German Emperor was a peculiar monarch. He was brilliant and could understand things quickly. He loved the modern technology and had a lot of energy. As such, he led Germany into the new century with courage and boldness. But there traits contrasted heavily with his tendency for rash decisions where thinking before acting was not prevalent.

In short, Kaiser Wilhelm was not the sort of leader you wanted in case of an international crisis. He was not a friend of democracy or peace, nor was he willing or able to manage a diplomatic crisis like the one that had surfaced following the assassination of the Austro-Hungarian heir to the throne. And if you wanted war, he was the perfect man to get it done.

"Your majesty," said General Helmuth von Moltke the Younger, the Chief of Staff of the Imperial Army. *"Yes, General,"* answered the German Emperor, yanked out of his train of thought. He had been busy thinking about what he would say to his third cousin Nicolas II of Russia once he'd won the conflict he was about to unleash (they were both great-great grandsons of former Tsar Paul the 1st and knew each other well). *"It's almost time,"* continued the military man, pointing at the pocket watch in his hand.

"General von Moltke," he started again, unsure of what he was about to do. *"Are you certain this is how we should play it? I mean, we could rein in the Austro-Hungarians to go back to their barracks. The Austrians can be reasoned with, I am certain."* And there it was again, he was hesitating, unsure. Moments ago, he had been so confident and decided. Von Moltke made a pained face. The top commander of the German Army knew his monarch and how to deal with his indecisions at the last moments. *"Your Majesty, the Habsburg's forces have been in Serbia since the evening of July 28th, and it's been reported they have started to shell Belgrade with their artillery. There is no avoiding war,"* countered the chief of the general staff, crossing his arms behind his back. There was no way the German military would back out now, and besides, thought von Moltke, he wanted war in order to put everyone in their place. It was about time he launched the war he and the German Army had been preparing for the last twenty years.

Kaiser Wilhelm hesitated for a moment, thinking about what he was about to do. There would be no turning back then. Von Moltke walked by him. *"I'll walk by you, your Majesty, and give you strength."*

And both men walked outside to the satisfied and enthusiastic roars of the Berliners. Wilhelm was almost taken aback by the show of love and enthusiasm but quickly recovered. He had many faults but could speak before a crowd.

He waved his arms in salute, to which they answered with even louder cheers. He then held his hands with open palms to appease them to silence. Everyone stopped cheering. After half a minute, the sound died, and he started speaking. *"I would like to start by thanking you for all the enthusiastic support you have shown me these past few days. We live in deadly, serious times. War is upon us, and we are united in facing it. Today, we are all Germans; we are all family. Our neighbors want conflict, and we will give it to them.*

The guns have been thrust into the forefront, and we must react. Tue Russian hordes are marshaling at the border and against our dear ally Austria-Hungary. We shall answer since we cannot bear the thought of letting the eastern invaders trample our beloved fatherland. In the west, Nicola's friends are also stirring, motivated by a revanchist attitude since we beat them in 1870-1871. The French are mobilizing like their Russian ally. We shall thus have to show them both what folly it is to defy us. The conflict about to be unleashed on the continent and the world will cost Germany dearly, but in the end, we will prevail."

He lifted his arm into the air, and the crowd responded with a tumultuous rumbling of satisfaction. The people wanted war and wanted to finish off Germany's adversaries.

The die was cast, and behind his resolute smile, Kaiser Wilhelm II of Germany had his doubts about the end result of the journey he was about to embark upon.

St Petersburg, Imperial Russia
Alexander Palace, August 1st, 1914

Tsar Nicolas II, the ruler of Imperial Russia, stood at his desk, trying to make sense of the momentous event occurring before his eyes. To his bewilderment, Russia was at war with Germany and Austria-Hungary. He'd tried to make it right, but the inflexible nature of the alliance and the position he was in as *"protector of the Balkan Slavs"* had forced events upon him.

That same day, he received the German declaration of war from its ambassador in St-Pe. Nicolas had been apprised of the situation moments later by his brother, who delivered the note to him personally.

He was in the portrait hall of the Alexander Palace, a magnificent castle where he and his family resided. The room he was in got its name from a large number of portraits of the Romanov family members, including Nicholas I, his four sons, Alexander I, and Catherine the Great. This was also the ceremonial room, decorated with the French Jacobean furniture, grand bronze chandeliers dating back to Catherine the Great, and exclusive parquetry in a diamond pattern.

Standing and looking into empty air just below an incredibly intricate crystal chandelier, he turned to face the painting of one of his illustrious ancestors, Alexander the 1st of Russia. The very man who had defeated Napoleon Bonaparte during the 1812 Invasion just a little over 100 years ago. He felt inspired by his ancestor's deeds.

The Alexander Palace (New Tsarskoselsky) was one hell of a luxurious place. When Nicholas became Tsar of Russia following his father's death, he decided to take residence in the collection of buildings and ordered it renovated by the best architects and decorated with nothing but the most luxurious. Thus, Alexander Palace became the home of the Tsar and his family. It was also where the ruler of the great country conducted many of the affairs of the state. It was also conveniently located in St-Petersbourg, the country's capital.

Beside him stood the Supreme Commander in Chief, Grand Duke Nikolai Nikolaevich, his very own uncle. *"Well, the die is cast, my Tsar,"* said the man. Nicolas took in a deep breath and crossed his arms behind his back. *"It appears so, Grand Duke,"* was the only thing he said. For a long moment, neither man spoke. And then Nicolas steeled his resolve to speak. *"Grand Duke Nikolaevich, fully mobilize the army, and let's run this thing to its conclusion,"* he started. Nikolai Nikolaevich stood straighter, happy with his Emperor's decision. It was no secret that the Russian military and many of the powerful people in St Petersburg wanted war. The buildup of forces and tension had increased and piled on itself for years. Every European Army was armed to the teeth and felt ready for a general conflagration. It was now time to finish this thing and put an end to German ambitions.

"Very well, sir, I will get the Army to prepare the offensives we have talked about, Your Majesty." At that, the Supreme Commander turned sharply, put his hand on his ceremonial sword, and walked out of the room through the large golden-gilded double doors.

Near the Belgian Border, August 4th, 1914
German 2nd Army, 4th Division, Infanterie-Regiment Graf Schwerin

By August 4th, 1914, the German 1st, 2nd, and 3rd Armies (a total of 34 divisions) were in the process of moving toward and through Belgium on the way to Northern France. The Germany Army was about to execute its Schlieffen Plan to the West against the French with seven armies, while an eight was tasked with defending Eastern Prussia from the Russian hordes. The Shlieffen Plan was the execution of a sweeping advance through Belgium into France, planned by former German Chief of Staff General Alfred von Schlieffen a generation ago.

For the offensive westward and through Belgium like the plan called for, Liege had to be taken. That task was entrusted to Field Marshal Karl von Bulow, the commander of the 2nd Army. Liege was the gateway into Belgium from Germany and then beyond into Northern France, where the Germans planned on outflanking the French Army.

The Belgian city was well-defended. It was ringed with twelve modern fortresses. With six sitting on each side of the Meuse River, they presented a formidable obstacle for the German forces. The entire defensive position stretched along a 30-mile radius and was considered one of the most heavily defended areas of Europe.

German soldier Oskar Dantz looked one more time at his Mauser rifle as he was instructed to by one of his NCOs. Oskar was part of the 2nd German Army about to attack the Liege Forts. He belonged to the German 4th Division and felt the weight of the world upon him before the battle.

The 4th Division was a unit with a long history going far into the past. Following its creation in 1818, it was involved in the Austro-Prussian War of 1866 and the victory at Sadowa. The division then fought in the equally victorious Franco-Prussian

War against France in 1870-71. Oskar's grandfather had fought in these wars and came back a hero of the Reich. The Regiment he was also a part of (Infanterie-Regiment Graf Schwerin) still had his father on the payroll as he was too old to be a frontline soldier, and his grandfather was still a known name in the unit.

He thus felt the weight of the world in hopes that he would be able to do as well as his illustrious granddaddy. He looked around him and found comfort in the fact that most of his comrades looked as white as he was. They were all conscripts, forced into the army by national conscription and did not really know what the future had in store for them. As it was, life was about to get very interesting for Oskar.

Following two successful wars in 1866 (against Austria and France (1870-1871) and helped by a very healthy military budget, the German Army was considered the most powerful land force in the entire world, and rightly so. It could count on over eight field armies, all well-trained and well-equipped. In the end, it could muster well over six million men once general mobilization was done.

Also, many organizational solutions used in the Prussian army and later in the German army (e.g., strategic railway lines or mobilization techniques) made it truly efficient compared to its European counterparts. As in the French and Russian armies, the largest number of armed forces in the German army in 1914 were infantry, like Private Oskar Dantz.

The German infantryman's main weapon was the successful and efficient 7.92 mm Mauser Gewehr 98 rifle, and on his head, he wore the famous pickelhaube – a steel arrowhead that highlighted every German soldier apart from other armies.

The German infantry uniform was much less colorful than its French counterpart. The German high command and the military in general had done their homework and studied the last few wars well. With dark grey uniforms, it was believed they would present less of a spottable target for the enemy. The events of the next few weeks would confirm they were right in thinking this, and every power in the conflict would soon follow suit.

"Done checking your weapon, Dantz?" said his sergeant with a sour face. The man had walked up to Oskar without realizing it. And no, he wasn't done. He'd been daydreaming and anticipating the battle to come in his imagination. *"Almost done, sir,"* he stammered back. *"Sure, kid,"* countered the sergeant. *"I'm going down there to inspect a few more men; just make sure you are ready when I come back."* *"Yes, sir,"* he answered as meekly as possible. Sergeant Wilhelm was not a nice guy, and not one of the guys in the nine-man platoon wanted to displease him.

The European powers in 1914
The nations who were about to fight the war.

Great Britain was the main power in Europe and the greatest empire in the world. The saying said it all: the sun never sets on the British Empire, meaning that its territory spanned globally. The Royal Navy ruled the wave with a powerful fleet, and London was the economic center of the world.

France was still a great power in 1914 but not as strong as it had been before the Franco-Prussian War of 1870-1871. It also possessed a world empire, with colonies in Africa, Asia, and the Caribbean. It possessed the second-largest army in Europe, behind Germany.

Germany was unified under one nation at the conclusion of the Franco-Prussian War of 1871. Ever since then, its economy had grown to be the first in Europe, and its army was rivaled by none on the continent. It was also busy carving its own little colonial empire across the world, with territories in Africa and the Pacific. It was also second only to the Royal Navy in terms of Naval power.

Italy had also been recently unified at the end of the 19th century. It was a second-rate power but, nonetheless, an important one, possessing come colines in North Africa. It also controlled the Central Mediterranean with a powerful and still-expanding fleet.

Austria-Hungary was a declining power in 1914. Including over twenty nationalities led by a German ruler, it was sort of an oddity in this Europe of burgeoning nationalistic movements. It possessed a powerful army on paper, but looks were deceiving. It was less well-equipped and had a lot of organizational problems.

Russia was one hell of a large country, with a lot of soldiers to fight the war it was about to get into. The economy had been growing for the last ten years, and the country seemed to be doing a lot better than following its defeat at the hands of the Japanese in the 1950 Russo-Japanese War. But again, looks were deceiving. The military and the country as a whole were plagued with badly equipped soldiers, incompetence, and corruption at all levels of the government and military leaders.

The Ottoman Empire (Turkey) was once a great power. In fact, it was the biggest of them all. But since the 17th Century, its fortune had been declining. In 1914, it was but a shadow of itself. With its military and the volume of strategic territory (the Middle East) it held, it was nonetheless still an important player in world affairs.

The system of alliances in 1914
How the world went to war

On the eve of the war, Europe was split into two blocs of powerful nations, covering most of the world with their respective empires. One side was the Central Powers or the so-called Triple Alliance, including the German and Austro-Hungarian Empire, with the new Kingdom of Italy. The other side was the Entente, including Russia, France and Great Britain.

France wanted revenge on Germany for the 1870-1871 Franco-Prussian War. Russia hated and feared Germany and Austria-Hungary. The British were feeling threatened by an aggressive Germany naval building program, pushing them to closer ties with France. Austria wanted to get rid of Serbia and expand in the Balkans, and for that they needed a powerful ally, in this case Germany.

The crisis following Franz Ferdinand's assassination in the summer of 1914 was one of many, and no one expected it to spiral out of control as much as it did.

International tensions mounted in the years leading up to 1914, and there was really nothing capable of slowing them down. The assassination of Franz Ferdinand stoked an already burning fire, and what was first seen as a local crisis exploded into a general war. The crisis spread as allies promised each other support for either the Austro-Hungarians or the Serbians. The Austrians knew full well that attacking Serbia was to trigger a war with Russia, claiming itself to be the protector of the Balkan Slavs.

Deciding on war, Vienna called its powerful ally in the Central Powers alliance on the 5th of July. Without a shadow of a doubt about what his action would trigger, the Kaiser promised the Austrian Emperor his full support in any action against the Serbs.

Russia and Austria both could not back down because of their fear of losing face and credibility, and thus, they played all the way to the last card and went to war.

Russia ordered its military to mobilize for war on the 30th of July to respond to the Austro-Hungarian offensive on Serbia. Berlin decided that it was an act of war directed against the Central Powers.

On the 31st of July 1914, Germany produced an ultimatum to Russia demanding it demobilize and send its armies back to their barracks or else face the might of the German Army. The next day, Tsar Nicolas II had not yet responded. The Kaiser signed the declaration of war on Russia and ordered its own general mobilization. The declaration of war against France soon followed on the 3rd of August since the plan was to attack them first and to outflank them through Belgium before they took care of Russia.

The German offensive into Belgium was too much for Britain, who anyway had no love lost for Germany because of its active fleet building threatening what they perceived as the security of the British Home Islands. On the 4th of August, London demanded that the Germans retreat out of Belgium. At the end of that same day, and with no answer, Great Britain declared war.

The entry of Britain and its empire made this a truly global war. Russia, France, and Great Britain against Austria-Hungary and Germany, with many of the still-neutral powers to follow soon.

And that was how one of the biggest wars in history started.

Strategic decisions
Oberste Heeresleitung (OHL), August 4th, 1914, on the eve of the offensive into Belgium

Ever since the French and Russians had allied themselves against Germany at the end of the 19th Century, the Reich was faced with the horrible prospect of a war on two fronts and, thus, a conflict of attrition it could only lose.

The German offensive plan called the Schlieffen Plan, was thought and prepared a decade prior to the conflict that was just beginning. The brainchild of the legendary Helmut von Moltke the Elder, it favored a strategy for the German Army to deal with the unavoidable two-front war that German would have to fight in case of conflict against France (West) and Russia (East). The idea was to wheel to the right on France and then advance on Russia once the French were done for.

The plan's basic premise banked on Russia taking six long weeks to mobilize its army and start attacking Eastern Prussia or Galician Austria-Hungary. During that critical time, Germany would stage an attack on Northern France by attacking through Belgium, a neutral country.

This route circumvented the border with France and presented a definite plus for the Germans since it permitted them to avoid the French armies and heavy fortifications. The follow-up to this northern attack was that the German forces were then to move southward, inflicting a severe blow on the lightly defended north of France through Flanders, Belgium, with the ultimate objective to storm Paris.

With the fall of its capital, German planners hoped the French would surrender, just like they did in 1871. If that could be accomplished, Germany could switch its forces East with its excellent and efficient railroads to deploy them against the Tsar and his men. General Schlieffen believed the Russian Army would take six weeks to mobilize and attack Eastern Prussia.

And so that was the gist of it and why the German high command met that day. Nothing was assured in war, and events were in motion. The Great Headquarters was organized by Wilhelm II on the day of the declaration of war in order to better coordinate the actions of the war and the two fronts (East and West) it would have to face. Within the Great Headquarters, a military section called the OHL was created. It was, of course, under the direction of the German Chief of the General Staff, General Helmuth Ludwig von Moltke.

The meeting that day was about the start of the Schlieffen Plan and other tactical considerations that faced the Empire. The people present were, of course, Kaiser Wilhelm and Ludwig von Molkte, the Chief of the General staff and commander of the OHL. Also present were his two deputies in most operational matters; First, Colonel Gerhard Tappen, the commander of the Operations Division, and Lieutenant Colonel Richard Hentsch, the leader of the Information Division.

Further present were the three men who would be in charge of implementing the Schlieffen Plan, or else the right hook into Belgium: 1st Army commander, General Alexander von Kluck, 2nd Army commander General Karl von Bülow, and 3rd Army commander General Max von Haussen.

General Maximilian von Prittwitz, commander of the German 8th Army, was invited because a decision needed to be taken on the matter of the Eastern Front defenses to offset any potential early Russian attack in Prussia. The Russian forces, according to German estimations, were supposed to take at least six weeks to mobilize, and yet, there were a lot of voices arguing for sending a little under 200,000 more soldiers to Prussia just in case. The 8th Army was very small and would not be able to withstand a Russian offensive if it ever happened before the French Army was done for.

"Thank you all for being here," started Moltke, then nodding at

the Emperor. *"Your Majesty, you honor us by your presence,"* he continued. Kaiser Wilhelm nodded nonchalantly. He wouldn't be part of the core of the discussions but might give his own opinion over matters.

"The offensive will start tomorrow, as agreed. 2nd Army," von Moltke gave the nod to General Karl Bulow, *"and the other troops will move around the city while it is being reduced."* Bulow lifted an eyebrow, obviously wanting to ask a question. *"Yes, General,"* answered Moltke. *"Will I have the planned heavy artillery needed to reduce those powerful forts?"* *"Indeed, you will, General. Once Liege is subdued, the army units need to make good speed on the outflanking movement we have planned,"* he stopped to give the nod to one of the staff officers roving around the table at which they were all sitting. The young man gave them folders containing their marching orders.

"Every one of the units you command has a specific direction, and I must insist that haste is the essence of the matter; the faster we smash across northern France to Paris, the better." All the military commanders opened their folders, and the Kaiser did as well, for what good it did him. Moltke looked at his sovereign for a moment and wondered if he understood the paperwork in front of him. The man wasn't the brightest light in the chandelier. With no more questions arising, he addressed the last part of what needed to be discussed today.

"General von Prittwitz, as commander of the 8th Army, and since you are responsible for the defense of Eastern Prussia by yourself, I believe you will have the most difficult job if the Russians mobilize and attack before we are done with the French." *"Agreed, General Moltke. I will make the best use of what I have to keep the Russian bear at bay."*

"Well, gentlemen," said the OHL commander as he sat up from his chair, *"You are all busy men and need to be back at your command. The attack starts at 0500 tomorrow. Good luck to all.*

CHAPTER 1
THE WAR IN THE WEST

Naval Pursuit in the Mediterranean Part 1
The epic journey of the Goeben and the Breslau, August 1914

(...) Pola, main Austro-Hungarian naval
base, August 1st, 1914 (...)

Admiral Wilhelm Souchon, the commander of the German Mediterranean Squadron, sipped his mug of scalding tea as he read the message announcing the declaration of war on Russia. It also stated that a state of war would soon be official with France. He made a face, part because the tea was hot and also because the orders created a mountain of problems for him. He was in the Mediterranean Sea, of all places, and would soon be surrounded by enemies since he suspected the damned British would join in with the Franco-Russians.

Souchon was the captain of the Goeben, a German dreadnought battlecruiser. His ship was flanked by the light cruiser Breslau. Both vessels were quite modern and powerful, but the problem would soon be the numbers arrayed against him if war started. The Goeben was not even two years old and sported over 30 guns of all calibers, with main 11-inch naval rifles. It was well-armored and a hell of a fast ship.

His ships were stationed at Pola, the main Austrian naval base in the Adriatic Sea. They had been sent there in 1912 by the Kaiser, further angering French and British interests in the area. His official mission was to try and disrupt the flow of troops and supplies from North Africa to France in the advent of conflict. Its only problem was some recurring problem with its boilers, and thus, it was the reason Souchon and his squadron were in Pola when he received the message. He was attempting to get more repairs done to his ship.

He wondered what to do for a moment but knew that his options were limited. Within days, the Royal Navy or the French Navy would probably blockade the Adriatic Sea, and he would be stuck there for the war's duration or until he sailed to confront the

British and try to force his way out.

He summoned his second in command, Vice-Admiral Hubert von Rebeur-Paschwitz, to his cabin. A few minutes later, the man appeared by the cabin's bulkhead. *"Sir,"* he said, saluting at the same time. *"Please enter, Vice Admiral,"* answered Suchon. The man did and walked by the small conference table in the Admiral's cabin. *"What can I do for you, sir,"* he said. Souchon winced as a large grating noise was heard, probably from the repair crews working on the boilers.

"War has been declared with Russia, and I have very good information," he waved the piece of wireless paper he had in his hand, *"that war with France will soon follow. High command is also pretty certain war with the British is likely."* Rebeur-Paschwitz was taken aback by the news, but it wasn't unexpected. Thus, he wasn't really surprised. His reaction was more related to the fact that this created a world of trouble for the German warships. *"Orders, sir?"*

Souchon took a deep breath and then spoke. *"Get the repair crews off my ship and get us on the open sea. We're breaking out into the Mediterranean to fulfill our mission when war with France comes."*

"Indeed, sir," answered the Vice-Admiral with a smile. Later that day, the German ships sped out of the Austro-Hungarian harbor.

(…) Meanwhile, in the Mediterranean Sea, Royal Navy (…)

Ordered by the end of July to cover the French transports ferrying troops from Africa to France, the Royal Navy's Mediterranean Squadron sailed near the Central Mediterranean. The fleet was pretty strong and included three modern battlecruisers (Inflexible, Indefatigable, and Invincible), eight cruisers (4 heavy and 4 light), plus a number of destroyers. The British commander was also on full alert and expected to be given orders to attack German ships within days since war with Russia was already declared and conflict between France and

Germany seemed imminent as well. From there, it wasn't hard to see where Great Britain would go since it had no love lost for Germany. When it was known that Souchon had sailed out of Pola (the British entertained spies in the area), the fleet was ordered to shadow the German battlecruiser and to blockade the Adriatic for Central Powers shipping if possible.

It was soon announced to the British squadron commander that Souchon and his two ships had been spotted near Taranto by Italian coast watchers, and the British consul there had relayed the information to the British Navy by telegram. Two of the three battlecruisers were promptly ordered back to Gibraltar to make sure the Royal Navy had ships if the Germans sailed westward in an attempt to break out into the Atlantic, while the rest of the squadron was ordered east and in pursuit of the Germans.

(...) August 2nd, 1914, Goeben (...)

After rounding up Taranto, where he was certain his small task force was spotted, Souchon had the Goeben and the Breslau sailed to the coast of Sicily. By August 2nd, the Germans were through the Strait of Messina and poised to make a run at the French embarkation ports in Algeria and Tunisia.

Souchon paced the bridge of his battlecruiser, pondering on the orders he'd just received. *"What do you want to do now, Admiral,"* said his second Hubert von Rebeur-Pashwitz. The German Admiral took some time to answer as he looked at the slowly dropping sun on the horizon. The red color reflected gloriously on the blue immensity, and it helped him relax. He'd always liked that time of the day. *"What are your thoughts, Vice Admiral"* he answered instead of giving an answer to his subordinate's question. He was of the mind to ignore the orders he now had but wanted to see if the Vice-Admiral was aligned with him. *"Well, sir, according to the latest reports that we received from the Italians, the Royal Navy is at Gibraltar, and there is no French fleet anywhere near our position. And, after all, we are not yet at war with the British; thus, they won't attack us just yet. I would change it and then sail for Constantinople as ordered."*

Souchon turned back once more toward the slowly and now fully orange setting sun. He had just been informed that Germany had signed an alliance with Istanbul and that the Turks would soon join the war on the side of the Central Powers. Part of the deal was that the Goeben and the Breslau would be sailed to Constantinople to beef up the Sultans' fleet. The orders were as clear as water. He was to abandon his pre-wars instructions, turn around, and head at best speed toward Constantinople. *"We are so damned close to fulfilling our mission, Vice Admiral, that I am tempted to make one run before we head for the Bosphorus and our new home."*

Von Rebeur-Paschwitz smiled. *"I agree, sir."*

The Battle of Liege Part 1
The fight for the forts, August 5th to August 16th, 1914

The Battle of Liege was where the land war began in August 1914, as German General von Bulow's 2nd Army attacked across the border into neutral Belgium.

The Schlieffen Plan had started, and in a broader sense, the First World War. Soon, the British would come in, following Austria-Hungary, Russia, and France. The British entry would drag other countries into the conflict, like the Japanese and the Ottoman Empire. The burgeoning war would soon engulf the entire world.

The initial German Army's goal was to storm and conquer Liege, the best entry to Belgium for its troops. The city barred the way just to the west of the Ardennes Forest, where it planned to start executing its outflanking move dictated by the Schlieffen Plan. It was, in a way, a highway for troops on campaign, a road used by invading armies from both sides since immemorial times. With Liege, the Germans could open the door for their forces to spill across the landscape, conquer the small neutral country, and spread into Northern France.

While the OHL and the plethora of German Army commanders expected a swift move through the area with little to no resistance, they had not verified if the Belgian Military was in agreement. Protected by twelve modern forts built on high ground at the end of the 19th Century, Liege was one tough nut to crack. The forts had a little over four hundred retractable guns, from all types and forms of calibers, all the way up to big 210mm mortars. The Belgian Army was a lot smaller than the wall of men the Germans were sending at it, and thus, the forts sort of compensated for it (Germany was sending well over 500,000 men while the Belgian Army was 70,000 strong). In short, it was one hell of a position to assault for the German Army.

The twelve modern concrete forts sat on a loose arc around the city of Liege and were well-spaced to cover every angle of approach over a large area. The purpose of the powerful defensive works was to create a line to delay or even stop any German attack and give time for the Belgian Army units to mobilize and get ready for the assault. The faced outside and toward the German border, while the side facing the center of Liege was a little less fortified as it was not believed Germans could encircle the position. Their reinforced walls could withstand big, high-velocity modern shells.

Overly confident in a rapid victory, the Germans attacked at night on the 5th of August with a small force of 30,000 soldiers but were repulsed with heavy casualties and without making any progress. This initial failure surprised the boastful German leaders.

They had elived theyr brave and superbly equipped men would just roll over the Belgians. However, this initial failure had nothing to do with the quality of their soldiers. It was all about the fact that they were fighting an unequal battle between the flesh, rifles against Belgian concrete walls, heavy guns, and machine guns. The night action lasted for several hours, but following that, the Germans retreated back to their starting positions.

As it became obvious infantry and their supporting field guns alone would not break the defenses, some heavier ordinance was called forth from the depots in Germany. The OHL had just the things on hand to smash the pesky Belgian forts to smithereens.

Fort of Barchon, Liege
Night of the 5th of August, 1914

(...) Infanterie-Regiment Graf Schwerin,
4th Imperial Division (...)

Private soldier Oskar Dantz was scared shitless by the ambient sounds of gunfire and artillery blasts. In fact, he was more than scared, he was completely stunned out of his mind. Come to think of it, he was lying on his butt and then looked at his hands. It was dark, and he saw they were covered with dirt. Or was it blood? He sort of snapped out of his predicament; his foggy mind sort of registered that he was in the middle of a battle.

He looked up, and there it was. Blossoming balls of fire from the German artillery shells were landing right on top of the Fort of Barchon. And yes, he was part of the Infanterie-Regiment Graf Schwerin, supposed to assault it. The next things he saw were the enemy machine gun bullet tracers rending the night, and then he realized he was in the open and could get hit at any moment.

He rolled to his side and luckily fell into some kind of ditch or depression, saving him from the direct fire of the enemy. He thanked God and his dead mother for the luck. Laying on his back, he was breathing hard. Trying to look inside himself, he tried to focus on his body, but there didn't seem to be anything wrong with it.

It was the dark of night; that much was obvious as he saw the black sky and the blazing tracers streaming above him from where he was. He started to register the yells and the sounds of gunfire. Damn, this was bad. He'd never imagined war would be so scary and terrible.

He suddenly remembered he was supposed to have a Mauser rifle. He'd lost it in the confusion. He still didn't know what had happened and wondered what had hit him.

As it happened, a Belgian 210 mm gun had fired near him, and the explosion, killing most of his platoon, had knocked him out without injuring him. Well, he was a little injured since his left ear bled.

He spotted a dead or seriously injured comrade (the man didn't move, so he figured as much) a few feet out of his small hiding place. With one of the powerful explosions came a temporary flash, and he saw that a rifle was right beside him. He crawled as low to the ground as possible and retrieved it before scurrying back into his little hole.

(...) Belgian 29th Regiment (...)

Belgian Soldier Jean Barries, a Private soldier in the 29th Regiment, moved the 1914 Hotchkiss machine gun, and his friend Edmond Sauniard chambered for the 8 mm Lebel cartridge on the side.

The Hotchkiss machine gun worked with a mix of gas and air-cooled systems, contrary to the German Maxim Gun, which worked with a coil that was cooled simply with water. Both weapons had their advantages, and the Berlgian were doing fine with the weapon.

The Hotchkiss' billowing smoke thus quickly clouded around the gun as they fired it. *"Hurry up, Edmond, the bastards are closing in,"* continued Jean as he tried to make sense of what he was seeing in the darkness.

The German troops had attacked in force as soon as darkness fell, but so far, things were holding. Jean, his friends Edmond and Jacques Pignant were holed up in Fort Barchon, the most northerly of the Belgian forts defending Liege.

The Hotchkiss machine gun was great in a fight where a soldier had to fire continuously. It could be easily and constantly fed by a team of three; each individual clip (or "strip") had twenty-four rounds of ammo. This was truly inconvenient to Jean as there were more Germans in front of him than he had bullets in a few strips. Edmond and Jacques got busy reloading the gun several times as they hosed the multitude of Germans streaming at them. He knew the German Maxim gun used a 250-round continuous cloth belt and felt bad for not having one with him. The Belgian Army used French weapons mostly but had also bought some from Germany. As he fired another burst the moment Edmond had closed the lid on the clip, he decided he would try to find one.

After he was done streaming the 24 bullets out, the empty feed strip was ejected automatically. Jacques didn't say anything and clipped another one in place, being careful not to touch the by now very hot barrel. "*Ready,*" he said to Jean, who nodded and pulled the trigger again. The staccato sound of the Hotchkiss spewed its stream of bullets once again.

The three men were in one of the most forward bunkers and were firing through an embrasure. As his tracers seesawed through the running and charging grey-clad and studded helmet soldiers, he had a fleeting thought about the fort designers and decided they'd done their job well. The embrasure had the perfect angle, considering the downward slope on which he was firing.

The scene he was firing into was chaotic. It was dark, but tracers blazed through the night while sudden bright flashes from the artillery shells landed all around. Then, the loud click of the weapon being out of bullets rang. He waited a few seconds while his two comrades worked their magic.

"*Go!*" said Edmond again as yet another clip was in the Hotchkiss machine gun. He pulled the trigger again, once more shredding German soldiers. But more and more of the bastards were streaming near their bunker, and bullets were slamming dangerously close to the embrasure, lodging themselves into the concrete in small puffs of smoke and dust.

He wondered how long they would hold.

(...) Aftermath, next morning (...)

As it happened, Jean didn't have to worry too much just yet. The German assault was beaten back around midnight, with the Imperial soldiers reeling backward in disarray after smashing themselves hard on the solid Belgian defenses.

The fact of the matter was that the OHL had underestimated the fort's capability to resist and had only attacked with 30,000 men. The next few days would be different in attempts but not in outcome. In the end, several large artillery pieces were called forth to the area to smash the bunkers and forts of Liege.

Germano-Ottoman negotiations and alliance
Constantinople August 4th, 1914

The Road to the Turco-German Alliance was simple yet complex. Following the Ottoman ousting from Central Europe in the late 17th century (after a string of defeats at the hands of Russia and Austria), imminent problems facing the Sublime Porte (another name for the Ottoman Empire) gradually changed. First, it was the loss of dominance over Europe, followed by a complete withdrawal from the Balkans. With the decisive defeat following the Balkan Wars (1912 and 1913), it was somewhat over for Turkey in Europe. In 1914, the main concern was the total collapse of the Empire, and the Turkish leaders felt that war was a solution to the myriad of problems for the Empire.

Hence, the leadership answer was to find a solid ally, and choose one of the two camps between the Central Powers and the Entente. With such a move, it was hoped the country would get back on the road to success in the military, economic, and diplomatic fields.

The events in Sarajevo and the following march to war between the European powers created a sense of urgency in Istanbul, and the Turkish leaders, with men like Enver Pacha in the lead, sought to find a quick solution since the Empire had not joined one of the two alliances yet.

The Ottoman leadership's first choice would have been Britain and France, but both of those countries were not very keen on close ties with Turkey for many reasons. The German Kaiser, Unlike the Anglo-French, was interested in making friends with the Ottomans. This was demonstrated by the German Fountain built in the heart of Istanbul in 1901, the agreement to construct a Berlin-Baghdad railway in 1903, the rapid rise in German financial investment, and the German military advisors sent to the Ottoman side.

Within Germany itself, the pro-Turkish attitudes of the German emperor, along with the strong ties the German military entertained with Turkish leaders such as Enver Pasha, increased the possibility for a Turco-German alliance.

In short, the Ottomans did not see they had any other option but to choose between the Central Powers because England and France were not interested. Germany did not have colonial ambitions in the immediate area where the Ottoman Empire was and was openly hostile to the Turk's traditional enemy in the Caucasus, the Russian Empire.

The Germans were also building main railroads spanning throughout the country, from Anatolia to Iraq, and helping the Ottomans reform and rebuild their armed forces. As such, public opinion and the opinion of the elite sided with the Germans. The Entente, on the other hand, appeared menacing. The British and French were right at the borders of Iraq and the Sinai and looked hungrily at the Middle Eastern territories. As seen by Cemal Pasha, the head of the Army of Palestine and the Sinai, *"We have already lost Egypt to the British, and there is no end to their appetite for our Middle Eastern lands like Mesopotamia, the Levant, and Palestine."*

It was in this context that both powers negotiated heavily from the end of July to the beginning of August 1914 and agreed on a formal alliance on the 4th. The Turks were supposed to enter the war immediately but hesitated as they were not ready and didn't have the necessary finances.

In general terms, the alliance was as such: Germany would give the modern battlecruiser Goeben to Turkey as a gift for their navy and provide gold for the Ottoman military. In exchange, the Turks were to close the straits to Russian shipping, attacking the British in Egypt and the Russians in the Caucasus. The Germans were also supposed to provide military supplies and support.

The Battle of the Frontier Part 1
Plan XVII and the French attack, August 7th, 1914.

It is my firm intention, regardless of any other considerations or circumstances, to go and meet the enemy at the border and to reclaim our lost provinces. We will attack in two areas. First, through the Vosges and the Moselle near Belfort; second, we will push hard from Verdun toward Metz and wrest it away from dirty German hands. Only the offensive can win this war.
—*Plan XVII, General Joffre, a year prior to the declaration of hostilities*

The initial French offensive of World War I was an attack on the city of Mulhouse in Alsace-Lorraine, a province that was lost as a result of the grave defeat in the Franco-Prussian War a generation before. The town was regarded as critical to the French war effort, allowing French troops to be well-positioned for further combat to the north, boosting French morale, and clearly stating France's intention to reclaim the lost territories.

Under the impetus of over-aggressive army commander-in-chief Joseph Joffre (Plan XVII), the French attacked over the heavily forested Vosges Mountains. At first, as they approached the city, the French troops only encountered surprisingly light resistance. They fought a few sharp, short battles with German troops that soon retreated in the face of their heavy numerical disadvantage. General Bonneau, the commander of the attacking French forces, suspected some kind of a trap, but on the first day, nothing came out of it. Even after he shared his worries with Joffre, the French commander-in-chief told him to march on to Mulhouse, where they found the city abandoned by the Germans. The OHL was busy executing the Schlieffen Plan and had not anticipated the enemy to attack so early in the campaign with such aggressiveness. But it wasn't like they wouldn't do anything about the pesky French attack.

The French offensive into Alsace Lorraine was a bit peculiar since it was obvious by the 7th of August that the main German effort was in Belgium. But its logic was rooted in the previous decades of military thinking and a resounding defeat. The 1871 war with Prussia was a tragedy for France. The Second French Empire was dissolved following it, Napoleon III was captured, and the Third Republic was born. The traumatic events of the military disaster still rang in French hearts and minds.

The economy was destroyed, and deaths, injuries, and other casualties numbered in the hundreds of thousands. At the war's end, Bismarck, the German chancellor at the time, forced France to supply a staggering sum in war reparations: five billion gold francs to Prussia, a quarter of France's annual revenue at the time. Germany took Alsace and Lorraine from France, moved its troops to the industrial area to ensure France would pay on time and promptly, and completed the humiliation by diplomatically isolating the French in the following years. The country was in shambles: Napoleon III's Second Empire crumbled to ashes. The people rose in revolt, and the Third Republic was born.

To French Army officers in the years that followed, an offensive mindset like the Napoleonic France of old held was the only way to victory. The French Army had developed some great weapons like the new rifle (Lebel Model 1886), or else a new artillery weapon, the Canon de 75 (75mm Gun). Coupled with the spirit of the offensive, the French military thinking at the time that the combination of both would bring overwhelming victory. Their forefathers had done just that a century before under the iconic Napoleon Bonaparte; hence, they believed that that offensive mindset still resided in the French soldier's persona.

The still-reeling-from-disaster French Army founded the School of War (École de Guerre) in 1875 to increase military skills across its officer corps and started to cultivate what they started to call the "*Cult of the Offensive*." The concept was rooted in old Napoleonic history and stated that the French will would overcome anything if properly harnessed. The "offensive officers" started to use a two-word theme called "*élan vital*," which had little immediate purpose in prosecuting a war, putting emphasis on morale and life spirit as an essential way to winning wars. It was a fine, romantic concept. It was not, however, very adapted to fend off machine guns, bullets, and artillery shrapnel.

Thus, out of this new strategic thinking born of the traumatic events of 1871, Plan XVII came to be. Plan XVII was an offensive plan for the mobilization, concentration, and deployment of the French armies in the extreme east of the country to make possible an invasion of either the lost Alsace-Lorraine province or, Belgium, or both.

Joffre's plan was for his move in hard and fast through the Ardennes and into Lorraine the moment war was declared. Since the German Army had the numerical advantage, the success of Plan XVII was taking into account the fact that the OHL would send a bulk of its forces east and would take some time to activate its reserves.

While an enemy sweeping attack in Belgium and then into Northern France was considered doable by the French high command, it was considered unlikely, even when the obvious was in front of Joffre, and three German armies battered at the Liege forts.

Doing the unexpected, the Germans high command (OHL) decided to gamble on Russia to mobilize slowly to devote its offensive power in the West, as well as immediately activate their reserves. Even when Russia did attack, they kept true to their original plan and continued pushing hard, almost ignoring the threat in the East to the point of being on the brink of disaster.

While the French troops were in Mulhouse, the Germans Army mustered a counterattack at the nearby town of Cernay on August 9th. Following a long, grueling day of battle punctuated by artillery barrages from both sides, bayonet charges, and thousands of dead, the French initiated their retreat in the face of by-then overwhelming German troops numbers.

The Battle of Cernay-Mulhouse
Alsace-Lorraine, near Mulhouse, August 10th, 1914

Armand Bonnier, a private soldier in the 14th French Infantry Division, fired his Lebel rifle as he turned back to try and fend off the German soldiers in hot pursuit. His sight was greeted by a madhouse of explosions, columns of smoke, tracers, and towering columns of dark earth thrown into the sky by enemy artillery shells.

He was dressed in the field-regulation blue top and red pants of the French army. He harbored a tired and scared face, dirty with black soot all over. He had blood on his uniform, not his own, but from one of his best friends, killed by one of the dreadful and overwhelming German attacks of the last few days.

As he turned back (he never stopped running to fire), he narrowly dodged a horse without a rider, stomping through the battlefield in panic. Looking left and right, his comrades continued to run. He again looked behind and saw the same thing, except that this time, he also spotted the outlines of the spiked helmets and the dark grey uniforms of the German soldiers in hot pursuit.

The 7th Corps, under the command of General Bonneau, entered Alsace on the morning of the 7th of August, triumphantly pushing aside the hopelessly outnumbered German frontier soldiers as they advanced. They bayonet-charged the light German opposition and cheered for their easy victory.

From Belfort, they marched inside the German Empire under the stunned gaze of peasants who were, for the most part, still French in their hearts. After all, some of them had fought the hated Huns in the 1870 wars. They were grandfathers now, but their hatred had not abated. The towns of Thann and Altkirch were taken from the light German defenses. By the evening of the 8th of August, the French were masters of Mulhouse, where they were overjoyously welcomed by crowds who saw them as liberators. And it was as they should be since Alsace was French, not German. The province was lost during the 1870-1871 Franco-Prussian War.

How Armand had rejoiced, as beautiful local girls had given him kisses on the cheeks and he'd received gifts from the local men. It had been a grand time. But now things were different, and they were being driven back by a powerful German counterattack. It was powerful because it was executed with at least four times the numbers in the 7th Corps. What had started as some minor skirmishes outside of town had quickly morphed into a full-fledged battle. Armand had been in a town square, enjoying some good local wine and the company of some of the residents, when the shells had started to land. At first, he'd taken cover and thought not much of it. But then, a lot more shells started to slam everywhere into the buildings around him. Soon, the entire area he was in was engulfed in a maelstrom of fire.

Half an hour later, he was exchanging fire with German soldiers, infiltrating the town from everywhere. The order to retreat had come quickly after that.

Just beside him, another of his comrades fell, hit in the back by an enemy rifle bullet. He barely looked sideways, trying to run as fast as he could. A large farmhouse was nearby, and he saw that several of the Division's soldiers were making a stand there and firing back at the advancing enemy. As he arrived at the large brick and wood barn, he noticed the border posts not far from the building, and his heart sank. They were back at the border, and it didn't look like they would stop there. "Allez, soldat," yelled a Corporal as he waved him inside the building. Beside the NCO, a couple of soldiers fired toward the enemy.

As he got in, he heard a loud bang just to his right, and then some smoke billowed near him. The unit defending the barn possessed the excellent and powerful French 75mm gun (Canon de 75 modèle 1897).

Armand was happy to see that the defense of the building and potentially his survival would be greatly helped by the amazing field piece. *"You go over there and find a spot to fire, soldier,"* *continued the Corporal.* "Yes, sir," he answered, gripping his Lebel rifle and moving to the right, where several blue-uniformed soldiers were already busy pouring fire into the advancing enemy ranks.

One tall and broad-shouldered soldier with a badly scarred face nodded to him. *"Here, my friend,"* said the big man. *"My name is Philippe Cren,"* Armand extended his hand. *"I am Armand Bonnier, 14th Division."* Cren smiled, *"Well, that's a first. Haven't seen any of your lot yet,"* he countered. Armand looked through the large hole in the wall and put his rifle level on the bricks to hold it still.

The fight was far from over, but before the day was over, General Bonneau would order all of the 7th Corps to go back into the Vosges and to the 7th Corps' starting positions. The entire probing offensive would amount to total and abject failure. General Joffre, the commander in chief of all French forces, threw a fit over Bonneau's obvious lack of offensive spirit and sacked him. The Battle of the Frontiers was far from over, but Mulhouse was back in German hands, where it would stay for the duration of the war.

Naval Pursuit in the Mediterranean Part 2
Central Mediterranean, August 3rd, 1914

(...) Goeben, offshore Philippeville Harbor (...)

The Battlecruiser Goeben was the second unit of the Moltke-class fast dreadnoughts of the Imperial German Navy (Kaiserliche Marine). Launched in 1912, it was one of the ships that made the German Emperor proud. Fast, sleek-looking, powerfully armed (11-inch guns) and well-armored.

Goeben was similar in design to the previous German battlecruisers, the Von der Tann Class, only it was an improved version, with better sped, more accurate range-finding guns and thicker armor.

Goeben was 25,555 tons at full load and thus packed a mean punch. Its guns were the excellent SK L/50 models, assembled in five twin-gun turrets for a total of ten; of these, one was placed forward, two were en echelon amidships, and the other two were in a super firing pair aft. It also sported powerful secondary guns and torpedo launch tubes. In short, it was one hell of a warship.

Thus, when it sailed just offshore the French-controlled Tunisian port of Philippeville on that fine day of August 1914, it was well-equipped to cause a ton of mayhem. The area was used by the French as a transit port to bring their colonial troops to Metropolitan France. Before Souchon received new orders to rally the Turks in Istanbul, places like Philippeville were Goeben's primary reason for being in the Mediterranean: to disrupt French naval transport to Metropolitan France in case of war.

"Fire," said Souchon with a wolfish smile. The small harbor before the Goeben was filled with transport ships, and the shells that exploded in fury from the German battlecruiser crashed amongst them, igniting large balls of fire.

Soon, the entire area was in mayhem, and large flames spread like wildfire. Earlier in the day, the Goeben and the Breslau had smashed the other small transit harbor of Bone. Satisfied, Souchon turned back to his people on the bridge. *"Helm, let's move us out of here,"* he said in a satisfied tone.

Souchon thought that things were all good, but he had no idea how dicey his journey would get on his way to Constantinople. The next day, the British Empire declared war on Germany, effectively morphing the situation from dangerous to disastrous. The entire Royal Navy Mediterranean Squadron was soon on the hunt for the two German warships.

(...) British Mediterranean Fleet, August 4th (...)

The German Mediterranean squadron's new heading was taking it toward the Royal Navy's task force, which cruised not far south of Italy. As far as Admiral Souchon was aware, the British were still neutral. Officially, they were. But in secret, they were getting ready to declare war on the Germans on August 5th.

Vice-Admiral Sir Archibald Berkeley Milne (the commander of the British Mediterranean Squadron) had received orders from London instructing him to find and track the soon-to-be-enemy ships since their breakout from Pola and into the Mediterranean on August 1st. But his orders were quite clear that he was not to engage in any way.

This state of affairs, combined with Milne's lack of initiative without clear instructions, saved Souchon and his ships from certain destruction. As the Royal Navy warships sailed toward Algeria, they were completely surprised to run into the Goeben and the Breslau's path sailing on a bearing straight for them. The Germans were returning from their quick raid in Philippeville, but Milne had not been notified of the deed, nor was he inclined to attack the soon-to-be enemy.

As they moved past each other, seemingly oblivious to their counterpart and without trying the customary peacetime salute, both fleets watched intently, with their guns cocked and ready to return fire if they were attacked. It was a very tense moment, but nothing came out of it save a few scares on both sides.

After passing the Kaiserliche Marine ships, the Indomitable and the Indefatigable battlecruisers were ordered to turn about and pursue the Germans. At four in the afternoon, Admiral Souchon sent orders down to his engine room to accelerate to battle speed in order to distance himself from the Brits.

His vessels soon started to pull away from the Royal Navy battlecruiser, but the intense speed tempo overheated the coal stokers (coal shovelers), many losing consciousness in front of the heat furnaces. As the German dreadnought got to full speed, machinery started to break down, and eventually, a partially ruptured steam pipe blew out, sending incredibly hot steam, killing seven sailors and four stokers. Goeben's speed then noticeably slowed down, but it was able to make it to safety in the neutral port of Messina. The Italians were part of the Triple Alliance but so far had wanted no part in the diplomatic wranglings concerning the burgeoning conflict and thus were not very pleased with Souchon's appearance in their harbor with a British fleet offshore.

The next morning, war was declared between the German Empire and Great Britain. Since Italy was still neutral, the Royal Navy commander, Vice-Admiral Milne, had to withdraw to international waters to avoid an international incident that could lead to Italy joining the Central Powers.

Both of his battlecruisers (Inflexible and Indefatigable), were were ordered to cover the northern shore of the strait, and cruiser Gloucester moved south to cut the othee escape route. Battlecruiser Indomitable was moved to Bizerte to get more coal instead of to Malta, which would soon have unintended consequences for the Entente trying to catch Souchon. The

British had not yet figured out what the Germans wanted to do and had no real idea Souchon was about to make a run for Istanbul. From Milne's point of view, Souchon's only option was either the Adriatic or Gibraltar and escape into the Atlantic Ocean. He was about to be surprised.

The Fall of Fort Barchon
The 4th Imperial Division assaults, August 12th, 1914

(…) Overall battle against the Liege Forts (…)

While the German infantry battered at the Liege Forts, a more amenable solution was on the way from Germany in the form of all the big guns the OHL could find. Everything that could be done had been done by the 2nd and 3rd Army during the last seven days. The gist of the matter was that it would take weeks to reduce the damned Belgian positions, and the OHL didn't have weeks.

The Germans had infiltrated the zones between the forts, stormed the trenches, and even encircled the forts themselves. Liege was also in German hands. But the forts themselves refused to surrender, and the Schlieffen plan's success relied on having control of the road they blocked to use it to move all the supplies they needed. The rapid execution of their outflanking maneuver in Northern France depended on it.

On the 12th of August, the Germans rolled one of the biggest guns in their large arsenal. The weapon was so impressive that it was even given a name. The nicknamed "Big Bertha," a 420mm gun, started firing its 500-kilo shells at the fort, with impressive (and shattering) results. The Austrians also sent a battery of 305 mm Skoda Mörser M. 11 mortars, with equally encouraging results for the Central Powers. The guns were already in Germany because they were on loan from the Austro-Hungarian government to the Germans, who knew they would need them for their Schlieffen Plan.

The road-transportable heavy artillery finally arrived near Liège, having taken two days to travel the eleven miles from the German border. Their travel was impeded by the Belgian demolition of railway tunnels and repeated mechanical breakdowns. In the early evening, one of the two monster Krupp 420 mm guns was set up to bombard Fort Pontisse north of the city.

At 6:30 PM, the gun crew (at a safe distance of 300 yards) fired the gun at Fort Pontisse for the first time. The shell traveled the two miles to the fort in sixty seconds but fell short.

Adjusting the aim of the gun, the crew slowly "walked up" the shells to the fort, firing about once every six minutes. The eighth shell hit the fort itself, doing considerable damage. The gun then ceased firing for the night but had found the appropriate range and would be ready to begin demolishing the fort in the morning, along with the other Krupp 420 which would also be in place. The eight Skoda 305s, borrowed from the Austrians, simultaneously were set up and began to open fire on the other forts ringing Liège.

The next day, the demolition work began, and Fort Pontisse would fall by the end of the next day. Within a few more days, the rest of the forts would fall.

(…) Belgian soldier Fort of Barchon (…)

Belgian soldier and machine gunner Jean Barries was getting worried. For the last hour, the big enemy shells had been creeping up toward his fort as the German and Austro-Hungarian gunners tried to find the range.

He knew what had happened first to Fort Pontisse and then to others, as they could tell the Central Power's big shells had exploded everywhere around them. The ground shook with light tremors every time one of the big shells fell on the ground.

Now, it would soon be the turn of his own position. He had not seen any German soldiers for days now, the enemy troops content to wait for their wonder weapons to do the job they couldn't do.

The characteristic whistling sound of the large shells flying over the fort was heard again. In fact, it was multiple whistling sounds. He figured that the enemy had decided Fort Barchon was the next target. He looked at his friends Edmond and Jacques. Both of them had the same resigned expression.

And then, two of Big Bertha's shells landed on top of the fort, and Jean's world rocked as if a volcano had exploded. Followed in quick succession, the shells from the Skoda 305s and the entire structure exploded in a fury worthy of the god of war of ancient legends.

Soon, a large billowing cloud of dust filled the corridors, and the bunker the trio of machine gunners was in started to crumble down on them. Jean was confused, and when the last salvo of rounds hit the fort, he was completely buried in what would be his grave.

(...) Private Soldier Dantz, Infanterie-
Regiment Graf Schwerin (...)

Oskar Dantz watched the numerous and powerful shells with glee. The things landed on Fort Barchon like the hammer of Thor himself. The blasts they produced were deafening and blinding, catapulting reinforced concrete, smoke, and dust in the air.

He could not help but yell with excitement as a quartet of four Skoda gun shells landed in quick succession on the crest of the fort. They blossomed with light and fire, obliterating the part of the fort he'd been trying to assault since the 5th of August. *"Let's go, you maggot,"* yelled one of the NCOs near him, *kicking a couple of the soldiers into action. "Get your gear ready and check your Mauser rifles. It's almost time to assault this fort and kill the bastards!"* Oskar gripped his weapon and steeled his resolve. He hoped the artillery had destroyed most of the dreadful machine gun positions, otherwise he might not survive the day.

(...) Overall battle against the Liege Forts (...)

The last of the forts surrendered on the 16th of August following very heavy fighting. While gutted and conquered, they had achieved the purpose of why they were built. They slowed down the Kaiser's armies, gave time to the French to organize and the Belgian Army to muster and assemble near Brussels, and gave the German Army a bloody nose.

Naval Pursuit in the Mediterranean Part 3
Battle of Cape Matapan, August 7th, 1914

When Souchon left Messina (following a few days of trying to get coal to refuel from the reluctant Italians), he was shadowed by the cruiser Gloucester, who could not face it in direct battle because it was too small. The German ships left under the guise of darkness, but there was a full moon; thus, the British ship was able to see and follow the Kaiserliche Marine vessels. The commander of the British vessel reported that the two German ships' heading did not appear to be the Adriatic or the Western Mediterranean. Instead, it looked like Souchon was going deeper east toward the Aegean Sea. Captain Troubridge (the Captain of the Gloucester) decided to head toward Greece at full speed, hoping to intercept the Goeben and Breslau to give enough time to the squadron's battlecruisers to catch up. The remainder of the Mediterranean Fleet (Admiral Milne) got the message and steamed eastward to try and intercept the Germans.

The shadowing went on for a full day, by which time both countries were at war. Souchon, knowing full well that with a British ship shadowing him, he would never shake the enemy pursuit, decided to make a stand off the coast of Greece at Cape Matapan.

Cape Matapan was the southernmost tip of mainland Greece and, thus, a logical place for Souchon to sail by as he headed for Istanbul. At about midday, the Goeben and the Breslau veered hard to port and to starboard in a wide circling move to kill their forward momentum and present their broadsides to the British cruiser. With Gloucester's lookouts taking their own time in understanding the extreme danger of the German maneuver for their ship, it was too late to do anything about the fact that Gloucester had got its T crossed.

In naval terminology, crossing the T of an enemy is when one has maneuvered his force so that his own line of ships can fire their full broadsides at an enemy line that is essentially perpendicular to his own (so resembling the shape of the letter T).

In the case of the beginning engagement, it meant that Gloucester could only reply with its forward-facing guns while the Goeben and the Breslau could fire with all of theirs. Within moments, the situation was completely reversed. The British went from hunters to hunted.

Goeben fired in anger at another ship for the first time in its career, and it was a magnificent sight. Its ten main 11-inch SK L/50 guns exploded in a blossoming fury of fire and steel. The German battlecruiser's first shot straddled the Gloucester, spraying water on its deck. Breslau continued to close in as its armament had less range. The Gloucester returned fire on Goeben and also missed by about the same margin as its opponent. The shells exploded just off the bow in a spectacular spray of foam and towering columns of water.

A few minutes into the exchange, Captain Troubridge tried to maneuver his ship out of the way and retreat toward the Greek coast, but the Breslau was able to flank it on that side, and the cruiser was trapped. And then disaster struck for the British. Four rounds of Goeben's 11-inch rounds slammed into the funnels and the funnel room and on the central part of the ship. A gigantic explosion rocked the smaller Royal Navy cruiser, and then a few moments later, a secondary explosion, this time larger than the 11-inch shell hits, blazed across the ship's deck, sending a long and dark column of smoke in the air. A gazillion pieces of debris flew from the stricken ship in every direction, showering down on the blue water of the Adriatic Sea.

Dead in the water and with most of its crew either dead or incapacitated, the Gloucester never saw the full broadside from Breslau that hit it, thus igniting the final cataclysmic blast to obliterate it from existence.

For a long time, Souchon and his men stared at the viewport, amazed at the result. Then someone cheered, and then the entire bridge erupted in raucous yells of enthusiasm.

Looking for more coal, the two German ships soon sailed out of the battle's vicinity in order to avoid any additional British ships and also because a rendezvous with a collier had been arranged near Greece. Coal-fired boilers where efficient, but it was quite easy to burn through a ship's supply when maintaining a high speed of battle tempo. Unlike oil in the next war to come, coal limited ship design range and made them easier to detect because of the dense smoke their funnels produced.

Stokers (also known as firemen) fed the monstrous boilers with shovels, and it was a hellish job. Most of the ships during the First World War were coal-fired, except for the Royal Navy, which had already started to switch to oil. Coaling stations were thus needed if a navy wanted to sail far and wide. The Germans didn't have the Royal Navy's world-spanning Empire dotted with coaling stations everywhere along a fleet's route. The Kaiserliche Marine thus employed allied ports or transport colliers for its ship to dock beside them and refuel at sea.

The coaling operation was done off the coast of a small uninhabited island in the Adriatic, during which time the German ships lost precious time. The coal collier, called the Cormoran, did its best to fill the two German ship's holds, and then Goeben and Breslau got underway once more. By then, Admiral Milne rounded the Greek island of Crete from the south and steamed northward in an attempt to intercept the German ships in the Aegean. The British Admiral had split his fleet into several parts, and he commanded the battlecruisers Indomitable and the Indefatigable.

One day later, they would be the ones facing the dreaded Goeben and its consort.

The Battle of the Frontier Part 2
Plan XVII and the French attack, August 7th, 1914.

While rebuffed and defeated during his first attempt at an attack across the border as per his plans, General Joffre kept the course with his dear Plan XVII. The goal to reclaim the Alsace and Lorraine Province was relaunched on the 14th of August, the moment he felt all of his forces were assembled for the attack. The French armies thus marched on the cities of Sarrebourg and Morhange.

The 1st French Army advanced with his troops through the Vosges and in the direction of the city of Sarrebourg, while the 2nd French Army (attacked just north of the 1st. Morhange in echelon to guard against a German attack from Metz, since not doing so would expose the french flanks to a dangerous enemy counterstroke.

By then, the German attack on Liege was drawing to a close, and the 1st and 3rd Armies had started to spill west of Liege and through the Ardennes. There was enough subject matter there to start getting worried, but General Joffre continued to discount reports of enemy movements in that area, instead keeping fixated on his own attack plans. His logic was that the Germans could advance on the northern flank all they wanted; if he broke through in Alsace Lorraine, then they would have to double back and defend, thus stopping their offensive into Belgium. To him, it was a simple matter to solve.

German 6th and 7th Armies barred the way of the French offensive, resolute in their stand. As per Moltke's defensive plans for the area, the German troops executed a flawless fighting withdrawal and took their own darn time in making the French advance as slow as possible. It was a *"bend instead of break"* type of maneuver. Joffre exulted, but reality would soon come to slap him back in the face. The Germans were far from defeated, and Joffre should have known better.

For several days, the Kaiser's armies continued to retreat, albeit slowly, fighting light skirmishes but not making any hard stand against the French advance. At the height of the French drive, some of their units went as deep as twenty-eight miles over the border and into Germany proper. A German regimental flag was taken and much fuss was made about it, Joffre asking to see it in person. It was brought at his field HQ (Vitry-le-François), and he made a solemn show about it, telling his staff officers that this was the result of French "élan" and offensive spirit.

The towns of Château-Salins, the Dieuze, and finally, on the 18th of August, Sarrebourg, were taken. Across all of France, the French people rejoiced in these territories. But then, the German forces snapped the lid shut and hardened their defensive positions. The party was over for France

Having received important reinforcements, Crown Prince Rupprecht (heir to the Bavarian crown) launched a powerful counterattack against his enemy on August 20th. What followed was an intense fight between the German and French corps over possession of the newly-"french liberated" towns. The French 8th Corps (in the River Saar near Sarrebourg) was overwhelmed; its artillery was outmatched by heavier enemy guns, and the German infantry used the opportunity of having a powerful shell umbrella to drive the French out of the area.

Heavy German guns did even worse damage to the 2nd French Army, struck by a concentrated bombardment along its whole front at dawn on the 20th of August. The 15th French and 16th Corps moved out of their positions under the infantry attacks that followed. Some of the French units did, however, hold firm and fight well. They were defending the French countryside and were commanded by General Ferdinand Foch, a military leader of exceptional talent and determination. While Foch soldiers clung on and fought like demons, the rest of the Army broke off contact and retreated to the Meurthe, the line from which it had begun its advance six days earlier. The Germans had nearly outflanked it, which would have resulted in irretrievable disaster to the entire Anglo-French position.

A little to the north and closer to Verun, Belgium, and the Ardennes, the French 3rd, 4th, and 5th Armies were supposed to launch their own offensive, but these plans were postponed because of momentous events with the Germans executing their Schlieffen Plan and starting to spill out of Belgium. On August 15th, after urging General Lanrezac (commander of the 5th Army) to move northward to intercept the Germans, engage, and destroy them, Joffre started to see the enormity of the problem he would soon have to face.

Seeking to gain the initiative and still only wanting to attack and avoid defense, Joffre directed the 3rd and 4th Armies to advance through the German-occupied Ardennes. Attacking on August 21st, they moved right up to face the German 4th and 5th Armies. A brief but intense day-long battle was fought and the French were beaten back, again because of superior German artillery, already unlimbered and ready for them, while the French guns were nowhere to be seen in great numbers. In the following two days, General Joffre tried to rekindle the forward movement of his troops and attack again, but his exhausted and beaten-back soldiers returned to their original lines a couple of days later. It was as if the French had never advanced.

While all of this happened, the British Army was getting ready to get into play. The British Army (BEF) had arrived via ships in Calais and was starting to be railed southward. General Joffre contacted Field Marshal French to move near the French 5th Army of General Lanrezac and to take a position to intercept the rampaging German forces.

On the eve of the twin battles of Charleroi and Mons, where the true urgency of the situation would then dawn on the Anglo-French, Joffre was forced by events to call a halt to his offensive attacks in Alsace-Lorraine. Casualties were very heavy, and he now had to give some serious attention to German movements in Belgium that would soon spill into Northeastern France.

Armand Bonnier
Morhange, August 20th, 1914

Private soldier Armand Bonnier was firing one round after the other at the enemy troops advancing in the farm field before him. His mouth tasted the acrid smoke produced by his Lebel rifle and the ones beside him. He was now up north and had participated, since August 14th, in the French attack toward the center. The war had started well for him and his comrade. They had won quick victories in ChâteauSalins, Dieuze, and Sarrebourg. He remembered those days fondly, but now they were but a distant memory since the situation was reversed, and it seemed the Germans had the initiative and were constantly attacking.

He was now in a small village named Morhange. Morhange was not merely a geographic location; it was the symbol of a complex past that interwove the destinies of two great powers: France and Germany. It was a legacy of the Franco-Prussian war, a grim reminder of the scars that the past had inflicted and the catalyst of a colossal clash that was to transpire. The French wanted it back, as it was stolen from them in 1871. The Germans had no intention to give any of it back. The battle that was raging was a testament to both side's sentiments.

The man right beside him was slammed with a German bullet right in the forehead and was pushed hard backward, but not before spraying brain matter and blood all over him and other French soldiers. *"Steady!"* said a Lieutenant just behind them as he saw some of the men wavering, as more and more of them were getting hit. Armand retched and almost threw up. He only kept his food in because he hadn't eaten in several hours.

He'd heard that the German counterattack was led by units of the Bavarian Royal Army under the command of Crown Price Rupprecht. The bastard looked different than the field gray of the Prussians he'd seen in the battle of Mulhouse. The most notable difference he'd seen on the dead bodies was the Feldmutze, the field cap. There were two circular cockades on it. The top was red, black, and white for Germany, but the bottom one was different for the Bavarians; it was blue. The Bavarian soldiers also had different buttons and belt buckles than the Prussian soldiers. The Prussians had an eagle, and the Bavarians had a lion insignia. He shook his head and wondered why he was thinking about such an unimportant detail at such a moment. He figured that it was some trick his mind was playing to keep him sane.

Since the start of the war, he'd seen so much horror and death to last a lifetime. And from the looks of it, it was only the beginning. If he lived, he suspected he would go through a lot worse. Or maybe it would get better over time? He just didn't know.

Reloading his Lebel, he then leveled it back on the sandbag and aimed. The Bavarians were getting very close, and he could sense his comrades' nervousness. The lieutenant and the other officers behind the makeshift trench line (they'd dug them very shallowly as they didn't have enough time to make proper defenses) were getting nervous at the unsteadiness of the soldiers and the enemy approaching.

The maelstrom of explosions, bullets zipping by, and the sight of the dead on the ground made a heavy, dark impression on the brave French soldiers, now outnumbered. They had faced this for hours on end, and they felt like they would all die in this dreadful place. Armand had no idea how he would keep up with the unrelenting tempo of battle.

They were eventually ordered to move backward as the position they defended was about to be outflanked and overwhelmed. The next hour was a myriad of actions, fighting and dying.

After a few more, Armand was out of Morhange as the French defenses had been completely shattered. As the fighting had devolved into street-to-street fighting and hand-to-hand combat, the German forces attacked relentlessly, pushing their French counterparts ever-backward. Only the murderous French artillery fire checked them as shell upon shell landed within their ranks.

They pushed hard with their bayonet-tipped rifles, and the defenders buckled, unsure of what they should choose between retreating or defending in place. Many officers were either dead or didn't know what else to do, as they were themselves without instruction from divisional command. The fields were covered in the bodies of the French dead and wounded.

Armand remembered the moment quite well. The moment he and his comrades had thrown their sanity to the wind. It was like a collective madness had gripped the French soldiers defending Morhange. One instant, they were fighting, going through the motions of obeying their officers, firing, reloading, and marching. The next, they were running, following some sort of mad rush backward. Armand didn't understand why they were going back and running, but he followed all the same, the situation in front not enticing to look at anyway. The Germans had only been too happy to push even harder as all forms of resistance crumbled to nothing.

Coupled with the fact that the Bavarian units were exhausted after hours of fighting, the French artillery was finally able to stop the irresistible German attack and

The French Alsace offensive was broken after the Battle for Morhange, and the entire line switched to the defensive as the focus (and the future of France) shifted to the Franco-Belgian border, where the first German units burst out and attacked.

Naval Pursuit in the Mediterranean Part 4
The Battle of Denusa, August 8th, 1914

"Open fire!" said British Admiral Milne. Indefatigable main batteries erupted as she poured fire at the German battlecruiser Goeben at 1,600 yards. The rainy sky and stormy sea became awash with tracers and heavy shells fired from both ships that were at close range. Rain was somewhat rare in these latitudes, but today, Mother Nature had decided it would have its say in the battle between the two British battlecruisers (Indefatigable and Indomitable) against Admiral Souchon's Mediterranean task force (Goeben and Breslau).

A salvo from the Entente ship immediately struck the Goeben. The British battlecruiser's broadside did little structural damage to the German vessel because its guns were loaded with explosives instead of armor-piercing shells. Regardless, it still wounded several sailors while shattering the deck with death and destruction. It also started a large fire that burned bright even in the relentless rain. On the Kaiserliche Marine ship's bridge, everyone, including Admiral Souchon, was knocked over and fell down on the steel deck. Most were in for a few bruises.

Not missing a beat, Goeben's main guns shattered Indefatigable armored sides, igniting large fires and internal explosions. The bow of the British warship buckled inward, and its forward-most turret blew up in a spectacular column of fire, smoke, and debris showering the sea all around the ship.

Breslau, engaged with Indomitable, did not fare as well as her consort. It was straddled by a few salvos from the powerful enemy ship and was able to land a few shots, igniting a fire on Indomitable. But when it received its first salvo, the rounds tore through her armored shell and created serious damage on the ship. The boiler room exploded with the impact, and the hull was cracked in several places. The ship came to an abrupt stop while fire blossomed across its deck, and smoke clouded the

British gunner's vision.

This battle was particularly violent because the ships fought at such close ranges. They could not really miss with these kinds of distances, even if the rain and bad weather blocked their view and spotting capabilities. From the moment Souchon had stopped for some much-needed coaling if he wanted to go the distance to Constantinople, the likelihood of a naval battle had been all but unavoidable for the Germans. Milne, the British Admiral, wasn't the best of naval officers but was just aggressive enough to get his ships in position, and then both sides' gunners and rangefinders did the rest.

The two task forces had spotted each other almost at the same time near a Greek island called Denusa. It was located 10 miles east of the island of Naxos and about 16 mi north of Amorgos. It was a small place (5.31 square miles), and its population was below 200. But it was destined to have its name in the history books because of the soon-to-be-famous battle raging off its shore. After all, it was the first official naval battle of the First World War.

The four ships fighting in a large and powerful storm was something to behold, and it created weird battle conditions. The next salvo from the Indomitable missed Goeben because the German ship had suddenly dipped in between two titanic waves. It was by no intentional maneuvers from the Kaiserliche skipper, but it saved the German warship from further harm. It was good old blind, naked luck that Goeben seemed to enjoy since the start of this adventure a few days before. The shells thus impacted the waves and exploded harmlessly.

The German battlecruiser prepared to fire its next salvo heading on a northeasterly course to try and vacate the area as it was firing at the British ships. All the while, Indomitable finished off the Breslau, who rapidly sank as it burned. At least, Souchon thought as he saw the burning hulk of his consort in the distant, rain-battered horizon; the light cruiser was helping his own ship escape. It put the Indomitable out of position to continue the battle as it would soon be too far.

As the Goeben crested over the giant rolling waves once more, the ship's gunners and range finders saw the enemy battlecruiser's superstructure in the distance and fired. Their aim was affected by the bobbing of the large wave, and the shells thundered well above the Royal Navy vessel.

The Indefatigable also fired a full salvo, but the distance between the two ships was increasing and missed yet again, firing well over the Germans.

Lady Luck wasn't done for the day and decided to give a little help to Souchon and his men. The forward turret fired a one-in-a-million shot and smashed right on the Indefatigable. "A hit!" yelled Souchon from his bridge as he saw the large ball of fire blossom briefly in the rain. The two shells from the turret smashed right onto the central island tower, plowing into the bridge and killing everyone there, including the captain of the ship. All the ship's control instruments were also obliterated.

He had a bleeding forehead that had spilled down his white uniform in a dirty red smear, a result of his fall minutes earlier. He looked like hell but had refused to go down and see a medic. One was on the way to the bridge to try and treat him as he directed the battle for survival his ship was fighting. Conditions on the German ship were less than ideal. Damaged and rocked by the storm, and with its deck splashed by high explosive shells, it was anything but looking brand-new. Added to his boiler problems, the ship would need some time in drydock eventually. The medics had not yet been able to make it to the bridge because of these reasons thus, Admiral Souchon endured without complaining.

As he was about to order a full broadside to finish off the stricken ship, the lookout officer yelled out of his lungs: "Captain! Large enemy ships spotted 2,000 meters to starboard! The lookouts think it's a battleship or yet another battlecruiser with many escort vessels!" A cold chill ran down the German admiral's spine. His vessel could not hope to match that much firepower. He reacted. *"Helm, what's our current speed?"* *"Sir, we are at 19 knots. Our boiler problems continue, and the choppy sea does not help."*

He turned in the direction the enemy ship had been spotted, just in time to see the telltale sign of a ship firing. The battlecruiser Invincible, heading the rest of the British Mediterranean Fleet, had fired three of its nine 12-inch guns at the Goeben. The ship continued to bob and slide on the large waves, and that saved it. The Royal Navy salvo exploded harmlessly where the ship had been a moment before. The dodge was no fault of the Kaiserliche Marine sailors; it was the storm making their ship an impossible target to hit.

"Full speed ahead! We need to get out of the area!" On the bridge of the newcomer battlecruiser Invincible, Captain Arthur Lindesay tried to stay calm and composed in the face of the enemy. *"Sir,"* said one of his bridge officers. *"The lookouts report that the enemy ship is increasing the distance between us. They also confirm it is the Goeben."*

"What of the Indefatigable and Admiral Milne? Have the signal people been able to raise them?" he asked in return. He was worried about the fate of his task force commander. After all, he'd seen the gigantic explosion during his approach: *"The battlecruiser is dead in the water, but an officer named Edelsten says he will be all right and should have the fire under control within the hour. He, however, confirms that the Admiral and everyone on the bridge are dead."* Lindesay's face darkened at the bad news. *"Very well. Send him my regards and tell him that we will dispatch some help."* *"Yes, sir,"* answered the junior officer. *"What do we do about the Goeben? It's escaping."*

Lindesay took some time to answer, hesitating. *"Sir,"* insisted the bridge officer, eager for orders. Time was of the essence, and the British commander knew he wouldn't have much time to destroy the enemy ship.

Already the distance was widening in between shots, and the damned German was very hard to hit because of the storm. *"Sir, the gunnery rooms all report that they have optimal fire but that the enemy vessel keeps stepping out of their given line of fire."* Lindesay ground his teeth. *"Just tell them to continue; we're bound to hit the bastards."* *"Yes, sir."* Lindesay then continued with more orders. *"Order all the destroyers in the fleet to render assistance to the Indefatigable.*

The two ship's dance of death continued while Indefatigable burned bright in the background, and the last part of the Breslau slid beneath the choppy waters. The distance continued to increase without Invincible being able to score a significant hit. Several near misses rocked the German ship hard, but nothing serious.

After several minutes, the range was getting near to the Royal Navy's guns maximum effectiveness, and Lindesay started to despair of catching the enemy ship. *"Where are you going, you bastard,"* he said, trying to figure out why Admiral Souchon was speeding up north toward the coast of Macedonia or... toward the Turkish Straits?

The storm increased in intensity as if the God of War did not want Goeben to be caught up. The combination of heavy rain and sea-level clouds caused Invincibles' lookouts to lose sight of the stricken Kaiserliche Marine.

A few hours later, Admiral Souchon was able to shake off his pursuer and head at best speed toward the Dardanelles and safety. The Goeben was let through by the Ottoman government, already in negotiation with Germany to join the

Central Powers.

By the time Goeben made it to the Turkish Straits entrance, columns of smoke from the British ships were visible on the horizon. Souchon, uncertain of how the Turks would respond, requested a pilot to be sent to the forts guarding the entrance (the old fortress of Kumkale on the Asian shore and the equally aging fort of Seddulbahir on the European side). After some tense discussion the Turkish commander decided to allow him through after he got things cleared up with the Ottoman leadership in Istanbul. In the same vein, the Royal Navy ships also tried to gain access to the Straits to continue their pursuit but were denied. The chase was done and over with.

In order to avoid any diplomatic problems (since the Turks were still neutral, after all) and anyway because they had agreed on giving the ships in exchange for the Ottomans to join the war, the German ambassador in Istanbul officially transferred ownership of the Goeben to the Turkish Navy.

Souchon and his men were also allowed to stay on the Goeben and to continue to handle the battlecruiser as the Ottomans didn't have the trained sailors to operate the great modern warship anyway. All of their newly trained personnel had gone into the two new dreadnoughts battleship's the Sultan's forces received a few months earlier from the British.

CHAPTER 2
THE WAR IN THE EAST
AND THE BALKANS

"For the first time in 150 years, German and Russian soldiers clashed in battle. The Russians proved they were good soldiers. Steady under fire, courageous, and hard to kill, they are well disciplined, well trained, and possess the same kind of modern weapons as our troops. This is not going to be easy.

German Colonel Rudolph Franz, in a message to the 8th Army high command following a skirmish with Russian troops on August 21st, 1914

Austro-Hungarian 21st Landwehr Division
The Battle of Cer, August 15th, 1914

Serbia's border with Austria-Hungary was surrounded by three rivers (the Save, the Rina, and the Danube). Directly behind stood the high mountains and rugged ground of the Serbian countryside. The entire area formed a powerful defensive setup for the Serbs. And the small nation had no intention of bowing to the giant arrogant empire just to their north. They would fight and fight dearly.

The last few years had been good for the Serbs, with two successful Balkan wars in 1912 and 1913. The Serbian troops were well armed, if not superbly equipped. They didn't have the modern guns the Austro-Hungarians had, but they were battle-hardened troops. After the assassination in Sarajevo, Radomir Putnik (the commander of the Serbian Army) expected an attack by the hated northern enemy and had thus positioned his troops accordingly.

The Chief of the Austro-Hungarian General Staff, Conrad von Hotzendorf, wanted to attack the Serbs with three full armies but was not permitted to do so by the Germans, who called in a favor for the Austrians to attack in Galicia to relieve some of the pressure on Eastern Prussia (by this time, the Russian offensive in East Prussia was in full swing). Austro-Hungary thus launched the attack on Serbia with only two armies, and that would prove to be insufficient.

It was in this setting that a Private soldier from Prague, Helmut Gottenburg of the 21st Landwehr Division, crossed the Drina River on the 13th of August. Two days later, they were approaching one more shabby-looking Serbian town called Valjevo, and Helmut was hungry. The unit had received little food and almost no water. Their commander (General Potiorek) was not the best logistician and had decided to disregard difficulties with roads and terrain. His plan – an overwhelming attack in western Serbia, rather than in the north, through Belgrade -- ignored complications of rugged terrain and lack of supply routes.

The result was exhausted, hungry, and hot soldiers attacking and marching uphill in 95 Fahrenheit temperatures carrying packs of 20 to 30 kg on empty stomachs. Helmut was grumpy like most of his comrades, and the outlook wasn't good.

The 8th Regiment (which he was part of) was positioned on the slopes of Cer Mountain, near the city of Valjevo, and he and his comrades were at the tip of the spear. They were the furthest soldiers in front of the Austro-Hungarian advance in Serbia. Helmut could tell things were shaky, as there were no real artillery units with them, while he knew the enemy was waiting for them near. He didn't feel like the entire invasion had been planned or else organized. The entire endeavor seemed to be one improvisation after the other.

Cer was a mountain in western Serbia, 18 miles from the city of Sabac and 70 miles to the west of Belgrade, and the entire area was heavily wooded. It was rich in the Turkey oak trees, and Helmut looked up at the peculiar branches above him, lost in thoughts.

As he busied himself trying to figure out the peculiar shape of one of the leaves ruffling in the light wind, it was snapped in two by a whistling bullet, and its too shattered parts scattered in the air. For a moment, his mind didn't register what was happening, but then whistling sounds started to fill the air. He instinctively ducked into the shallow trench he'd dug with his comrades of the 8th Regiment.

The unit had dug its trenches in the area as it was sloped and looked down on the valley floor below. Brown shapes were making their way up toward the Austro-Hungarian positions. A lot of brown shapes. Helmut was no expert and hadn't gone to school for long, but he could see that the number of enemy soldiers coming at them was too great. They all yelled a peculiar sound and fired as they moved forward.

Then, the first artillery shells started to land in their midst, and the ground shook like crazy. The Serbian army fielded the modern "French 75 1897", a fast-firing anti-personnel cannon that did not require re-aiming after each shot. It was the best of what the French had on the Western Front as well, and the weapon would go down in history as one of the best field guns of the First World War.

Austro-Hungarians did not have anything similar in their inventory and, in fact, did not have artillery in numbers anywhere near sufficient to offset the Serbian's superiority in artillery on the battlefield. Helmut could not see the French 75 below the slope but could tell they were used as direct-fire weapons since they were fired from point-blank range. The combination of soldiers charging, thousands of bullets whipping above their heads, and the explosions of the French 75 guns had a deadly effect on the Austro-Hungarian soldiers, who started to die in droves, but it shattered their already low morale and willingness to fight.

At that critical moment when they should have stood their ground, the main weakness of the K.u.K Army (K.u.K. stood for kaiserlich und königlich, in English: imperial and royal) was revealed. While the unit Helmut was part of was mainly ethnic Germans (the 21st Landwehr Division), most of the remainder of the invasion army of Serbia was a multi-ethnic hodgepodge of nationalities. There were Serbs and Croats from Bosnia and Croatia, Czechs from Bohemia, and other Slav nationalities. Many had been mobilized by force, and equally, many were not truly motivated to fight against Serbia or to fight at all.

And so, most of the non-German units broke and ran. They were hungry, badly led, without proper artillery support, and attacking through difficult terrain.

For his part, Helmut soon started to see the backward movements of many of the soldiers in the Austro-Hungarian line and was swept in the panic of the rout. Within minutes, the entire K.u.K. defensive position disintegrated and fell back.

(...)

A few days later, the entire K.u.K. invasion army was back over the Drina with severe losses to show for itself. The Serbs had just won the first Allied victory of the war and stunned the world with an upset no one had thought possible.

The Battle of Gumbinnen
The Russian Offensive in East Prussia August 20th, 1914

The artillery opened up with an ear-splitting noise and started to shatter Germans running and charging the field of battle. For the attacking soldiers, the entire area transformed into a maelstrom of blasts of fire and shrapnel. The well-arranged lines of grey-uniformed soldiers were torn to pieces, bloodied, and tossed about like rag dolls. In several sectors, the advance was shattered, and deaths amounted to thousands and then ten thousand. For hours on end, the shelling lasted, and it seemed to the poor grunts on the ground that the world had ended.

Suddenly, the shattering noise of the guns stopped since the Russians ran out of ammo. Finally freed from the blasting out of the enemy artillery, the German 1st Corps moved ahead and attacked the Russian 28th Division, decimating it in the process. The Battle of Gumbinnen had started.

The Russian invasion of East Prussia was two days old, and the fight was already inside the Second Reich. The ambitious Russian war plan envisioned nothing less than a double envelopment and the complete destruction of the German forces in Eastern Prussia. With the majority of the Kaiser's army tied up in the west, the capture of the eastern parts of the German Empire would be a critical blow to the enemy. The Russians were still a long way from Berlin, but with enough luck and aggressiveness, there was a chance they could pull it off and storm the German capital while most of their troops were engaged in the West.

Close to twenty days ago, a state of war was declared between the Russian and German Empire. Both sides had been enthusiastic and had clamored for their respective sovereign as they'd declared war from their palace balcony.

Both countries had their plans. The German's analysis was that Russia would take six weeks to mobilize and get going. But the

Russians had decided not to cooperate.

Completely derailing the German plan, over three million Russian soldiers had crossed the border between Poland-Lithuania (into Eastern Prussia) and Galicia (in Austrian Poland). By the 19th of August, the situation was dire and the Germans had to try and stop the enemy offensive.

The paltry German 8th Army, under the command of General Maximilian von Prittwitz, could count on 205,000 men and about 1,500 guns for the defense of Germany's eastern borders against the Russians. It was a powerful force, but unfortunately for them, the Russians were bringing a lot more to the fight. Three times the numbers, in fact.

Russian General Paul von Rennenkampf's 2nd Army was made up of some 310,000 soldiers. His mission was to attack from Lithuania and head for Konigsberg while attacking any German forces foolish enough to cross their path. At the same time, the 1st Army, some 306,000 soldiers strong and under General Alexander Samsonov, launched an offensive from Poland, attacking in large outflanking moves around the Masurian Lakes. The general goal of that action was to outflank and get into the rear of the engaged German forces.

The Battle of Gumbinnen was initiated following a premature Germans counterattack toward the Russian 2nd Army under General Rennekampf. It wasn't a bad move on their part since they had to do something for the too-fast-advancing Russians. Following limited but encouraging initial success, the German forward impetus soon slowed down because the Russians kept fueling the battle line with fresh troops and outnumbered the attacking troops by a factor of four to five to one.

Some Kaiser's units tried to attack and press forward, and, out of several assaults, they succeeded in penetrating some of the enemy defenses, bayonet-charging their opponents. Blood flowed like a river, and both sides fought fiercely for victory.

While the Germans were well-trained and tough soldiers, the Russian peasant-soldier was one hell of a son-of-a-bitch gutter fighter. The shattered Germans were forced to give way one battle after the other. The shelling was so heavy (before the Russians ran out of ammo) that some of their formations never even got near the Russian lines. Some Tsarist shells landed on ammunition wagons, heightening the confusion and terror by igniting gigantic blasts of fire blossoming into larger-than-life fireballs. They only reached their enemies when the poor Russian logistics failed to resupply their numerous guns.

The Germans were tough, but not invincible and with limitless morale. They were beaten badly and eventually broke. At first, it was just a few scattered groups, but then whole units started to pull back.

The Russians were pushed hard in the battle's beginning, but by the end of the day, it became clear the fight would end up being a Russiam victory.

All across the border from Poland to Lithuania, the invading Russian armies went on a rampage of epic proportions, and General Maximilian von Prittwitz (the commander of the German 8th Army) was soon in real danger of being overwhelmed. In addition to the 2nd Army's victory at Gumbinnen, the First Army under General Samsonov spilled everywhere from the south, winning quick engagements at Offelsburg and Allenstein that left them masters of the towns.

Then, Nicolas II's troops were slowed down by their strenuous-at-best supply lines because of the Russian broad-gauge rail line. Russia did not have the same width for its trains and thus couldn't use the German ones once in East Prussia without having to widen them.

This widening of the gauge was mandatory prior to any rail lines in Europe could be used with Russian trains. This problem had been taken into account in pre-war planning, but that didn't mean it was easy to execute. It involved the movement of a large, technically capable workforce and equipment on the same trains that were supposed to be used to bring food and supplies to the fighting troops. In short, this was an opportunity for the Central Powers to take a breather.

And a breather they needed. The situation was quite desperate for them, and something would have to be done, or else things would continue to deteriorate.

The German defeat at Gumbinnen dropped a cold shower of worry in Berlin and at the OHL, which then had to do something about it and react in some way. Panic started spreading across East Prussia and the civilian population.

OHL, Berlin
German high command meets on the Eastern crisis, August 22nd, 1914.

"This is unacceptable," said Helmut von Moltke the Younger, chief of staff of the German Army, as he stormed into the room with the other members of the OHL. Everyone but the Emperor rose and gave him the military salute. He moved to the chair at the head of the large oak table in the map room they were all in and gestured them to sit. He had just hung up with the commander of the 8th Army, responsible for the defense of East Prussia and currently embroiled in heavy fighting against the Russians. He was getting weary of trying to prop up the man's morale.

With the lightning-speed offensive of the Russian 1st Army from Poland and of Rennenkamp's 2nd Russian Army's almost-stationary action toward Konigsberg (following the defeat in the Battle of Gumbinnen), General Prittwitz (the commander of the German 8th Army) ordered the troops to retreat hundreds of miles behind the Vistula. This meant that the man was abandoning over 150 miles of pristine Prussian territory to the enemy. *"That is unacceptable, General, if you may,"* countered the Kaiser, Wilhelm II. *"Maximilian von Prittwitz had just told me a few minutes ago that he was about to give the order for a general retreat behind the Vistula, Your Majesty."* The room suddenly went silent. These proud men could not comprehend nor accept the possibility of abandoning the cradle of the Prussian state, the very territory conquered over the Slavs by their ancestors, the famed Teutonic Knights.

The people present for the meeting of the OHL were the German Emperor, the Chief of the General Staff, Helmut von Moltke the Younger, and General Erich von Falkenhayn (Minister of War for the Reich). Hermann von Stein, the Quartermaster General (Generalquartiermeister in German), was also present since he would be the man to make things happen if troop movements were decided during the discussion.

The anxiety he conveyed to Moltke via telephone over his withdrawal decision had caught Moltke by surprise, but he was now back on his feet and ready to act. He'd also spoken with the Kaiser earlier in the day on his misgivings concerning von Prittwitz, and they'd already pegged a name if it was decided to replace him.

"I have decided upon a command change for the 8th Army to send reinforcements to the East, and the Emperor agrees." Eric Von Falkenhayn, Molkte's rival and the one most likely to replace him if a change was ever needed at OHL, spoke up. *"Well, General. I am all ears as to who you have chosen to replace him,"* he said with a thin smile.

"We will recall retired General Paul von Beneckendorff und von Hindenburg. The man is well-known in the army, a solid commander with a long and storied career. He has even fought in the Austro-Prussian and Franco-Prussian wars," countered Moltke, giving a quick look to the Kaiser, who nodded silently.

For once, Falkenhayn seemed in agreement with his rival. *"Well, I like it, General Moltke. It is even said the man has known the gardener of Frederic the Great himself."* As it seemed the matter would be approved since no one else spoke up, he continued. *"But, what and where, if I may, will you conjure up those reinforcements you mentioned you want to send to the East?"*

"I propose we transfer the 11th, 12th, and the Reserve Guard Corps along with the 8th Cavalry Division to the East immediately." The assembled generals in the room stirred uncomfortably. They all knew where those troops were at the moment. Quartermaster General Hermann von Stein spoke up. *"But General, I may say, aren't those units already engaged or about to be into the offensive in Northern France? These forces are needed to make sure we keep up our advances."*

General Moltke stayed silent for a moment, trying to convey his answer as best he could. He understood that General Prittwitz needed to be replaced and that the man had become almost unhinged in his fear and discouragement over the Russian offensive. But he could also not help to think about the defeat at the battle of Gumbinnen. For him, it was obvious reinforcements were necessary and that he urgently needed to take a sizeable portion of his offensive force in the West to defend Eastern Prussia.

He also knew he had the backing of the Kaiser. Eastern Prussia was where Prussia was born. It was the land of the legendary Teutonic Knights, the land of famous battles. It was the embodiment of the Germanic fight against the Slavic hordes. It could simply not be given away without a real fight.

"It is necessary to send them, or we will lose Eastern Prussia, and that cannot be permitted," he answered his audience confidently, giving a quick glance toward Wilhelm II to signal to Falkenhayn and the others not seemingly-so-excited-about-his-proposal that this was approved by their supreme commander.

But Falkenhayn had no intention of weakening the Schlieffen Plan and of letting this decision to reinforce the East slide by. *"I do not think this is a good idea. We should stick to the plan and let that new commander of yours fight it out with the Russians and win us some time to execute the Schlieffen Plan to its conclusion."* General Hermann von Stein nodded. *"I agree with General Falkenhayn,"* he said.

For the next twenty minutes, the men argued, and what came out of it since they could not agree was that Moltke deferred to the German Kaiser for a final decision, being confident that Wilhelm would continue to support him. But the German Emperor, always the ambivalent one, had listened to Falkenhayn's and von Stein's arguments and now wavered. What did it matter that people complained about the Russian invasion? Prussia could always be liberated at a later date once the French were destroyed and brought low. The most important strategic aspect here was to smash the French, and then they would have all the time in the world to move their troops to the East and finish the Russians.

"Your Majesty," said Molkte with a confident tone. *"The decision rests with you,"* he continued as he tried to force the issue. For a moment, the Kaiser stayed silent, not wanting to displease Falkenhayn or his chief of the general staff. And then he spoke.

"I know that we have a real problem in East Prussia, General Moltke, but at the same time, we are committed in France; thus, I agree with General Falkenhayn and von Stein. We keep the troops we have in the West, and we hope Hindenburg can stem the Russian tide."

And that was that. There would be no troop transfers to the East, and the Schlieffen Plan would continue as planned.

2nd Russian Army command
Three miles west of the town of Gumbinnen, August 22nd

General Paul von Rennenkampf, commander of the Russian 2nd Army, looked once more at the operational maps his staff had just updated for him following their victory at the Battle of Gumbinnen. As he basked in the glory of the first Russian military victory in a decade, he felt confident, yet he was weary.

Rennenkampf was a well-experienced officer, having fought in wars as far in the past as the one with China in 1900. During the Russo-Japanese War of 1904-1905, he commanded a cavalry division and showed enough bravery to be commended, and following the troubles of 1905, he went up in rank rapidly. He remembered the battle with the damned Japs quite well and had kept a form of hesitancy born out of a wish not to be too rash in his actions. His former commanders had not taken the eastern enemies seriously and had advanced too fast and too hard. He was determined not to repeat the errors of the past.

Following the serious beating and resounding defeat it suffered in Port Arthur in 1905, the Russian Army was left in shambles and forced to make serious changes. While many new weapons had been brought in, new training and more modern ways of making war adopted, the underlying aspect of the new changes did not modify the Achilles heel of any modern army: logistics. This much explained his current predicament since he was waiting for his supplies to catch up before resuming his advance westward. He had the men, the guns, and everything in between, except food for his soldiers and ammo for their weapons.

Rennenkampf had assumed command of the 2nd Army on the mobilization for war. The strategy called for an invasion of East Prussia by his forces and Alexander Samsonov's 1st Army, and the goal was to attack hard and fast to, perhaps with enough luck, take Konisberg, East Prussia, and threaten Berlin.

"General," said one of his aides. He was under a field tent as the weather outside was quite lovely. August was a beautiful weather month in Eastern Prussia. Around him hovered several staff officers, most of them harboring their dirty uniforms and ceremonial swords as proper Russian officers should. Around them, the mayhem of troops hovering about was activating itself. A squadron of Cossack cavalry thundered by, and a column of infantry marched to the sound of the drums. Many of the troops were mobbing westward to new temporary defensive positions. *"Yes, Colonel Primosrsky,"* he answered. *"As you have requested, the rail gauge widening teams are in place to work on the line from Ragnit to here."* Rennenkampf grunted in satisfaction. *"Very well, Colonel. You are dismissed." "Sir,"* answered the man, *putting himself at the ready and giving the military salute before leaving the vicinity of the tent.*

He'd called a meeting with his field commanders near Gumbinnen to discuss what would follow next. The enemy was in retreat and defeated, but at the same time, his forces were suffering from a chronic shortage of supplies. His goal was to reassure his unit commanders that everything would be fine, even if it was obvious that it was not.

"So, as I was saying, gentlemen, we will wait for our supplies to catch up, and then we will resume the advance." One of his officers, General Savarin, spoke up. *"Sir, what of 1st Army's offensive? Won't we support them in their advance? It is reported they are making good progress north."* Rennenkampf looked at him before answering. *"General Samsonov will have to make do without us for the moment, gentlemen,"* he replied, but to everyone at the same time. He knew his officers wanted to resume the attack and pursue the enemy. However, the unavoidable logistical problems could not be avoided. The men and the horses were already hungry, and his guns were out of ammo. It wouldn't do to go about gallivanting and fighting the Germans on barebone

supplies.

The Battle of Gumbinnen was a great victory, but Rennenkampf would advance a a snail's pace while von Pritwitz, the commander of the German 8th Army, would continue to retreat until the German high command (OHL) did something about it.

St Petersburg, Imperial Russia
Alexander Palace, August 23rd, 1914

Tsar Nicolas II felt better than he'd had since the beginning of his reign. Things finally seemed to be looking up. The Emperor of Russia was sitting in his work office in the Alexander Palace. The place was richly decorated, as with anything relating to the Romanovs, the ruling dynasty in the country. It was said that Nicolas II was the richest man in the world; the room he was working in said as much. Gold-braided walls, expensive rugs from Persia, paintings from illustrious Tsar like Catherine the Great. On his desk lay paperwork and it was surrounded by gold. A gold pen, gold box for letters, gold everything. A Fabergé egg also stood in the right corner.

The news of the Gumbinnen victory had come as a breath of fresh air for the Empire. The timing was good, and he was now inclined to believe in his people's arguments about the usefulness of a war to fix some of Russia's problems. His own brother, Grand Duke Nikolai Nikolaevich (the supreme commander of his armies), was amongst them.

The declaration of war by Germany was followed by great demonstrations of enthusiasm across the Empire. It was sort of refreshing to see the people finally aligned behind him.

He remembered mobilization for the Russo-Japanese War quite well, and the current situation was very different from then. His people were enthusiastic and wanted to fight the Central Powers, especially Germany.

He'd read the reports on the stories about many of the *"to be mobilized reservists"* in faraway territories and cities showing up even before the recruitment officers sent them a letter or paid them a visit.

The Russian people were rising to the challenge, and he was proud of it. The workers and the peasants, both traditionally opposed in their views and reactions to the Russian monarch, came to the army with the same dedication to duty. Nicolas believed that Russia was rising to the challenge and in the defense of its rights to support him and his dynasty. Thus, he started to hope again for his children and the future of the Romanovs.

Nicolas smiled to himself. The scenario he was going through could not have been written any better. Things were looking up for Russia. The news from Galicia was also good, and the fighting there was also taking a turn for the better. Never in his wildest dreams would he have asked for so much. *"Papa papa!"* said the young Tsarevitch as he barged in at a run into his father's office. *"Nicolas, what are you doing here,"* said the Tsar. *"Come play with me, Father,"* answered the young boy. And the Emperor smiled. The world could wait for a little.

War in the Black Sea Part 1
Golden Horn, Ottoman Fleet, Constantinople, August 23rd, 1914

Following the harrowing British Royal Navy chase of Admiral Wilhelm Souchon's Mediterranean Squadron, the German battlecruiser Goeben had been permitted to enter the Dardanelles Strait, preventing the British from destroying it. This event caused much embarrassment for the Turkish government as the Ottoman Empire was still neutral and had yet to declare for the Central Powers or the Entente. After all, the negotiations between Berlin and Istanbul had not been over yet at that moment in time.

As always, Souchon had his own plan: if the Turks vacillated, he would have forced the Straits anyway. He would have been able to circumvent the Turkish minefield because one of his flag officers had been stationed the year before in Istanbul with the German military mission to the Ottoman Empire. The old forts at the entrance (Kumkale and Sedulbair) were also no match for his top-of-the-line armor, so Goeben would have sailed right past anyway, and Souchon would have fulfilled his mission.

But none of that maverick type of maneuvering was needed. The Turks relented rapidly under the impetus of their very influential Minister of War, Enver Pacha. The man was deeply involved in the Germano-Turkish negotiations and had already decided to join the Central Powers. Thus for him, it was even better with Goeben since the ship would now with for the Ottoman Navy.

As he walked the deck of his powerful battlecruiser (now called the Yavuz Sultan Selim), the ranking officer of the Turkish fleet was now Admiral Wilhelm Souchon. The German officer was thoughtful but resolute with the order packet he'd just received from Berlin that very morning. Despite donning the fez and raising the Ottoman flag, the Goeben was still very much a

Kaiserliche Marine ship crewed by German sailors. His orders were clear. Sail into the Black Sea and bombard the Russian cities of Odesa and Sevastopol to force the Ottomans into the war. Enver Pacha, the Turkish Minister of War, was enthusiastic enough, but other ministers in the Government hesitated.

Enver had given his go-ahead for Yavuz and the rest of the Turkish fleet to steam out of the Bosphorus by late August. Souchon crossed his arms behind his back and gave a good look at the ships he would soon command for the mission. His eyes obviously went directly to the most powerful vessels in the harbor.

The Ottoman fleet of 1914 had just been reinforced in June of that year by two pristine and brand-new dreadnought battleships built in England. Sultân Osmân-ı Evvel was one hell of a modern and powerful battleship. It was armed with fourteen BL main guns in seven turrets. The design was new. Fourteen guns on one battleship was a first in the world. Next was the Resadiye, the second battleship built in England. It was a single ship class and another modern dreadnought. Displacing 22,000 tons at full load and sporting 13-inch guns, it was no pushover and would fight well for the Ottomans.

Both ships had been launched at the end of 1913, and, following a brief period of uncertainty when the British government (with Winston Churchill in the lead had wanted to confiscate the warships to add to their own), they were delivered to Istanbul by a British crew.

Ottoman Navy- Admiral Souchon	
BB Sultân Osmân-ı Evvel	CA Hamidiye
BB Reşadiye	CA Mecidiye
BC Yavuz Sultan Selim (HMS Goeben)	8 DD
Pre Dreadnought BB Barbaros Hayreddin	
Pre Dreadnought BB Turgut Reis,	

For the rest of his fleet, Souchon could count on two pre-dreadnought battleships. While slow and less armored than the newer vessels, the two warships were nonetheless good gun platforms and would do fine against the light Russian Black Sea Fleet. They were named the Barbaros Hayrredin and the Turgut Reis, both honoring famous Ottoman admirals of the 16th Century. The fleet also had two cruisers (Hamidiye and Mecidiye) and eight aging destroyers.

With this kind of task force, Souchon was confident he would be able to do some damage to the Russians and bring the Turks into the war.

The next day at sea (August 24th), Souchon informed the other captains of their orders.

A day later, on August 25th, the fleet shelled the major Russian naval base at Sevastopol in the Crimea. He then sailed at full speed to proceed to attack Novorossisk. On September 4th, it was the turn of the port of Feodosia (Theodosia). On the way back, Admiral Souchon made a "quick stop" in Odessa and tore the city asunder.

His daring raiding mission not only enraged the Russians, who would prepare their Black Sea Fleet for action, but it also brought the Ottoman Empire into the war on the side of the Central Powers.

Back into Austria-Hungary
Scapegoat, September 1st, 1914.

Private soldier Helmut Gottenburg spit on the ground in frustration. He was bruised and still battered from the ordeal of the Cer Mountains. He still wore a large bloody red and crusty bandage wrapped around his skull, thanks to a bullet injury during the retreat back into Bosnia. He had also received a parting gift from a tough Serbian rogue with whom he'd had to fight in a bayonet duel. He'd killed the bastard, but not before the Serb had badly mangled his left cheek. He felt pretty bad about the injury, but his friends and comrades (the ones that survived anyway) joked that it would greatly help with the ladies back in Prague. Young and beautiful girls were suckers for scarred soldiers, according to them. While he liked to think about that, the burning sensation on his face reminded him that it wasn't fun to be injured.

The Cer Mountain offensive had ended in disaster, and the entirety of the Austrian forces had been beaten back out of Serbian territory. He felt shame and discouragement and didn't know what to do, for the Army seemed to be looking for a scapegoat, and the 21st Landwehr Division was one of them. They had broke and ran in the face of overwhelming Serbian forces, and there was no cleansing of the shame of it all. The entire world took note of the Austro-Hungarian military weakness, and the result played a great part in the aggressiveness with which the Russians launched their offensive on Galicia during that same time period.

Unknown to a lowly private like Helmult, General Pitiorek, the commander of the Austro-Hungarian forces invading Serbia, was trying to put the blame on others for his utter failure. The man was bad at planning, couldn't command properly, and was arrogant. Thus, he'd started to put the blame on the lack of equipment and the non-ethnic Germans in his force.

The small group of soldiers was huddling around a warm fire as the day was over and darkness had fallen. The soldiers spoke in hushed tones, and they got busy eating their paltry rations. But not many of them portrayed happiness. The entire affair was truly bad for their morale, now at rock bottom. Helmut wondered if the Division would ever get the chance to prove its worth once again.

While Helmut liked to have been singled out as brave and considerate by the rest of the division because it soothed his hurt pride (he had been commended by his superior and put in for a medal for saving a wounded comrade), he resented the treatment reserved for his comrades in the Division. From what he'd seen, they were as brave and with as much fighting spirit as the rest, Germans or not. The Division was camped a little off from the rest of the Army, another sign of its disgrace.

Helmut took a bite of the loaf of bread he'd acquired from the Regiment's quartermaster earlier in the day and dreamed of revenge on the Serbs and of another chance to prove his worth to the Empire.

The Battle for Galicia Part 1
The twin pyrrhic victories of Krasnik and Komarow on August 25th and 27th, 1914

On August 18th, 1914, Russia launched a major offensive into Galicia. The offensive objective was nothing less than to knock Austria-Hungary out of the war. What was to follow was a military campaign of epic proportions. Millions of men fighting across vast expanses of territory and often not even finding each other because of the distances involved. The area where the fighting was going to happen was so large that the armies had to march hundreds of kilometers to even fire a shot at each other.

The fighting started off innocuously enough for the Austrians, as their border units fought off small Cossack recon units and other small battalion-sized units. They were soon to be flooded with angry Russians spilling out everywhere.

In the case of war with the Central Powers, the Stavka (Russian High Command) had two plans at its disposal. The first was a concentration of forces on the border with Germany (War Plan B), while another, called War Plan A, planned a concentration on the border with Austria-Hungary. Having considered the fact that the Germans had sent most of their forces across Belgium into France, Grand Duke Nikolai (the overall commander of all Russian forces) decided to implement Plan A and attack the Austro-Hungarians. The risk of being defeated by the Germans was rather small because they were busy westward against the Anglo-French, and he decided he could use the time to knock the Austrians out of Galicia altogether and perhaps move beyond the Carpathians and into Hungary proper. Thus, he sent the majority of his army of millions in the direction of Galicia and only two field armies into eastern Prussia.

After the Austro-Hungarian armies had taken up their planned positions along the rivers San and Dniester by August 23rd, a wall of Russian men was soon seen, and the immensity of the danger in the situation slowly materialized: three full Russian armies, over two million strong, marched on the 1,5 million Austro-Hungarian soldiers.

In the given situation, when it was clear that an attack would be futile, Conrad von Hotzendorf decided (wrongly) to meet the Russians in an all-out offensive. The 1st Austro-Hungarian Army, which had occupied the position at the confluence of the rivers Vistula and San, and its adjacent 4th Army were instructed to thrust into north-eastern Russian Poland and encircle and destroy the two incoming Russian armies in the vicinity of Lublin.

What the Austro-Hungarian General Staff did not know was that there had been, at least, one further Russian army (the 9th) behind the approaching two. Due to poor reconnaissance reports, the Austrian 1st Army marched headlong into the Russian 4th Army and was poised to get one hell of a bloody nose.

Even with ineffective artillery attacks, stupid bayonet charges, and very high casualties, the Austro-Hungarian forces still managed to turn the battle (which lasted three days) into a victory.

Oblivious to the reality of war, Austrian General Dankl's victory at Krasnik was praised across Austria-Hungary. Ironically, the military attributed the victory to its tactical superiority over the Russians, declaring that their armies had penetrated the enemy's lines at several key points, while the Russians presumably adhered to a *"primitive style of fighting."* The local newspapers described the Russian army as barbaric, while they considered their own to be a civilized one that fought against the *"Asian destructive passion."*

East of Krasnik, a second battle was fought, and there again, the Austro-Hungarian forces mastered the Russian ones. As the Austrian 4th Army moved right up to the throat of the Russian

5th, a fierce battle was initiated. The fight was intense and lasted a day and a half, ending with the Russians retreating in disorder.

The Battle of East of Krasnik (called the Battle of Komarow) put a recurring weakness on both sides of the field of battle: A general lack of knowledge of what the enemy was doing. It was hard for the generals on both sides to locate and accurately pinpoint the enemy forces as the distances involved were so great and the terrain so rough. As a result, many a fight happened because one formation walked right up to the other. In the case of the Battle of Komarow, the two opposing forces were roughly equal, but there were many instances where smaller units encountered larger ones and were obliterated.

As for the Russian Empire, these defeats at Krasnik and Komarow were anything but fatal. Contrary to what was being hailed as a war-winning campaign in Austrian newspapers and military leadership circles in Vienna, things were not doing well. Not doing well at all. A few hundred kilometers to the south, the Austro-Hungarian armies east of Lemberg were disintegrating.

Russian 4th Army
Fighting in the Battle of Krasnik August 25th, 1914

The Russian 4th Army and the Austrian 1st Army met at a small town called Krasnik in Galicia, igniting the first of many battles between the two in the area.

And, unfortunately for Private Soldier Dimitri Fedorov, he was in the middle of it. He was looking warily to the sides and in front of him as his unit marched across the small town of Krasnik. The Russian Imperial forces were strung out in a long and winding road column, without many or any units on their flanks. He wondered why they had not been warned of the enemy troop's approach. He had no idea his superiors were incompetent. Well, not yet anyway.

He could see the Austrians were across the bridge his unit had been advancing toward a few moments earlier. Their numbers seemed considerable, and he wondered what would happen next. Right after the bridge was a few large farm fields, and then it was the town of Krasnik, where he was along with the rest of his unit. It was his first battle of the war, and he was incredibly nervous and anxious at the same time. He made a quick prayer to God in the hope the almighty would listen to him and help him survive this day.

He was also moving to the side of the road and into the small buildings or any cover in the town as per the orders they'd received from the NCOs and the officers. They had also seen the enemy approach. Krasnik was a town in a small valley, surrounded by tall ridges on the east (Russian-occupied) and on the west (Austro-Hungarian-occupied).

He ran toward the orchards as he'd been instructed to find shelter and tried to find the biggest tree to get under and also to use its trunk as a shield from the bullets that would soon be shot in anger toward him and his comrades.

Once he was deployed along with his comrades, Dmitri started to hear the pounding of hooves seemingly coming from all around them. The enemy cavalry was charging Krasnik, and right behind ran Austrian soldiers. Fedorov didn't know it, but he was about to face Slovenian soldiers from a relatively unknown province in the Austro-Hungarian Empire.

"Get ready," yelled one of the officers beside them. He was so nervous he almost threw up, but by some miracle, he kept his dinner in. Perhaps it was because he'd barely eaten since there was not a lot of available food. Russian supply was terrible.

"Our cavalry's coming!" yelled someone behind him, and he turned his head to see a few squadrons of Cossack cavalry charging with their sabers high. He cheered them on as they streamed on the road, in between him and his comrades and across the village. Soon, they clashed with their Austro-Hungarian counterparts.

Due to their speediness and maneuverability, the cavalry units were the first to clash. These first moments– similar to those on the Western Front happening in France at the same time– were fought only with cavalry, and these early engagements were reminiscent of the Napoleonic Wars: swords, lances, and pikes clashing in loud steel clangs. The two forces clashed with one another, and Dmitri decided it was a grand sight. Then the Austrians broke and ran, quickly followed by the Russians, eager for slaughter.

But as they galloped toward the marching enemy infantry, the whole picture changed; things went from Russians attacking to Russians dying in droves. Machine guns, rifle fire, and artillery blossomed all across the field they'd been fighting in, shattering the Russian cavalry force. The proud and self-confident cavalry was shattered, and they fell back toward Dmitri and Krasnik. A minute later, the tattered survivors had zipped past the infantry in the town and were fleeing. He was amazed at the number of bodies of horses and men lying on the battlefield. Modern war was truly appalling, he thought for a moment.

Then, it was time to fight as bullets started to slam into the big tree's bark he was using as cover. He went from observer to fighter in moments. Bullets started to blaze by, with the tracers crisscrossing everywhere.

About ten minutes into the battle, the order came down from command to fall back toward the center of Krasnik and even to continue. Dmitri felt pretty good about what was in front of him, as his unit was keeping the enemy at bay. But the larger picture was not looking good for the Russians as they were getting overwhelmed by the Austrian's superior forces.

Dmitri fought on for hours on end but, eventually, the enemy pressure was too great, and the unit broke and ran. He was one of the panicked soldiers trying to get out of Krasnik as fast as his legs permitted him, and he prayed to God once more.

A new General
Hindenburg and Ludendorff arrive at 8th Army HQ August 23rd, 1914.

"*I am ready,*" said Paul von Hindenburg, an old and retired military commander now living in Hanover. He said the phrase matter-of-factly, just as he would be ready for dinner. The Chief of the German General staff hung up the phone and gave a weary smile to his Kaiser, Wilhelm II. "*Let's hope he is our man, your Majesty.*" Kaiser Wilhelm raised an eyebrow in skepticism. "*Well, yes, my dear General. I have heard of the man, but isn't he a little old?*" "*We'll just have to see, Your Majesty, we'll just have to see...*"

Sometime later, in the early hours of the morning and still in darkness, a towering and solitary figure in full general uniform stood on a railway platform at Hanover, Germany, waiting for his ride from Berlin to the East. While he did so two Russian armies laid waste to East Prussia. He wasn't sure about what the future had in store for him, but he knew he would prevail over the enemy hordes. He just didn't know how yet.

Hindenburg had seen much during his 53-year-long career. He'd fought the Austrians at Sadowa (1866), the French at Sedan (1870), and even met with the then-captured French Emperor. He had also been part of the forces sent to China to put down the Boxer Rebellion.

Half an hour later, the train rolled in, stopped, and one of the front railcar doors opened. Out stepped a figure as tall as Hindenburg. The man strode confidently down the small steps to the railway platform. It was Hindenburg's recently named chief of staff, Eric von Luddendorf. "*General,*" started the man with a top-notch military salute. Hindenburg responded with the same, and the younger man continued. "*Sir, I am your new chief of staff. I have been instructed to ride with you to 8th Army HQ,*" he gestured for Hindenburg to step inside the railcar. "If you would, sir, your cabin is ready, and I have a full assessment of the situation as we understand it at the moment in Eastern Prussia." Hindenburg Smiled since he decided he would like this man's efficiency. "Indeed, General," he simply answered before stepping onto the train. A minute and a half later, the engines were started up again and the train was off to bring the two future great men to their destiny.

The very same day (in the evening) and without much sleep, both men were in the German Army East Prussian HQ in Elbing near the Bay of Danzig, and things did not look good. First of all, the reinforcements that had been discussed were canceled and were kept for the Western offensive. *"This is unfortunate, General,"* said Hindenburg over the matter of the troops that would never get here. *"I agree, commander,"* said Ludendorff, knowing full well that the 180,000 soldiers would be sorely missed.

They were in a nondescript room in the bunker building in Elbing where the army had its HQ; it was some kind of regional military office before the war. The two men were looking at maps laid on the table. There was another man in the room, going by the name of General Max Hoffman. The man had come to meet his new commanding officers in person and also to propose a bold offensive plan.

"What you propose, General Hoffman, cannot be done without those reinforcements," continued Hindenburg, putting both his knuckles on the table and over the map. Hoffmann was yet another experienced German officer, having been a military advisor during the Russo-Japanese War of 1905. He'd seen firsthand what modern war was. He was a dynamic and aggressive unit commander and had attempted to convince the 8th Army's commanding officer, General Max von Prittwitz, not to retreat backward and instead attack.

While Hindenburg had no intention of abandoning East Prussia to the Russians, there was a world of difference between that and launching the offensive toward Samsonov's Russian 1st Army and trying to outflank and destroy it. Without the fresh troops, they just didn't have the men to execute such a maneuver. Max Hoffman, ever the tactician and the strategist, knew his new master was right. *"I agree, General Hindenburg. But why won't OHL send the necessary troops to smash the Russians?"* Ludendorff grunted and then took a deep breath before speaking. *"I have heard that Molkte was overruled by the Kaiser upon the urging of von Falkenhayn."* Hoffman knew of the two men's rivalry for the top position in the German General Staff.

"And now that Rennenkampf has started to move forward again, the plan is even less practical," continued Hoffman. *"We will just have to deal with the cards we have been given,"* countered Hindenburg calmly.

Ludendorff agreed with his commander. *"Let's make a new plan, General Hoffman. One that emphasizes on defense, without our predecessor's propensity to retreat too far and too fast."*

The three men went to work and, the next day, had agreed on a course of action. The German 8th Army was about 200,000 men strong, while the combined Russian forces were about half a million men. There wasn't much they could do about it but try and defeat them in detail, just like Napoleon Bonaparte would have done. The plan was thus to march the bulk of the troops toward the south, where the closest Russian Army was advancing. There was no fancy maneuvering to outflank the Russians, but just a good old *"let's give them a good bloody nose plan."*

The decision had also been taken to leave Konigsberg to fend for itself. The city was a powerful fortress, and Hindenburg left 40,000 men to fight and man its defenses. The goal was for the great city to occupy half of the Russian force (Rennenkampf's 2nd Army) until such time that they'd either dealt a decisive blow on Samsonov's 1st Army or else received enough reinforcements to attack across the entire front. The plan was also sent and approved by the OHL, even if the Kaiser and other nobles in the German Empire didn't like the Russians trampling all over eternal Prussia. And just like that, events were in motion for the first truly large battle between the Russians and the Germans on the Eastern front at Tannenberg.

War in the Black Sea Part 2
The Battle of Cape Sarych, September 4th, 1914

Following the Ottoman raids (led by the Goeben and the rest of the Ottoman fleet), the Russian leadership was enraged at the deed and declared war on the Ottoman Empire. The Russian Black Sea Fleet was up and about and wanted to have a go at the pesky Ottoman Navy.

However, what they proposed to accomplish was a tall order because they didn't have the necessary firepower to face the Turks on equal terms.

At the end of the Russo-Japanese War in 1905, there were only two words to describe the Russian Imperial Fleet, either in the Baltic or the Black Sea: gutted and all but inconsequential, while there was no more Pacific Fleet to speak of.

This was mainly due to two important occurrences ten years before - the destruction of both the Far East and Baltic fleets in the Russo-Japanese War and the mutiny/loss of the flagship of the Black Sea Fleet - the Battleship Potemkin in the following civilian troubles and "almost civil war" in 1905.

These momentous events dropped the Russian Navy from third in the world (Behind the UK and Germany) to sixth (behind the US, France, and Japan). Russia never recovered its former standing in the world. Even with ten years between the Russo-Japanese War and the current conflict, there simply wasn't a chance of rebuilding much of anything in the decade prior to 1914, and with the rise of the Imperial German fleet in the interim, there was little meaningful chance at successful naval operations or planning.

So, the Imperial court did little of either and only made half-hearted attempts at getting something done and afloat. By the time the war started, there were some dreadnought battleships (finally) in construction, but none were ready by the start of

World War One. Two of them (the BB Imperatritsa Mariya and BB Imperatritsa Ekaterina Velikaya) would eventually be ready for Black Sea operations since they were in the final stages of completion at the naval yards in Nikolayev. However, none were available in the meantime, and the Russian Black Sea Fleet was thus entrusted to fight off the Ottoman fleet with what it had. Russia needed its sailors to put an end to the shelling of Russian ports all over the Black Sea.

Russian Black Sea Fleet August 1914	
Vice Admiral Andrei Eberhardt and vice-Admiral Kolchak	
Pre-Dreadnought BB Ioann Zlatoust	3 CA
Pre-Dreadnought BB Evstafi (flagship)	13 DD
Pre-Dreadnought BB Panteleimon	
Pre-Dreadnought BB Tri Sviatitelya	
Pre-Dreadnought BB Rostislav	

The Black Sea Fleet that sailed out of Sevastopol, thirty kilometers away from Cape Sarych, would have been considered very powerful in 1900, but in 1914, it was a great unknown how it would fare against dreadnought battleships.

It included twenty-one ships, with five Pre-dreadnought battleships, three aging cruisers, and thirteen destroyers. It packed a punch but lacked the modernity of the three Turkish Dreadnoughts (BB Sultân Osmân-ı Evvel, BB Reşadiye, BC Yavuz Sultan Selim)

Pre-dreadnought battleships were warships that came before the HMS Dreadnought, and dreadnoughts were the warships that came after. Prior to 1906, it wasn't possible to control the gun armament of a warship from a centralized position. Guns were individually laid by hand and fired locally. This meant that it wasn't practical to fight a battle with large caliber weapons since they couldn't fire fast enough at the short ranges used to be effective, and large numbers of smaller, quick-firing guns were much more effective at disabling the enemy ships. The large guns were to be used to deliver the coup-de-grace when the enemy had been silenced by the rain of fire of the smaller weapons. Armored cruisers were regarded as being just as effective as the battleships since their secondary armament was as numerous and effective as those of the battleships, while their armor was adequate to defeat the smaller weapons, and their greater speed was very useful in gaining a favorable tactical position. The Battle of Tsushima was fought in this way in 1905.

By 1906, centralized fire control, with spotters at the mastheads, had been developed by the British, and suddenly, a fast ship with many large guns was practical. The first such ship was Dreadnought, hence the generic name. She was much faster and more seaworthy than her predecessors, with her higher freeboard and her turbine engines, and was, in fact, much closer to what would be called a battlecruiser than a battleship. Compared with the pre-dreadnoughts, she could be expected to be able to choose the range and overwhelm any enemy without getting hit in return. As a result, Great Britain had an overwhelming advantage for several years before other nations, particularly Germany, caught up.

By 1914, the Dreadnought herself was pretty much obsolete as both Britain and Germany built much more powerful warships with much heavier armament or armor (respectively) and similar speed. The new ships began to be called battleships, with a faster but less armored variant also built called battlecruisers, like the Goeben.

There were many proponents of both, and the consensus was pretty much that a dreadnought would master any pre-dreadnoughts in a one-on-one fight. But there still remained people who believed the big gun platforms on the pre-dreadnoughts could do some damage.

After all, the five Russian battleships were armed with two or three 305 mm guns and three to five 203 mm guns. While they could not fire together nor had any centralized control system, their caliber meant that they would do damage if they managed to hit something.

(...)

On September 2nd, 1914, Admiral Souchon ordered the Ottoman fleet on a foray to repeat his bombardment mission against Russian ports. The first stop was Odessa, and his powerful task force shelled Odessa for a few hours and burst the city into flames, wrecking harbor and hangar facilities. Odesa was a very important commercial and military port for Russia. While 90% of the Russian trade came from the Dardanelles, now closed since the war between the Ottoman Empire and Russia, there remained enough trade inside the Black Sea for Odessa to retain a grand importance.

Ottoman Navy- Admiral Souchon	
BB Sultán Osmán-ı Evvel	CA Hamidiye
BB Reşadiye	CA Mecidiye
BC Yavuz Sultan Selim (HMS Goeben)	8 DD
Pre Dreadnought BB Barbaros Hayreddin	
Pre Dreadnought BB Turgut Reis,	

After a few hours of bombardment and blasting everything they could see to oblivion, the Ottomans and Germans decided that there weren't any worthwhile targets they could see anymore (everything was clouded by raging fires and huge black smoke columns) and decided to sail on toward his second objective, the main enemy military base in the Black Sea, the city of Sevastopol.

Souchon sailed with the confidence of having the most powerful fleet afloat in the entire theater of war; thus, he never in his right mind imagined the Russians would actually sortie to challenge him.

The Russian commanders (Vice Admiral Andrei Eberhardt and Vice-Admiral Kolchak) were under orders to intercept and sink the enemy fleet. Not having the most confidence in what their ships could do against the Ottoman's brand-new dreadnought warships, they nonetheless sortied out of Sevastopol to intercept the enemy fleet a bit away from the city and harbor to try and avoid damage to it.

The two fleets spotted each other about 19 miles away to the northwest from the city of Sevastopol, at a place called Cape Sarych. It was a headland located on the shore of the Black Sea in the Crimean Peninsula. It would now be the place where the first major naval battle of the war would occur.

The Russian force was steaming toward battle and in a tight battle formation, with the three cruisers -- Pamiat' Merkuriia, Almaz, and Kagul – on a screening line several miles ahead of the Russian fleet.

The five old Russian pre-dreadnought battlewagons were led by the flagship, Battleship Evstafii. The aging but proud warship was flanked by the Ioann Zlatoust, the Panteleimon, the Tri Sviatitelia, and the Rostislav.

The escorting ships (destroyers) sailed on their flanks facing outward, watchful of enemy submarines and other threats. At about midday and as the Russian fleet sailed around Cape Sarych, the cruiser Almaz reported seeing smoke in the distance. Admiral Ebergard, the Russian fleet commander, ordered his battleships to increase their speed and prepare for battle.

The screening forces of both fleets sort of spotted each other simultaneously. The Hamidiye and the Mecidiye sighted one of the enemy cruisers to their portside, while the Almaz saw its counterpart from their starboard side. Both of the screening cruisers then sailed back to their fleet's main body and prepared for battle. Their part in the action was done, and now it was time to fight.

Believing he had the upper hand and knowing the enemy didn't have any dreadnoughts in the Black Sea, Admiral Souchon ordered his Battlecruiser (Yavuz, formerly Goeben), dreadnought battleships Resadiye and Sultan Osman-I Evvel and the two pre-dreadnought battleships (Turgut Reis and Barbados Hayreddin) to move at battlespeed and to intercept. It didn't take long for both sides to close in on the other. Admiral Souchon described the feeling of impending battle in his diary, found after the war in Constantinople: *"Finally, my wish to meet with the enemy with overwhelming strength had come."*

It was now time to fire, as both fleets crossed each other's paths, enabling them to fire their broadsides like the naval battles of old. Russian pre-war exercises had been practiced, and its sailors trained to attack from a long distance and to concentrate the firing of many warships on one target at a time. These tactics resulted from the Russian naval disaster at the Battle of Tsushima in 1905, where Admiral Togo, the Imperial Navy commander at the time, was able to concentrate its ship's gunnery fire on the leading Russian battleships with devastating effect. The need for concentration of fire became especially urgent when the two Turkish battleships arrived in Istanbul, greatly upsetting the balance of power in the area.

The concentration of fire by several ships on a single target was a difficult business as the technicalities and communication challenges to coordinate the action were complicated to execute. The Russian method was based on gunnery control by a "master ship" -- ideally, the center ship in a three-ship group. In the case of the battle of Cape Sarych, it was the flagship battleship Evstafi that executed the gunnery maneuver.

This Russian flagship passed initial range finder information from its gunnery control to the other ships in the squadron by radio; the other ships in the group then started to apply the coordinates and the corrections to fire in conjunction with the flagship. The concept was relatively simple yet hard to make a reality: get the five old battleships in the group fire as one single entity. It was a kind of decentralized "dreadnought" with the respectable armament of twelve 12-inch guns.

On the other side of the battle, the German and Ottoman sailors didn't need to do any fancy coordinating as they had three dreadnoughts on their side. The three fired independently, and their salvos landed with great effect on the Russian ships.

The Central power fire thus arrived before the Russian one ever got organized. Battleships Resadiye's five twin 13.5 in (343 mm) guns slammed hard on the battleship Ioann Zlatoust in one hell of a lucky first shot.

The damage on the ship was extensive. First, on the port rear casemate, killing the entire one main gun's entire crew complement destroying the turret in the process. Second on the casemate armor, piercing the 127 mm thick hide, setting a large fire inside the ship. Shell exploded in the mess and caused many casualties, with some damage on the decks above and below. The third shell fell short of the ship at the waterline and slammed the hull hard. It only buckled, but some water started to rush in as cracks appeared on the hull. Ten officers and forty-three crewmembers died immediately. The last of the shells zipped over the boilers and exploded harmlessly into the sea.

Battleships Sultan Osman-I Evvel and battlecruiser Yavuz missed, each landing straddling shots on battleships Panteleimon and Tri Sviatitelya. Their next shot would count, but not before the Russian salvo arrived.

The Russian Vice-Admiral in command, Andrei Eberhardt, decided to concentrate the fire on the Resadiye. It was struck by three 12-inch HE from Evstafi, Panteleimon, and Rostislav. As predicted by the most enthusiastic armchair admirals of the time, the three shells did some good damage. The first one landed on port, a 15 cm casemate, which penetrated sturdy armor and opened it outward in a great burst of fire. Fifty-seven sailors and officers died on impact. The next shell hit the Turkish battleship just above the waterline, but the armor shrugged off most of the damage. The last shell was a plunging hit right on the deck between turret no. 1 and turret no.2. The entire deck planking catapulted in the air in a million pieces of debris, and a large column of black smoke rose in the air.

Great cheers erupted on the Russian ships, but their excitement and joy would be short-lived. Yavuz (Goeben) was able to slam a full salvo of the 11-inch /50 SK gun shells into the Panteleimon. The old ship buckled under the relentless power of the multiple impacts, and a large ball of fire replaced the sight of the ship for a moment. When the fire dissipated and was replaced by smoke and debris falling in a star-like fashion everywhere, the ship was in three parts and sinking rapidly.

Sultan Osman-I Evvel was the next to hit, and its salvo of powerful 12-inch shells slammed on the bow and the central boilers of the Tri Sviatitelya. The results were much the same. The thinly armored (comparatively speaking) vessels did not resist the ordinance, and they plowed themselves deep into the bowels of the ships. A catastrophic horizontal column of fire burst out of the Russian battleship, and a fire engulfed the inside of the ship like a rolling wall of fire, killing 80% of its crew. The shell that hit the boilers added to the catastrophe, and the ship was dead in the water, a floating burning hulk moments later.

Resadiye's fire was less effective because of the hits it had just received, but nonetheless hit the Rostislav with two 12-inch shells, destroying one main gun and severely damaging the rudder with a hit on the stern.

Vice Admiral Andrei Eberhardt decided to order his ships to increase the range, but not before sending one last salvo at the Resadiye in an attempt to damage it further. With fewer battleships now that two were destroyed and with a third unable to align to fire, his aim was less effective, and his shots only straddled the Turkish battleships.

Just as the Russian admiral thought he would be able to increase the range to avoid getting hit again, the two slower, old, pre-dreadnought Turkish battleships, Turgut Reis and Barbaros Hayreddin, cut his retreat. Their slower speed (14 knots) had them enter the battle quite late but at an opportune moment for the Germano-Turks.

The two ships, in fact, old German vessels sold to Turkey in 1910, poured their 11-inch guns (four each) into the turning and maneuvering Russians, hitting Evstafi (flagship) and Ioann Zlatoust as they tried to veer to port. Their shells splashed on the decks of both ships, killing over a hundred sailors on each. The Evstafi lost 2 main guns and several secondary guns, while the Ioann Zlatoust boilers were destroyed, killing its speed completely. It would soon surrender instead of being destroyed as, without speed, it became an instant kill if it decided to continue the fighting.

The Rotislav also pulled up the white flag because it could no longer flee with its rudder damage problems. The only Russian battleship that escaped was the Evstafi.

The Battle of Cape Sarych concluded in a stellar Turkish victory and another naval disaster for Russia. Souchon, happy about the results of the battle, decided to head back to Constantinople to avoid further damage, as he suspected enemy submarines and the smaller ships could further damage the Resadiye.

The Battle for Galicia Part 2: The Fall of Lemberg
Austrian catastrophe in Gnila Lipa, August 24th to 30th, 1914

On the morning of August 26th, the Austro-Hungarian 3rd Army collided with the Russian 8th Army, more than twice superior in soldiers (250,000 soldiers with over 700 guns compared to 115,000 men with 260 guns for the Austrians). What had at first been a misguided Austro-Hungarian offensive soon morphed into a reeling backward defeat because of overwhelming Russian numbers.

The epicenter of the battle took place about twelve miles west of Solotschiw, where the 40,000 men of the Austro-Hungarian 3rd Corps came into contact with the main force of General Ruski, well over 120,000 strong. There, a road that connected Lemberg to Solotschiw divided the terrain into two geographically completely different shapes. To the south extended a hilly and wooded terrain, whereas northward from the road began a lowland area with marshes, which significantly impeded larger manoeuvers.

On such terrain, the outnumbered Austro-Hungarians stepped into an unequal battle. At 9:00 am on the 26th of August, the ground beneath the front-most units of the army shook with tremendous force. After a few moments, the soldiers were bombarded with shells by powerful artillery fire. Russian guns soon flooded the marshy ground with fire and death.

Almost simultaneously (to the left of the Austrian 3rd Army), underwent a similar baptism of fire. Its commander, Major General Ludwig von Fabini, blindly pushed the 6th and 28th Divisions into a general offensive along the road towards *Solotschiw*. The entire affair was completely misguided, but he obeyed the stupid orders from the overall commander, Von Hotzendoff (to attack at all costs).

The Austro-Hungarian forces were subjected to a storm of fire, fire, and soldiers. Almost immediately, the forces at the front buckled under the tremendous pressure. Within the first three hours of the fight, the Russians overwhelmed two Austro-Hungarian divisions, opening the flanks to more attacks with artillery and machine gun fire from the surrounding hills.

The K.U.K forces withstood the enemy pressure until the late afternoon when a general retreat was sounded. By then, all Austrian field commanders were under no illusion about his force's chances to stop the overwhelming enemy and disregarded the unrealistic orders from high command too far away from the front.

The outcome of the day was catastrophic for the K.U.K forces. The heavy fighting put to light the long list of their weaknesses and did nothing to further their aim of winning.

Due to a general lack of reliable battlefield intelligence of the surrounding area and reconnaissance units, most of the Austro-Hungarian forces did not know where the enemy was or where it was attacking from. There was a lot of confusion, and no orders or instruction came from high command; thus, the divisional commanders were left to their own devices. In short, they were not even aware that superior forces attacked them until it was too late. The 3rd Austrian Corps, for example, had no overview of the situation as it got encircled and crushed by four Russian corps in the span of only a day and a half north of Lemberg. It was an improvisation of the worst kind and the prelude to a disaster of epic proportions. The Austrians, by way of their over-enthusiastic commander-in-chief Franz Conrad von Hotzendorf, had bungled themselves into defeat.

Outdated military tactics by the Austrian high command and field officers, which employed numerous and reckless bayonet charges by the infantry, produced terrible casualty rates. The account of the baptism of fire of the 26th LAndwher Division (for example) exposed all of these weaknesses while at the same time offering an insight into the gruesome reality of war in general: The soldiers drove into enemy fire in an almost parade-like formation, screaming *"Morgenrot, Morgenrot, leuchtest mir zum frühen Tod!"* (Morning sun, morning sun, will you illuminate an early death?). Not half of them survived to tell the tale, the rest littering the field in a gory spectacle of blood and death.

On August 28th, there was no major change in the overall situation. The Austro-Hungarian forces achieved a bunch of meaningless, pyrrhic victories, but these were completely nullified the very next day when the defining battle broke out east of Lemberg.

While General Dankl's Austrian 1st Army continued to make progress in the direction of Lublin inside Russian Poland to try and grab some pipe dream and unreachable glory, the Austrian 3rd Army defending Lemberg to the south was on the brink of disintegration. Even though its 3rd Corps much-needed reinforcements on that day, its offensive capabilities were gone. The adjacent Austrian 11th Corps had already disintegrated, and its surviving men were fleeing to Lemberg. Everywhere, the Russians spilled into Galicia, and there seemed to be no end to the disaster in the making for the Austro-Hungarians.

The local Galician Army Command came under enemy artillery fire and saw its forces reeling backward in a streaming line of retreating and panicking soldiers. These men dropped their weapons, their guns, and everything in between for the believed safety of the rear. Some of the remains of the Austro-Hungarian 3rd Corps were able to hold the line for a couple of days near a town called Peremyschljany on the outskirts of Lemberg but eventually relented. Both its northern and southern flanks collapsed because the rest of the army was disintegrating around it. The commander of the unit had thus no other option but to call for a full retreat. Three days after that, Lemberg fell to the Tsarist forces. The event sent panic shockwaves and dread across Europe, particularly in Berlin and Vienna.

Austria had lost a major battle, and it seemed its armies were completely defeated.

CHAPTER 3
The war in the West

"I am being pressed very hard on my flank. The center is buckling. Next to impossible to move units around; they are all pinned down by the enemy. I am attacking."
French General Ferdinand Foch during the battle east of Paris.

The leadup to Mons and Charleroi
The fight to August 21st, 1914

August 2nd-7th, 1914: Germany invade the Low Countries except the Netherlands, that are neutral. France launches an offensive across the border with Alsace-Lorraine. The British Expeditionary Force (BEF) arrives in France. They are under the command of Marshall John French.

August 4th-15th, 1914 - The battle for Liege ends in a German victory following the German attack on the twelve Belgian Forts defending the city. The remnants of the Belgian Army retreat northward toward Antwerp as the German westward advance continues, and the Belgian Army prepares for the final unequal battle.

August 7th-21st, 1914 - The French offensive in Alsace-Lorraine blunders into disaster and is defeated by superior German forces in well-defended positions. The French Army suffers heavy losses.

August 7th-10th, 1914 - Battle of Mulhouse. German victory, French in retreat.

August 12th, 1914 - Battle of Haelen. German victory, French Army in full retreat.

August 14th-25th, 1914 - Battle of Lorraine. German victory, French in full retreat.

August 20th, 1914 - German troops occupy undefended Brussels, the capital of Belgium, following a big battle south of the capital between its tiny army and the German 1st and 2nd Armies. The Belgian forces are shattered and in full retreat toward Antwerp. The German Schlieffen Plan continued, and the main outflanking German armies (1st and 2nd) wheels westward and invade France. The giant counter-clockwise movement aims for Paris and the destruction of the French Army's left flank. The Germans' goal was to beat the French in six weeks so they could wheel their force around to the East to deal with the Russians.

August 20th-21st – Battle of the Ardennes. German victory, French retreat again, and then it starts to dawn on General Joffre that there might be a big problem in the north.

French field HQ
Joffre plans a new offensive on August 21st, 1914.

"As you can see from the recon report, sir," continued the staff officer, trying to point out to General Joffre where the Germans were at that moment. The map was dirty as the writing used to update it had been used and erased many times. The Germans were advancing at a blistering pace toward France. Joffre grunted. *"Well, there aren't many more options left to keep the Huns out of France,"* he answered, putting his fingers on his mustache and turning them slightly.

"What are you thinking, Commander," answered the man on the other side of the small table. General Charles Lanzerac was the commander of the troops that would now be facing the German Juggernaut, as it was positioned north of the Ardennes, right on the path of the approaching enemy troops.

Fifth Army was deployed away from the Ardennes invasion to face any potential German attack from the north, first because it was sensible to do so, but also because its commander was advocating prudence and defense against the Germans. In short, he had been sort of sidelined from what Joffre had thought would be the war's main show in Alsace-Lorraine. But now things were different, following the drubbing the French troops had taken during their ill-fated invasion across the Germano-French border. Lanzerac's 5th Army was the only true unit in a position to block the rampaging Germans while the rest of the Entente forces moved backward and into position to face the large enveloping movement the enemy looked to be executing.

They were in a small manor outside of the town of Mauberge, requisitioned for the occasion. The French officers present in the meeting, always thinking of the offensive even after their (very) serious setbacks during their execution of Plan XVII, kept the same state of mind when they looked at the advancing Germans. Well, with the exception of Lanzerac, who advocated a different stance. Where there should have been some defensive reasoning was only offensive and attack.

Four of Joffre's main commanders were present at the meeting since he'd recalled them for consultations following the reports (that he was now finally taking seriously) of large German forces approaching France from Belgium.

First, there was General Pierre Ruffey, Commander of the 3rd Army, positioned between Saint-Mihiel and Verdun. The man was already heavily engaged against the German forces pushing hard from the southern Ardennes and Metz. He was to hold the line as well in his defensive positions. The city was seen as the pivot of the German attack; thus, the French could not let it fall.

Then there was General Fernand de Langle de Cary, Commander of the 4th Army, between Saint-Dizier and Bar-le-Duc at the rear of the front. It was the last troops held in reserve in the Argonne Region. Joffre had not thought of initially needing the troops, but now that the Germans were bursting out of Belgium in force, things looked quite different.

Also present was André Sordet, Commander of the Cavalry Corps, positioned near Verdun. The man's purpose in Joffre's original Plan XVII was to advance into the Belgian Ardennes in case of a German attack on Belgium. That was what he had done at the beginning of the war. General Joseph Joffre, the French Commander-in-Chief, had anticipated the main enemy attack would be directed at Verdun, but when Germany demanded passage of her troops through Belgium, he ordered the cavalry unit into the Belgian Ardennes region to execute some recon on the 5th. Over the next three days, the cavalrymen combed the area located east of the Meuse and as far as Liege, scouring an area 110 miles wide. They approached as near as nine miles of Liege and also moved to Charleroi, but found no evidence of the enemy trying to cross the Meuse. It was a failure of epic proportions since it failed to predict the large enveloping

German movement through Belgium.

And then, there was General Charles Lanrezac, Commander of the 5th Army, between Hirson and Dun-sur-Meuse, right where the main German forces were barreling down in France. The very man that would be the main factor in the battle to come.

"General Lanzerac," continued Joffre, not leaving his eyes from the dirty map laid in front of him. *"You will attack in force at Charleroi as we discussed earlier,"* he continued, knowing what the man he gave the order to would say. *"But General, can't you see the Germans are in force here? My army will be overwhelmed. The Germans are certain to have superior numbers."* Joffre stayed silent, still playing with his mustache and looking at the map as if he were searching for a treasure. His apparent dismissal of Lanzerac's words only emboldened the 5th Army commander and made him even in a worse mood than he already was. The two men had been clashing together on the matter of Belgium and the fact that Lanzerac, contrary to Joffre and the rest of the French General Staff, believed that the main enemy effort was through there. From his point of view, they should have switched to the defensive and moved more troops to northeastern France.

"Sir, I must insist that we need to avoid attacking the German forces prematurely, at least until we know their full strength." *"I thought Frenchmen were brave and all about the offensive spirit,"* said the only officer wearing a field brown uniform. It was Field Marshal John French, the commander of the British Expeditionary Force (BEF). The man's troops were finally arriving at the frontlines, and he was ready to fight. *"Marshal,"* started Lanzerac, ready to again argue with the British commander. The French General felt he was the only clear-headed man in the entire room.

"Enough!" said Joffre in a loud voice, hitting his fist on the table. *"General Lanzerac, you will launch the attack tomorrow morning toward Charleroi. Your mission is to push the German forces back*

and send them reeling toward Belgium." Joffre didn't give any opportunity for Lanzerac to answer. *"Marshal French, when are your forces ready to attack?"* The British officer smiled. He was happy he was getting what he wanted: to fight the Germans. *"Sir, we should be ready to move to Mons very soon, and if God is willing, help General Lanzerac to push the bastards back home."*

And just like that, General Joffre was sending the 5th Army to fight over twice its numbers in Charleroi, and the same would soon be true in Mons as well. The strategic implication of the twin battles about to come would be immense in the following weeks.

25th Brigade Royal Field Artillery
Arriving in Mons, August 22nd, 1914

After Great Britain declared war on Germany on August 4th, the British Expeditionary forces under Field Marshal John French started to land at Calais just a few days later. It asse

The troops, after concentrating near Le Cateau and then Mauberge, France, had moved up to Mons on August 21st and 22nd and were in position to meet the advancing Germans and to protect the Allied left flank. They arrived just in time to witness General Lanzerac's 5th Corps ill-fated attack on Charleroi.

Artilleryman Archibald Totenkam was a member of the 113th Battery RFA (Royal Field Artillery) within the 25th Brigade, a component of the 1st British Division. He was a gunner in his unit. It was one of the (rare) permanently established Regular Army divisions in Great Britain. Consequently, it was one of the first to be sent across the Channel and right into the First World War.

Archibald was yet another poor orphan from London's slums and had not been lucky enough to get to know either his father or his mother. Raised in an orphanage where violence was prevalent, he joined the Army at 16, lying on his age to escape the dreadful life. And ever since then, he'd found his purpose in life. Military discipline was harsh, but at least it was just, unlike what he'd come to experience as a youngling. He was now twenty years old (officially 22 by the Division's books), and he was now a seasoned artilleryman. When war broke out with Germany, he was ecstatic to get a chance to be one of the first soldiers to go to France to fight the Germans.

The trip from Southampton to France and then the assembling of the unit in Mauberge went swiftly enough, and then they were shipped by rail to the front lines. The 113th Battery had arrived a day before, and they were ordered to move up to Mons right on the line of battle. The Germans were fast approaching, and the BEF was needed to support the impending French attack from the 5th Corps.

Be as it may, the unit's morale was quite high, and everyone looked forward to facing the damned Germans. At last, they felt they would be able to put the Huns back in their place.

As he pushed his 18-pounder guns to the encouragement of his Lance-Bombardier NCO (Corporal in the RFA), he grunted hard but kept his good mood up. He was eager to fire his first rounds in anger. He would soon learn the horrible reality of war is quite different from what he'd envisioned. They were only trained to fire directly at targets; thus, it explained why they were setting their weapon up from a low farm wall facing a large farm field. The British had no real knowledge or training in counter-battery fire, but they would soon learn their trade.

Once they were done setting up their weapon, one of the guys in the unit thought he'd heard the distant rumble of explosion and artillery. "Can you hear this?" he said, and everyone listened to the sound. To them, it was an exciting sound. But soon, they would learn that avoiding it was the best way to stay alive. War was no fun, contrary to what they were told or believed.

Into the Charleroi Maelstrom Part 1
Fighting and dying in Charleroi August 22nd, 1914

Private soldier Armand Bonnier, now attached to the 5th French Army, grunted hard as he ran under the relentless fire of the enemy. He'd been moved to Charleroi along with a few of his comrades, including his best friend, Philippe Cren, as reinforcements for Lanzerac's attack.

The tracers blazed all about him, and he was tempted to simply lie on the ground and hide, for it was the sensible thing to do. Enemy fire was so thick that the French soldiers around him and Philippe fell like cattle to the slaughter.

"Merde!" said Philippe, pulling Armand by the arm and pushing him into one big hole that had just been blasted by the enemy artillery. Armand was about to protest and tell him that the sergeant would not like it but remembered that Sergeant Ivard was dead. He'd received a bullet in the throat. Then, the next one, Lieutenant Bambin, was also dead, killed by artillery shrapnel. His mind quickly registered that it was not so bad to finally find some shelter because they were getting seriously hammered.

Both the French and the Germans were very offensive-minded in the fall of 1914. Their doctrines were born out of the belief that only the attack could bring about a swift and decisive victory, just like the Franco-Prussian War of 1870-1871 or the Austro-German War of 1866.

On a tactical level, the situation was slightly different, which meant a world of difference for poor blokes like Armand and Philippe. The Germans were bloodied troops since they had fought hard during the battle for the forts and then against the Belgian Army. They were now accustomed to the reality of modern war and understood the shattering power of artillery over human flesh, no matter how determined a soldier could be. The French had yet to learn this lesson.

On 22nd August 1914, General Charles Lanrezac was ordered to attack the German 2nd and 3rd Armies frontally. Without any artillery support, the French soldiers, with their bayonet-tipped rifles, were just supposed to march up, use their "élan," and shatter the more numerous enemies advancing relentlessly in front of them. Just as the General had predicted and argued about with Joffre, the French commander-in-chief's bad decision was coming to fruition. He had attacked right into a wall of men and guns, completely outnumbered.

The "run and gun doctrine" so favored by the French military establishment of the time deployed itself in its full glory. It was all about the will of the offensive spirit and how French arms and men would mater the mindless eastern hordes. Only things didn't work out that way. The poor French soldiers were quickly slammed with lead, bullets, and death.

And that was why Philippe had pulled his friend into the large blasted-out hole. Loud whistling sounds were making themselves heard in an overwhelming crescendo, like blaring sirens. Armand had not heard them because his rifle had numbed his ears to almost deafness since the start of the fight. He had fired a lot of shots, and the ringing in his ears had just taken over. Philippe's capability to recognize sounds was better because he'd fired fewer shots and thus had heard the shells coming down on the valley they were stupidly charging into.

Moments later, the first shells started to land and to rock the ground in a catastrophic display of fire, smoke and catapulting earth into the sky. The entire field blossomed in balls of fire, and French soldiers died in droves. It was a terrible massacre. The shelling went on for ten minutes, and when the German guns stopped, the field was covered in dead and horribly wounded. Only the smartest (Philippe and Armand) and the luckiest (those favored by extreme luck) were unscathed.

With the bombardment over, both men cautiously peered their

heads out of the hole they were in and were suddenly privy to the macabre sight of their dead and shattered comrades. There were bodies everywhere, but that was not the worst of it. There were plenty of body parts and red meat sprinkled with blood everywhere, evidence that some of the French soldiers had been hit and shattered to pieces by the explosions.

"*Can you hear it,*" said Philippe, still with better ears than Armand. "*What?*" answered Armand, barely able to get what his friend was telling him. The ringing in his ears was terrible. "*It's the fucking Germans, they are coming,*" he said nervously. And just as if he'd called them forth, a line of grey-clad and spiked helmet soldiers burst out of the swirling smoke and midst of the artillery bombardment, yelling out of their lungs with bayonets fixed to their rifles.

"*We need to go!*" said Philippe, and Armand didn't argue with him. They sprinted out of the hole and ran in the opposite direction, where they figured some semblance of a French line of defense was surely being set up.

The battle was not going well. Not going well at all.

The Battle of Charleroi
The French bungle into disaster, August 22nd-23rd, 1914

The Battle of Charleroi was fought in Belgium from the 22nd to the 23rd of August 1914 by a lot of men and equipment: 755,000 Germans against 322,000 French, with hundreds of guns on both sides. Just as General Lanzerac predicted (in an argument with Joffre a few days before when he was ordered to attack instead of putting himself in a defensive stance), his French 5th Army ran into a wall of bayonets and guns.

The Battle of Charleroi was a result of the French and German armies' movements during and after the Battle of the Frontiers and was rendered unavoidable by the conquest of the Liege Belgian forts.

While the defensive construction had certainly been a formidable obstacle, the hunkered-down and well-armed Belgian soldiers could not do anything against the flood of 140,000 German men and over a thousand guns that splattered them for days on end until they got obliterated. When the town and the twelve forts fell, it opened the entire road to the German forces and they marched with great speed into Belgium and then northern France.

Although the so-called "Battle of Charleroi" was perceived as being one battle, it was indeed a plethora of smaller skirmishes making for a bigger-scale battle. These fights were not in any specific way by either side but instead resulted from actions launched piecemeal by many marching units with contradicting orders. In a sense, the movements of the two armies made them meet in the middle at Charleroi.

Seeing that they were clearly outnumbered, the French decided to use their good old "elan" (offensive spirit) and attack regardless. French Bayonet charges were thus promptly shattered by German machine guns and artillery bombardment. This way of doing war was a lot better than the French tactics from another war.

Unfortunately for them, their army and its old officers were ready only for a replay of the Franco-Prussian conflict and had not learned the lessons offered by the more modern seen during the Russo-Japanese War of 1904-1905. In short, General Joffre and his acolytes within the General Staff were a war too late.

This resulted in heavy losses for their forces. By the end of the day on the 22nd of August (for example), the 25th Infantry Division registered 2,000 losses alone, and the 49th Infantry Regiment registered 350. It was a slaughter of epic proportions, and that was when artillery shells didn't make an appearance on the battlefield. Then, it was even worse.

But the French fought on with reckless bravery and thus also caused serious casualties to the German troops. The OHL had not expected such resilience from the French in the area, and they paid for this lack of preparedness with their own blood.

Fighting continued on the 23rd of August and again to the German's advantage because the French forces in the area started to retreat backward, reeling backward under the pressure. The German 3rd Army moved across the River Meuse and slammed on the French right flank. General Lanzerac's Fifth Army's line of retreat was thus almost blocked, but the swift counterattack kept the line open. Added to the German capture of the Namur fortress and news of the defeat of the 4th French Army in the Ardennes, Lanrezac, very aware of the danger, ordered his forces to withdraw. The entire point for him was to avoid being outflanked and isolated. The German army was victorious.

Lanzerac's decision turned out to be highly controversial, although it saved the French Army from imminent defeat and destruction. Joffre, not being one of his best fans, sacked him and replaced him with a more *"offensive-minded"* officer.

Into the Charleroi Maelstrom Part 2
Retreat August 23rd, 1914.

Armand and Philippe ran as fast as their burning legs let them. They were flanked by many of their blue uniform-red trousers comrades, trying to extricate themselves from the Charleroi area. The order to retreat had been given a few hours earlier, and now the entire affair had the smell of a rout.

But the French soldiers (in general) kept their cool amidst the blast of earth lifted by the enemy artillery and flurry of tracer fire zipping by. Armand almost fell, as he had not seen a French dead soldier on the ground, but Philippe helped him keep steady. The big, broad-shouldered man had been a lifesaver since the start of the battle. He smiled. *"Come on, Bonnier, you don't die on me just now."* *"Sure thing, Cren,"* he answered. They had become good friends over the last two weeks of intense battle they'd fought together from Mulhouse to Metz to now in Charleroi.

The battle was terrible. Armand figured that their Regiment had lost well over 40% of its number. He remembered the stupid bayonet charges amidst heavy machine gun fire. How ignorant had that been? He wondered if those *"bold generals"* would feel the same if they had to feel the brunt of a German division. He doubted it. He doubted it very much.

A truly large explosion about fifty meters away reverberated loudly, and the ground shook hard. He turned his head just in time to see a big mushroom of dark earth catapulting in the air. "Keep going," said one of the sergeants around them. *"It's one of those Karl-Gerat mobile mortars the Krauts have. Don't worry about it."*

"Easy to say," mumbled Philippe in between two heavy breaths. Indeed, it was easy to say not to take notice, but when an explosion simulated the end of the world like that one, it was hard not to turn the head and take notice.

They were getting truly winded with all this running and being fired at. Armand spotted a large farmhouse made of brick and wood on the right side, and he tugged his friend. *"Phil, look over there. Let's head to the place; we can shelter for a moment and rest and breathe a little."* Cren didn't say anything in response and just followed Armand.

The field they ran on was a maelstrom of fire and steel. Enemy ammo crisscrossed everywhere while fireballs blossomed all around them from the enemy artillery exploding. Armand and Philippe felt truly lucky to be still alive. Many of their friends and comrades had not been that fortunate.

They ended their sprint just as they rounded the corner of the building to finally shelter from the withering enemy gunfire because the barn protected them. They found a large bunch of French soldiers already huddled behind it. Some more were inside the structure, firing at the advancing Germans. Not one of them took notice, as men were constantly streaming out and into the area. It was a madhouse of running Frenchmen and of death.

Winded, they both put their hands on their knees and took several slow, hard air intakes. *"Damn, that was a hell of a run,"* said Philippe, slapping his friend on the shoulder. *"Yeah, buddy..."*

"Get ready! The Germans are upon us!" yelled a Captain somewhere inside the big barn. The staccato of fire, quite loud already, increased its tempo by a few notches. The two comrades looked at each other and decided that this place was not where they would make their stand. It was not their unit, and they had no standing orders, nor had any officer at the barn given them any. *"Let's make a run for it, Armand,"* said Cren. *"Agreed,"* he answered, not looking forward to being winded again. The constant running was hard. They started sprinting once more in the same direction as the rest of their comrades.

The general order was to assemble south of Charleroi at the village of Florennes, a couple of kilometers down the road. Then, they both guessed someone would give them fresh orders and that if they were lucky, the damned Krauts would be out of sight for a while.

The Battle of Mons
The BEF's baptism of fire, August 22nd to August 24th

'I want you to concentrate and will your action… on one and only one objective,
and that is to put everything you have in terms of skills and power to exterminate
the damned Brits and destroy that little, no-contest army of theirs.'
Kaiser Wilhelm II – 21st of August 1914

As the French Army threw away its armed forces (in vain) in head-on assaults against the German forces across the Alsace-Lorraine border and insisted on attacking to retake its lost province, the great German offensive (Schlieffen Plan) swung hard north and west, slamming on the Allied left. It fell into too small a segment: the Entente forces, the French 5th Army, and the British Expeditionary Force.

The first to feel the full might of three German armies was General Lanzerac and his 5th Army. By the end of August 23rd, the French were in full retreat, and their only hope in avoiding a rout was the British Expeditionary Force (BEF) on Lanzerac's left. The small French town of Mons was the pivotal point on which the Entente forces could retreat if the Brits held long enough.

The BEF included much of Britain's tiny regular army, a rather small force of four infantry divisions and five cavalry brigades. When one compared it to the large continental armies it was almost a non-issue on paper. The German troops barreling down on them from Belgium looked like they would flood them with a storm of steel and might.

Nevertheless, the British troops, unafraid of the ratio difference, moved east toward the advancing Germans, marching across the storied grounds where their ancestors from another age had defeated the French two centuries before (under the command of Malborough). Not far from there was also a famous field where history had been made called Waterloo.

The Commander of the BEF (Marshal John French) eventually confirmed the enemy's intentions when the battle was joined in Mons, and Lanzerac retreated in disaster. The German came at him with so many troops that it was obvious he had positioned his men too far forward and would soon be in a very difficult position.

Just a little under two days before, the British officer had been mad at General Lanzerac for not wanting to go to the offensive once again. He soon understood why his French counterpart, probably the only clear-headed Allied officer before they finally understood the nature of the German threat, had advocated defense.

The first heavy fighting happened in the dreary industrial area of the town, pictured by old, worn-down houses and industrial buildings and grey, dirty surroundings. There, on Sunday, August the 23rd, and, as the French were backing up in disarray, The British 1st Corps (under the command of Sir Douglas Haig) got bloody-nosed hard by the German forces (on the Conde Canal). The Conde was a disgusting industrial-human waste sludge that stank badly. It wasn't large, but it was what the British had to defend. In the end, it proved large enough, and no German soldiers were willing to move into the green, stinky, and disgusting liquid.

Haig's units, stretched thin on a large stretch of land 21 miles wide, were rapidly attacked all along the front, and their defenses buckled, almost snapping. Although the British were badly outnumbered, their massed firepower, including their excellent Royal Field Artillery, stopped the Germans cold.

The fighting continued for another day, and then, when Lanzerac's forces were somewhat disengaged from the Germans, Marshal French ordered his forces to fall back and execute a fighting retreat.

Near the Conde Canal, British 1st Division, 113th battery
Artillery fire and counter-battery fire, August 23rd, 1914

Archibald Totenkam went through the motion of loading a shell into the gun and then moving toward the pile of ammo to pick up another as the team's 18-pounder fired one shot after the other at the mass of gray-uniformed attackers on the other side of the Conde Canal. The stench was terrible, as the Canal was polluted and clogged with human feces, combined with coal residues and other chemical products. Unfortunately for the British, the wind was blowing south, bringing them this nice fragrance.

"Fire," said Lance-Bombardier Henry Stimms (the equivalent of a Lance-Corporal in the infantry), and the gun spat yet another shell. The British 18-pounders were field guns, and most of the BEF's training was in direct fire. Thus, the blazing round flew a few meters above the troops lined up along the Canal and flew in a relatively level line toward the incoming German horde. The shell slammed into the grey mass, and a powerful explosion shattered a few infantrymen to pieces. Body parts, smoke, and dirt flew in the air. *"Reload,"* yelled Stimms, but he didn't have to; Archibald was already at work with his colleagues. The shells were heavy, and he was helped in the loading operation by one of his comrade gunners.

The loading mechanism was relatively simple and efficient. *"Loading,"* he yelled as per his training. He inserted the shell. He then did the rest of his movements, locking the shell in place and closing the breech. *"Ready!"* And the 18-pounder fired once more, its muzzle brightening briefly with fire, and the shell thundered down to slam on the line of German soldiers advancing on the Conde Canal.

The cannon was a great tool for the British and would go on to serve the Entente Powers faithfully for the duration of the conflict. The weapon was designed to work with indirect firing, and thus, it meant it was supposed to fire directly at the enemy he could see on the battlefield.

A time would come when the BEF would practice indirect fire with the very same weapon, but for now the 18-pounders was what it was, a field artillery support weapon during battle. The gun itself looked great and menacing. It had an imposing steel barrel resting on a well-designed bronze cradle. It was heavy and looked powerful.

As he moved backward to get one more shell, Archibald took the time (a few seconds only, but it was enough) to give himself a view of the battlefield. To his left and right, 18-pounders in line fired one shell after the other, their round flashing in the sky as they recoiled backward from the blasts. German bullets blazed by everywhere, and artillerymen were getting hit by the dozens. The 18-pounder had a steel faceplate for protection, but it wasn't large enough to cover the gunners as they went about their business. He also noticed a thin veil of smoke or more like a mist. The rumble of battle was overbearing, as if a powerful summer storm unleashed its fury, only it never stopped, and there were no time lapses between the rumbles. The ground shook with permanent slight tremors, proof that explosions were blossoming everywhere.

And then he was back through the motions. The shells were in a hole dug beside the gun in order to avoid the gunners being hit by direct fire. While it was a good precaution, it wasn't any protection against indirect and plunging fire. The British had learned that the hard way the day before, when a battery of German guns had taken the 113th as a target, Three guns were destroyed.

And it was just about to happen all over again. "*Incoming*," yelled Lance-Bombardier Stimms as loud whistling sounds made themselves heard. The enemy had put artillery in place (they had the high ground, after all) and were now launching counter-battery fire on the British. Archibald knew what that meant. He ran to one of the nearby shallow trenches they'd dug in the early morning when it was still dark. Plunging hard into it, he arrived just in time as the enemy shells started to land around them. He lost his breath as he hit the ground hard, but at least he was protected from the deadly, indirect damage of shrapnel and debris falling everywhere when someone was in the middle of an artillery bombardment.

The ground shook, and his ears ringed. The concussion power of the blasts was so great that he was almost knocked out. But he was unscathed, as the only way he could be killed was by a shell landing directly into his small hole. He yelled to his mother, cried for some, and then curled into a ball, praying to God to survive the ordeal. And then, it was over.

When a relative calm presented (it was still a battle, but shells weren't landing right on his position), he peered his head out. What he saw was utter devastation. While his own gun was still standing without any apparent scratch, the gun on its right and on its left were gone. One was shattered to pieces, and the other was gutted, with one wheel still standing, but the rest of the weapon crumbled to the ground. He saw a few body parts around, and he figured that many of the men had not survived the ordeal. A thin veil of smoke hung over the ground, and a stillness hung over the scene. The British artillery had been silenced, and as he watched the German guns in the distance on the high ground, it was a stark reminder that if they fired again, they would only call another strike on their position.

The officers above them also got the message, and the order soon went out to move the surviving 18-pounders back toward the rear. War was a terrible business. Not long after the RFA (Royal Field Artillery) was gone, the infantry along the Canal was also ordered to pull back. By the morning of the 24th of August, the British were gone from Mons and in full retreat toward Paris and the West.

Attacking Mons
2nd Army, 4th Division, Infanterie-Regiment Graf Schwerin

Private German soldier Oskar Dantz felt a little weary. In the last few weeks, he'd seen the worst of all the destruction modern war could bring about. Shattered body parts, burnt houses, tens of thousands of casualties, and the rotting smell of death. It seemed to him that then everything was becoming senseless and that the war he was now in was a lunacy, a horribly bad joke about people and their history.

He had set out in a rain of flowers to seek the death of heroes. Like many in Germany, the war had been (before he fought in it) a glorious affair, where he would march to the glory of victory, everyone in his hometown seeing him for what he would be: a hero. He used to think there was no lovelier death in the world. For him and his comrades, it was a hell of a lot better than staying at home and being a coward. His fevered thoughts had considerably cooled ever since he'd faced Fort Bachon in Belgium. He now knew the folly of war.

And yet, there was reason to rejoice. German forces were victorious everywhere. First, they'd stormed Liege and then trampled all over Belgium. Oskar himself has basked in the glory of it all when he entered the Belgian capital in triumph. The defenses in Alsace-Lorraine were holding, and the French were reeling back with heavy casualties.

He was weary, especially today, as he marched toward the stinking Conde Canal, some wretched place near a French town called Mons. He'd heard the Captain talk about the place, and the area was famous for a few historical battles, something to do about yet another Englishman or else Napoleon Bonaparte himself.

He was about to rehearse a battle all over again, with its follow-up dead and wounded. He didn't even know if he would survive. Loud noises whistled above their heads, and some of the soldiers around him (probably new soldiers, replacements sent from Germany) cheered loudly. German artillery was firing on the British position on the other side of the Canal. He knew better. The killing would soon start, and it wouldn't be pretty.

Oskar could feel the enemy bullets zipping by, with a noise reminiscent of a large fly or a bee flying close to one's ear. Only these noises were a byproduct of something a lot more lethal than harmless insects. He was not in the front ranks moving toward the Canal, and thus, he and his comrades weren't receiving the brunt of the attack, but he knew that ahead of him, it must be hell. He remembered being at the forefront of a battle, and it wasn't pretty. The tracers, the explosions, the dying.

Anyone with a minimum of sense could tell that the large blasts of earth, smoke, and fire catapulting in the air ahead of the platoon didn't forecast anything good for them once they got to the same spot. He hoped that by the time they got there, perhaps things would be a little less dicey.

Moments later, they all started to hear the chain explosions of their own artillery guns blasting, and Oskar decided they must have fired at something close because, normally, artillery fired at the rear of the attacking columns. *"Steady, lads,"* said crusty Sergeant Wilhelm as he walked beside them. *"If anyone wants to know why our gun boys are firing so close, it's because we are about to face British troops, and their cannons are right up to the frontline and firing at point-blank range on our troops,"* he continued. A line of concussion blasts as high as hills was seen by the troops, even the ones in the middle of the formation like Oskar. It was an awesome display of firepower, and the new recruits cheered yet again. Smoke rose following the shelling.

For a moment, Oskar wondered how the hell the man knew that and figured it must have been explained to him in the briefing he was having with the Lieutenant and the Captain. He shook the thoughts out of his mind, as he had better things to do than think about trivial issues. After all, he was kinda wanting to survive. He thus concentrated on the front of him.

As they walked, the ranks thinned, and they got closer to the enemy line, and he finally saw the enemy defenses. They were laid right at the Canal's western side. The British soldiers were lying down flat on their bellies, using the concrete lip of the Conde Canal for cover, while having their rifles leveled horizontally at the attacking German troops.

The orders then came down to hurry the pace and to charge. He noticed the enemy artillery had stopped fighting. Now that he was almost in the open field covering the distance between the canal and where the German troops were, he saw that the enemy's scattered fire was slackening. He even saw figures running back. The bastards were retreating!

And indeed, the British were. The German artillery had shattered their field artillery, and now it was time for the BEF's men to try and survive for another day. He shouldered his rifle to fire a couple of rounds at the enemy and then kept advancing. He was quite happy that things did not go too awry for him and his comrades this time.

Battle of Heligoland Bight Part 1
Prelude, September August 28th to September 6th, 1914.

Heligoland Bight was a semi-circular expanse of water that was part of the North Sea, enclosed by the north-western coast of German and the western coast of Denmark. The Kaiserliche Marine (German Navy) had a base there, located on the island in the center of the semi-circle (called Heligoland Island). If there was one strategic spot near German waters, it was there. The base itself was a major threat to the Royal Navy because it could be used as a staging area for a full German fleet attack in the North Sea. It was also an early-warning system of sorts for the Germans as they operated patrol in the area to intercept any enemy ships approaching the German coast.

The British Admiralty had planned an attack on German vessels patrolling near the Heligoland Bight base, but it had been limited in scope. At that time, Great Britain had been busy with other tasks. BEF troops were transferred to France; thus, the ships were needed to escort and protect the transport vessels used to bring the 200,000 soldiers to battle. The Battle for Belgium was just beginning, but then things got a little more complicated. The idea was thus to send some cruisers and fast battlecruisers and confront the small recon squadrons based on the island. It was a well-known fact the Germans maintained a fast, light cruiser squadron. Thus, an attack there was considered a low-risk-high-reward for the British.

From the British point of view, the war was not going well. The Germans were advancing across the frontline and seemed unstoppable. By early September, the Entente forces were in full retreat toward Paris, and there didn't seem to be anything stopping the German Army. London wanted to do something about it but didn't have the troops yet to confront the Germans on the ground. But they had ships and ships they would use.

But the real clincher for the British to want to make something bigger out of what was originally a small operation was the situation at sea. The Allies were still reeling from the terrible Russian defeat at Cape Sarych in the Black Sea. The German dreadnought battlecruiser Goeben and a fleet of Ottoman ships (including two brand new battleships built in England) had sunk no less than five pre-dreadnought battleships. While the Royal Navy had not been involved in any of it, it did suffer a setback during the pursuit of the Goeben and the Breslau. It was thus time for the English navy to clean away what was perceived as a smear on his reputation.

The British were gifted with an aggressive First Lord of the Admiralty in Winton Churchill, a man of action. For him, there was no compromise; the island and the base needed to be neutralized and British Naval primacy re-affirmed. The man had been stung and stung badly by the mad dash by the Goeben, the ships Souchon had first sunk in the Aegean Sea, and then in the Black Sea against the Russians, and then in general because he saw British pride hurt, and he felt it was bad for the nation's morale. The way he saw it, the Kaiserliche Marine needed to be put back in its place.

It was with this state of mind that he met with Admiral John Jellicoe, his brand-new commander of the so-called British Grand Fleet. The orders for the Navy were clear: destroy the base and come to Heligoland Bight with enough force in case the German Navy decided to make a scene about it.

The original plan was scrapped, and instead of sending only the 1st Battlecruiser squadron with cruisers and destroyers (Cruiser Force C, First Light Cruiser squadron, 3rd and 1st destroyer flotilla), Churchill upped the ante by attaching the Grand Fleet 1st Battle squadron that contained no less than eight dreadnought battleships.

Grand Fleet 1st Battle squadron	
Adiral Lewis Bayly	
BB Marlborough	BB Neptune
BB Collingwood	BB St. Vincent
BB Colossus	BB Superb
BB Hercules	BB Vanguard
Grand Fleet 1st Battle squadron	
Vice Adiral David Beatty	
BC Lion	
BC Princess Royal	
BC Queen Mary	
BC New Zealand	

Cruiser Force C (Seventh Cruiser Squadron)	First Light Cruiser Squadron
Euryalus (Rear-Admiral Christian)	Southampton (Commodore Goodenough)
CA Bacchante	CL Birmingham
CA Cressy	CL Falmouth
CA Hogue	CL Nottingham
CA Aboukir	CL Lowestoft
CA Amethyst	CL Liverpool

Third Destroyer Flotilla	First Destroyer Flotilla
15 DD	16 DD

The original mission, planned for the 28th of August, was thus postponed by a week for the 1st Battle squadron to reposition and join the rest of its comrades in the Firth of Forth near London, where Beatty's battle cruiser and raiding force had been assembled. The powerful British raiding fleet then made its way toward the Heligoland Bight.

On the other side of the North Sea, the German Kaiserliche Marine didn't have any plans to attack the British, but it was indeed committed to making sure its forward base survived. The base's naval defense was normally ensured by a squadron, including six light cruisers (Mainz, Strassburg, Stralsund, Kolberg, Danzig, and München).

Heligoland Bight squadron	
CL Mainz	CL Kolberg
CL Strassburg	CL Danzig
CL Stralsund	CL Munchen
1st Scouting Group	
Admiral Franz von Hipper	
BC Seydlitz	BC Deerflinger
BC Moltke	BC Won Der Tann

If the British had attacked the base on the 28th of August as originally planned, they would have found only the light cruisers, and the engagement would have been a sort of footnote in the history book as a minor naval battle. Instead, Beatty and Bayly arrived just as the German 1st Scouting group, under the command of Admiral Franz von Hipper, sailed in the vicinity.

At about noon on the 6th of September, Beatty's battlecruisers, along with Cruiser Force C and the 3rd Destroyer Flotilla, ran right into the six light cruisers of the Heligoland Bight German Squadron. The two groups of ships immediately opened fire on the other while the numerically inferior Germans turned back toward the German coast.

The German 1st Scouting Squadron wasn't far and thus Hipper ordered his ships to reach the battle area as soon as possible, while the British commander of the Grand Fleet 1st Battle Squadron did the same.

Everything was set for the first real naval battle between Germany and Great Britain.

Charleroi and Mons: Aftermath
Early September 1914

From August 20th to 24th, the entire French frontline was blazing with battles, known to history by the name the Battle of the Frontiers. From south near the Swiss border in Lorraine to the northern French plains, the war was in full swing.

By the morning of August 20th in Lorraine, the French 1st Army and the 2nd Army had battered themselves bloody against the prepared facing the German defenses. The *"Elan vital"* concept found its limit facing the German defenses, backed up by industrial power and the technology of artillery, machine guns, mines, and barbed wire. The 1870-1871 war was over, and the French should have paid more attention to the bloody fighting of the Russo-Japanese War of 1904-1905. There, the inklings of the impacts of modern weapons on tactics and maneuvers started to become obvious to the few and sharpest, among them several other German officers and very few Franco-British ones.

In executing the tactics of bayonet assault, the French military doctrine dictated that in twenty-five seconds, the infantry line could cover fifty-five meters prior to the Germans having time to get ready to fire their weapons. The reality of the battlefield could not have been further from the truth.

All these gymnastics, so painfully practiced at maneuvers, were for naught when the battle was joined. No Frenchmen could run faster than the German machine gun bullets or protect themselves against the powerful artillery shelling.

The doctrine also stated that shrapnel fired by French artillery support would eliminate the enemy defense and keep it pinned down. The opposite happened, just like it had in the Russo-Japanese War of 1904-1905. Any infantryman could keep fighting, firing, and surviving if well protected behind sandbags, a parapet, or a trench.

But the French weren't the only ones still in love with the concept of the offensive. Following the successful German counterattack across Alsace-Lorraine and the French being booted out of every inch of imperial territory, the OHL decided to modify its plan. Perhaps, after all, the German Army's might would win over modern defenses?. Had they not smashed the French and could do the same while the bastards retreated?

Perhaps the fortified French towns of Epinal and Toul would be weak enough to fall as quickly as the Liege forts. Perhaps the two armies of the left wing, so recently basked in the glory of their successful counteroffensive, could succeed in breaking through the enemy defense... In cooperation with the troops executing the Schlieffen Plan toward the French North, both sides of the pincer could realize one of the greatest encirclement in history, like at Cannae.

This was the scenario that men like Moltke at the OHL were starting to think possible as the battles of Charleroi and Mons ended victoriously for the German forces. Like the temptation of the proverbial apple in Eden, the prospect of a truly glorious victory overcame years of focused planning for a decisive attack on the right wing. At that moment, the famed General von Schlieffen must have turned on himself in his grave at the folly of it all.

The German 6th and 7th Armies were thus sent on frontal attacks upon the French fortress line, and the battle increased in intensity just as the fight for Mons was ending on August 23rd. Joffre (of course) counterattacked as he still saw the best defense was the offense in the area. General Joffre was adamant that Plan XVII was the French Army's only option. The French leader could simply not contemplate the other possibility, which was to immediately switch all his troops and units to the defensive. For the spirit of the French military doctrine and all the officer corps brought up in the last thirty years, this was unthinkable, except for Lanzerac, who was punished for proposing it.

In the following days, the German 6th and 7th Armies fought frontal battles against the battered but still fighting men of the French 1st and 2nd Armies. And then the roles were suddenly reversed. It was the turn of the French to shatter the German attacks, backed up as they were by the guns of their fortress in Belfort, Toul, and Epinal. Epic clashes were fought where casualties were heavy, running in the hundreds of thousands. It was a butchery of epic proportion, with no gains on each side.

Following the twin battles of Mons and Charleroi, Belgium was a wasteland in shambles, and the Germans advanced, victorious toward France. And over it all lay a smell. It was the smell of half a million unbathed men and a field littered with dead, rotting corpses. The was no time to bury the dead as the troops were busy advancing and fighting. Or else the enemy was firing at them; thus, they could not venture to pick up the fallen.

After all the carnage, the dead, the attacks, the hope, and the defeats, the Germans still advanced toward Paris, while hundreds of thousands of men fought and died in the still-going Battle of the Frontier. The fate of the Entente Powers hung in the balance, and French offensive dreams were broken.

Mauberge
August 25th, 1914, 1914

"Sir," said the young French staff officer. General Joffre, the commander-in-chief of all French Armies, nodded nonchalantly. *"Your car is ready to go, and the train stands ready to bring you to your new HQ,"* continued the man, saluting sharply. *"Humpff,"* grunted Joffre. *"Very well, Lieutenant,"* he continued as he looked at the long and thick columns of smoke rising to the north. He could also hear the rumble of the guns; obviously, it was getting nearer. And, of course, it was.

Joffre, towering above with his offensive spirit doctrine and his own wishes for glory and victory, wasn't ready to accept reality. The responsibility for the catastrophe rested upon him and his offensive stubbornness. The borders of France were breached (the situation was very serious, indeed), and none of his offensive plans or attacks had worked. Facing the Alsace-Lorraine province he so long sought to liberate, the 1st and 2nd French armies struggled mightily to contain the hordes of German troops attacking with abandon. Things were not going well.

And yet, he remained steadfast in his thinking and planning. By putting the fault on men like General Lanzerac, who had only tried to execute his stupid attack, he was able to keep fooling himself into thinking that it wasn't the plan that was working; it was the men executing it. As he did so, he put forth the conditions by which the calamitous days ahead would unfold.

Beside him stood his faithful chief of staff, General Jean Cabes. *"You know, Jean,"* he started, resting his hand on his ceremonial sword pommel. *"We can't inogre the obvious; we might now be forced to go on the defensive and to rely on our fortified lines. As we wear down the enemy, we must take the next opportunity to attack in force."* *"Indeed, sir,"* answered the man who could not have said otherwise because he was supportive of his commanding officer.

"We need to rearrange the lines of retreat to prepare the regrouping of our forces to get the necessary strength to counterattack whenever the opportunity presents itself." He paused, turning toward his staff car as it was time to evacuate Mauberge and go to an HQ further back into the rear. *"Where do you think we can hold a line while we reorganize, Jean?"*

The ever-faithful yes man answered what his commander expected. *"As you have said, sir, we should be able to establish something solid on the Somme."* *"I agree with you, General,"* said Joffre with a nod of the head. They walked some more and eventually arrived at the black staff car on the side of a dusty road where French troops marched westward in columns. The men looked battered and worn, many of them with bloody and dirty uniforms. But at the sight of their commanding General, they cheered. Joffre smiled. *"You see, Jean,"* he exclaimed as he lifted his arm to make a perfect salute. *"The men are still in good spirits."* *"Yes, General,"* answered Cabes.

Joffre still believed in France, in himself, and in ultimate victory. He had been encouraged by a recent telegram from Russia announcing several victories in Eastern Prussia. The Tsar's armies were plowing deep into East Prussia, and the sensible thing to do was to send them reinforcements. They would soon threaten Konigsberg and could be on the Vistula within weeks. This entire state of affairs comforted him in thinking that the Germans would forced to send reinforcements to the East to deal with the threat, greatly weakening their offensive power in their current offensive.

Unfortunately for the French commander, the OHL had already decided to go through the Western offensive before doing anything about the East.

A soldier standing beside the car opened the door for Joffre on one side, and another man did the same for Cabes, who entered from the other side. They both removed their hats, gave the salute to the two soldiers, and made the signal for the driver to get going.

They continued their discussion in the car. *"We should have won already, Jean,"* he started with a frustrated voice. *"In spite of the numerical superiority which I thought we had secured for our armies." "As you said earlier, sir," countered Cabes." It has to do with a lack of offensive spirit."*

Joffre looked through the car window, still to the north, where the large columns of smoke prevailed. *"We need to get a note for all armies that the field regulations have not been followed to the letter. Assaults were initiated from too great a distance and without proper artillery support; thus, we suffered heavier losses from fixed defensive weapons such as machine guns that should have been destroyed by our mighty guns."* Cabes quickly fished his notepad from the small briefcase in the car. When the General spoke, it was always good to take notes. Joffre continued unabated. *"You get this, Jean,"* he said, and when the chief of staff nodded, he went on. *"Entrenchments must be dug. The capital error has been a lack of coordination between artillery and infantry, which needs to be rectified. The 75s must fire at maximum range."* Cabes changed the page, still writing furiously.

Whatever else were the French General's faults, he wasn't totally blind to the now-prevalent role of the defensive in warfare. But he still wanted to win the war, not create a stalemate and only defend in place.

And then, Joffre stopped speaking, losing himself in thoughts and his own self-awareness. When he truly looked deep down at the very bottom of his soul, he knew that he was partly – at least – to blame.

On August 24, as Joffre was busy dictating new instructions for when his armies would go back to the offensive, it was clear the Entente forces were starting a full retreat westward. The full extent of the potential disaster for France was not yet understood, but with the fall of Namur, announced by the Germans at the end of the day, it started to dawn on the Allies that things were not going well.

The news shocked the Entente and the rest of Europe. It had been claimed by many a newspaper and military expert that Namu could withstand a siege of at least six months; that claim could not have been further from the truth: it had fallen in five days.

On August 24th, the Germans felt an immense surge of confidence, while the Anglo-French were wary of where they would stop retreating and if they could turn the situation around. And their commander-in-chief, General Joffre, was not so certain of the final outcome as he had been only a week earlier when he sent his glorious bayonets on the attack.

Battle of Heligoland Bight Part 2
The slugging match, September 6th, 1914.

A few minutes before 1100 AM on the 6th of September 1914, one of the German light cruisers guarding Heligoland Island was sighted by the British lookouts about three and a half miles to the southeast.

Vice-Admiral Beatty, commander of the 1st Battle Cruiser Squadron, ahead of the main force along with the 3rd Destroyer Flotilla and Cruiser Squadron C, sent his escort ships (destroyers and cruisers) to confront the enemy squadron. He didn't want to commit his entire force yet, as the Grand Fleet's 1st Battle Squadron was still some miles behind him; thus, he wanted to take no chance if he encountered a powerful enemy force.

The four British destroyers came upon the rest of the German light cruisers (six of them), and consequently, the naval battle began. Both German and British warships started to fire their guns. The range, however, was too great to be effective. The Germans switched from being defensive to aggressive while the four destroyers turned tail and ran. It didn't take more for both sides to call in the big boys. On the German side, Admiral von Hipper (four battlecruisers) received the frantic calls and ordered his ships to sail toward the coordinates where the battle was being fought, while Beaty (four battlecruisers) and Bayly (eight battleships) zeroed in as well. All was set for a great naval battle, and neither side had a clue what the other was bringing to bear.

As Squadron Cruiser C closed the range and started to engage the German light cruiser task force, lookouts from the Seydlitz and Von der Tann, and both the Lion and Princess Royal spotted each other roughly at the same moment, their towering columns of boiler smoke churning out as they were at battle speed, visible for miles around.

For the first time since the Germans had started to build up their navy, both ship builds and effectiveness would finally be tested against the other.

The British concept of the battlecruiser was a ship with high-speed, heavy firepower but relatively weak armor protection. The theory was that a battlecruiser could chase and outgun any kind of cruiser but be fast enough to run away from a battleship.

So Royal Navy battlecruisers weren't ever intended to slug it out with battleships, nor really even supposed to slug it out with other big-gun ships. They were supposed to use their speed to run away from that kind of risky encounter (and report back the enemy positions to the main fleet of battleships).

In contrast, the German design of both battlecruisers and battleships emphasized armor protection and survivability - at the cost of comfort and practicality for long-range missions. They weren't building ships needed to protect the sea lanes of a global empire - they built ships for short raids into the North Sea, hoping to catch small enemy squadrons and narrow the overall gap in numbers and firepower.

It wasn't really a one-dimensional "*which was more powerful*"; the British battlecruisers were excellent ships for their intended use (albeit with some flaws in being too vulnerable to magazine explosions and lighter armor), and the German ships would have been horrible on a long cruise. However, they sported accurate gunnery and good armor protection. Consequently, it was argued they were more effective in their intended role in the North Sea. The entire affair would be settled.

Unfortunately for the British that day, the battle that was beginning was to fit right into the German design scope – at least initially until the eight powerful dreadnought battleships of the 1st Battle Squadron arrived.

As the German ships were spotted, Beatty had, of course, no intention to back down and slink away from the fight. The Royal

Navy prided itself on being the dominant naval power on the globe and also with the *"offensive spirit of Nelson and its other forebears."*

Both forces thus opened up on the other at long range but sought to close the distance to score real hits. It was a four-against-four fight, and shells started to fall everywhere around the big ships, straddling each other, but no one scored any hits in the first few minutes. All the while, the smaller ships battled it out (the German battlecruisers also had some destroyer escorts), and it was soon obvious to the numerically inferior Germans that they needed to sail away or be destroyed. When the light cruiser Kolberg exploded in a spectacular fashion (hit by a full broadside from the cruiser Cressy), the rest got the message and veered to port to return to Heligoland base and use the fixed naval guns for added protection.

While this was happening, Admiral von Hipper was ecstatic at the first hits scored by his vessels. Von der Tann, Seydlitz, and Deerflinger all scored on their opposing numbers, while Beatty's also jubilated with vessels slamming a few shells on the Kaiserliche Marine ships.

After a few straddling salvoes, the Seydlitz gunners connected with the New Zealand and blanketed it in fire. Seven shells out of its twelve 280 mm gun salvo landed at a plunging angle right on the ship's deck and armored turrets. The damage to New Zealand was very serious, with two main guns damaged and out of commission and two large fires, one above and one below deck. It wouldn't take much more to cripple the vessel after that hit.

Next to be hit on the British side was the Lion (by Von der Tann), with three impacts below the waterline, opening parts of its hull to water and causing some stern damage. The Princess Royal (targeted by Deerflinger) was also seriously hit, with three shells slamming on the boilers, diminishing its speed to a scant seven knots, plus starting a severe fire below deck.

But the hit of the day would belong to the Molkte and its four shells plowing through the deck of the Queen Mary, finding their way right into the magazine room. The resulting explosion was something to behold. One moment, the battlecruiser was there. The next, it was replaced by a bright, expanding ball of fire. The concussion wave it produced sent a giant circular ripple across the sea, and the ship shattered to pieces, showering the other British ships around and causing additional damage.

The British also scored hits: The Seydlitz, von Hipper's flagship, shook with a powerful boiler room explosion after being hit with two shells from the Lion. The Molkte received a straddling salvo from Queen Mary before it died. But its thick armor belt shrugged off most of the damage. Deerflinger was taken under fire by the Princess Royal and the New Zealand and got one main gun destroyed and over sixty sailors killed in the following fires.

(...) Seydlitz, German flagship (...)

On the deck of the German battlecruiser, everyone cheered as they saw the Queen Mary explode in cataclysmic fury. But their celebrations were destined to be short-lived. Admiral Hipper was about to order the ships to continue to close in when a towering wall of water twice as high as the Seydlitz catapulted into the air. Large columns of water also rose behind, aft, and near the stern. The ship shook from the near impacts. Just beside it, the Moltke was slammed by what seemed the hammer of god, and a series of powerful shells hit it in succession as if fired by a giant machine gun until it was but a ball of flaming inferno. *"What the hell is that!"* yelled von Hipper. But the man knew what it was; those shells weren't from battlecruisers. They were the telltale signs of something terribly bigger, just like the British 340 mm dreadnought battleships were armed with.

"Turn the fleet around," he yelled to the helm and the communication officers. A few destroyers were flanking the battleships, and they quickly put up a large smoke screen to try

and avoid more of the British fire.

As the fleet turned, the British were able to riddle the Deerflinger with more hits. It was, as a consequence, seriously damaged, and that killed its speed. Within under a minute, it was but a floating hulk. It would be finished off by the Royal Navy a few hours later.

(...) Bridge of the Lion, Beatty's flagship (...)

"We've got them," said the Admiral with a wolfish smile. The pain of losing the Queen Mary to enemy fire was quickly dispelled as success replaced it. The British Fleet was so superior in numbers that the Germans would not hope to win, even if their battlecruisers were more armored compared to his. Against a full dreadnought battleship squadron, the bastards stood no chance.

(...) Aftermath, British side (...)

As the British ships bombarded the Heligoland Naval base to oblivion, Admiral Beatty looked at the maelstrom of fire that was the island he'd come to destroy in the distance. It was now dark, and the entire place was awash with destructive explosions.

The plan had worked and the enemy base would be destroyed. No longer would the Kaiserliche Marine be able to guard the entrance to the Bight with the effectiveness it had with the island and its small light cruiser squadron. And to boot, they sunk two battlecruisers (Deerflinger and Moltke) and a light cruiser. And even better, a ton of damage was inflicted on the other German vessels.

The price they paid was high as well, but from his perspective, it had all been worth it. The Queen Mary battlecruiser was gone, and his ships were badly damaged. But it was good to savor the victory.

(...) Battlecruiser Seydlitz, at main German
naval base of Wilhelmshaven (...)

Admiral Franz von Hipper skulked on the damaged bridge of his flagship, battlecruiser Seydlitz. The German Navy had just been handed a severe defeat, losing three ships (including two dreadnoughts) and had also lost a base. While there wasn't much he could have done against so many enemy ships, he still felt a pang of guilt at having lost the fight. He walked through the bridge hatch giving way to the exterior ramp and looked down on the very serious damage his ship had sustained. It was impressive how much of a beating a Kaiserliche Marine dreadnought could take. The entire surface of the ship's deck was blackened out, a main turret was stuck in position as the steel melted from a shell impact, and one of the two large boiler chimneys was hanging sideways. At least the fires were out, he thought.

He crossed his arms behind his back and vowed to himself that he would get his revenge, British naval superiority or not.

The Battle of Le Cateau
The RFA and the BEF try to survive, August 25th-26th, 1914.

The horse-drawn gun bobbed up and down as British artilleryman Archibald Totenkam looked at it nonchalantly. He was sitting in the gun cart and felt every jolt, bump, and rock on the broken road. *"Where are we again, Lance-Bombardier Stimms,"* he heard one of his comrades say to their NCO. *"We are somewhere south of Cambrai, about fifteen miles out of Mons."* *"What is this town called,"* continued the soldier. *"Le Cateau, soldier. Now, stop asking questions and shut up,"* countered Stimms. Archibald turned his head toward the scrawny little village in the distance as the cart hit another large pothole, sending everyone in the cart into a ragdoll dance.

The dwelling didn't seem to look like much. He could see the church and a bunch of dreary-looking buildings, some streets but nothing spectacular. *"Yet another French town in the middle of nowhere,"* he thought.

The bumpy road they were on was leading them up to the small town, but they were still some distance out. To his left, there was a forest. In the distance (eastern horizon), the rumble of the guns and battle could be heard. The infantry rearguard action the BEF infantry was executing was getting nearer and nearer. The fucking Germans were not far. He thought for a moment about his earlier enthusiasm for war. He'd lost all the notions of romanticism he'd harbored before Mons. Now, he knew better.

A column of happy and singing soldiers marched right beside their gun procession to the side of the road. They were British soldiers and were going toward the rumble of the guns. *"Who are they, Thorpe,"* he said to the man beside him in the cart. William Thorpe was one of the men in the gun team, and Totenkam usually asked him for info as he seemed to be well-connected somehow. *"They are from the 4th British Division and fresh off the boat, obviously,"* he answered. Archibald laughed. *"Yeah, but soon they'll be like us."* He returned the smile like the enthusiastic smiles one of the soldiers gave him as he walked past. *"We'll give it to them,"* he went on. *"They are happy and willing."* He spat on the ground in a sign of disgust. *"Poor chaps,"* said Thorpe, shaking his head in disbelief. *"They don't have a fucking clue. To think we've been like that. It's sickening."*

Archibald stopped talking and turned his head away from the soldiers. He felt bad for these happy men. By the time their first fight was over, a ton of them would be dead. He thought for a moment about the situation. Archibald was happy to be alive and unscathed following the Battle of the Conde Canal. A lot of gun teams had either seen their weapon destroyed or had lost many men. His team was intact, and he was grateful for it. But apart from that, a quick analysis of the situation didn't seem to give the Anglo-French troops a chance of reversing the situation.

Archibald had no clue about what was happening in the grand scheme of things, and he hoped his commanders knew what they were doing. At a glance, it didn't look like they did, and the entire affair had the smell of a giant clusterfuck. The French and the BEF forces were retreating – no, running away more like- and he had no idea what the plan was. He would have been appalled if he'd known the extent his commanders were improvising as the Entente troops reeled back in disarray across northern France.

There was no real plan apart from falling back in the face of the overwhelming German offensive. Sir John French's goal was to move southward toward a small French town called Le Cateau, but even that was simply a stopgap to try and halt the Germans from pursuing. Defeating them or pushing them back would give his force time to disengage.

To move into the town, he first had to circumvent the Mormal Forest, as there was no trail going through it. At one point, he would have to face the music and stop marching to fight the Germans, getting nearer since, by going around, the enemy troops would eventually be able to catch him.

The Forest of Mormal was bounded on its western border by the old Roman Road, which ran straight from the small town near Le Cateau called Bavai in a south-westerly direction, crossing the road from Le Cateau to Cambrai.

Field Marshal French ordered his 2nd Corps to march west of Mormal, with the Cavalry Division on its western flank, and directed the 1st (the one Archibald was part of) east. Then, the troops were to set defensive positions at the forest edge to try and bludgeon the German advance,

Archibald didn't have the names, a map, or any idea of what was happening in the grand scheme of things, but he obeyed the orders coming down to start setting up in the forest. The goal was for the 113th Battery to get in a line at the edge of the forest to use it as cover. The rearguard was retreating soon, apparently, and the Royal Field Artillery would be there to help them dislodge themselves from the pursuing enemies. They worked feverishly to get everything ready, as with each minute that passed, the loud sounds of battle seemed to approach faster and faster.

(...) The next morning, Mormal Forest (...)

A loud whistling sound whipped in the air, and the enemy round slammed hard on a tree near the gun position. The trunk exploded, and bark splintered everywhere in a shattering sound. The man just beside Archibald was hit by a large piece of wood that pierced his neck. Blood splattered everywhere on the gun and on Lance-Bombardier Stimms. Aghast, Archibald stared at his NCO, who just made a face. *"What a fucking mess,"* he yelled. And then he noticed the rest of the gun team was looking at him. *"What are you looking at, you maggots,"* he continued in an even angrier tone and pointed toward the field from where the Germans were firing. *"Put your fucking attention to the Krauts, not on me!"*

As everyone was afraid of the crusty man, they got back to work once a quick check of the injured gunner confirmed he had been killed on impact. They worked amidst the thick smoke and the smell of cordite. Fires were raging all around them as the enemy guns had lit a few with their exploding ordinance. Once again, Archibald felt he was at hell's doorstep.

Going through the motion of firing the 18-pounder, he pulled on the lever to unlock the breech. *"Loading,"* he yelled as per his training. Thorpe inserted the shell into the chamber. Archibald used the same lever to insert the breech screw. The lid snapped shut. *"Ready!"* The cannon shell thundered out of the barrel while the weapon recoiled hard backward in a loud blast and a flurry of smoke and fire. As with the last few rounds, Archibald didn't even check where the shell went, instead concentrating on getting another round in.

The 113th Battery, along with a few others, were arrayed at the edge of the forest, some dug in where it was possible (it was hard to dig trenches with tree roots), and others behind wood and sandbag fortifications. Many were destroyed or else operated with diminished crews. The rear was already full of newly injured artillerymen, and the ground beside the gun position was littered with dead bodies, blood, and body parts. It was sickening.

The German artillery was busy softening them up as the enemy infantry seemed to hunker down below a small elevation in the ground. The soldiers were thus impossible to hit with direct fire. While they weren't trained in indirect firing, they had started doing so anyway because there was nothing else they could do. *"Nothing better than training in the field,"* had said their crusty Lance-Corporal, Henry Stimms.

The German drive to Paris and the French retreat
Soldiers fighting on the ground in early September 1914

(...) Facing the Mormal forest (...)

The Captain's whistle blew, and then other whistles were heard going down and up the line, and the German soldiers rose up from their hiding positions and walked up, bayonet-tipped rifles in hand, over the small ridge they had been hiding behind to avoid the deadly British shrapnel fired by the line of guns installed at the edge of the forest near them. Some men started to yell, others just grumbled, and a bunch, like Oskar, stayed silent. Not everyone had the same way of dealing with extreme danger and stress. Because there was no mistake about it. There was mortal danger over the lip of the ridge. The British artillery and infantry awaited them to make a killing.

Amongst the German troops lay Private Soldier Oskar Dantz of the Infanterie-Regiment Graf Schwerin. The man had a stony face, stubborn and cold. After weeks of heavy fighting and facing death, he was sort of numb from it all. He didn't care anymore about anything. He just went through the motions of obeying orders, advancing, and killing when he could.

He'd faced and survived impossible odds already and had accepted his fate, like most of his stoic comrades. And his attitude wouldn't be disappointed again this time. The moment he was over the lip of the ridge, a maelstrom of fire seemed to hit the area. The British gunners, seeing that their enemies were finally within their direct sight, quickly traversed their guns down to fire at the long line of gray-uniformed soldiers that suddenly appeared.

An enemy shell filled with canister exploded about ten meters right in front of him, and the result was a carnage of epic proportions. The metal shards and the small steel balls shredded through bodies, uniforms, and everything in between. For a moment, the concussion from the blast dropped a circle around the impact zone, and Oskar fought to stay upright.

The same scene repeated across the line to his left and right. And yet, many of them survived, and more came behind. Soon, the gray-uniformed soldiers had reformed a line, and the mass started to run toward the forest.

Hundreds upon hundreds of puffs of smoke erupted all across the edge of the forest, proof that the Brits had infantry waiting for them as well. More soldiers fell.

But as they charged, they also fired and killed enemies. German artillery shells whistled loudly above them and slammed the forest relentlessly. Soon (Oskar was about two-thirds of the way to the forest), the enemy fire (either artillery or rifle) had slackened considerably.

The British were already moving the guns that could be out of the area. Archibald and Lancer-Bombardier Stimms were running backward into the forest through one of the small trails, since their gun was already destroyed. There was no point in staying where they were, and the rest of the gun team was dead.

Then, Oskar was at the forest edge, filleting an enemy soldier with his bayonet. He yelled out of his lungs, happy and sort of ecstatic at having again survived the terrible odds. The British line disintegrated before his sight.

(…) 14th French Division, somewhere south of Le Cateau (…)

The 14th French Division was executing a desperate fighting retreat, and Private Soldier Armand Bonnier was trying to survive as best he could. The French 5th Army was in full retreat toward Paris and the West following the battle of Charleroi.

Armand fired once again, moving up from his cover position behind a destroyed staff car. The bullet he fired slammed into the chest of an enemy soldier. He'd heard they were Bavarian soldiers. To him, it didn't make any difference since they were

Germans.

"Got the bastard," he said as he crouched back, smiling at his friend and comrade, the broad-shouldered Philippe Cren. *"My turn,"* answered the man, moving to the side between the shattered door and the broken window. His rifle spat a round, and the bullet raced to find a German head, exploding it in a spray of blood. Cren came back behind the staff car, smiling.

They were at the edge of a large town square in a French village west of Mauberge, the town that used to be the French HQ. *"They're everywhere, Phil,"* said Armand. And indeed, they were. The German 2nd German Army was overbearing because it attacked with twice the men the 5th French Army had. Cren busied himself on reloading his Lebel Rifle with his usual dedication.

A few enemy bullets slammed into the staff car's hulk, sending a few small splinters near them and some puffs of dust. The ground beside the broken vehicle was also peppered by enemy rifle fire. *"They're on to us, mon ami,"* answered Philippe. *"Where are we, anyway,"* he finished, slamming the reloaded gun chamber shut. *"I have no clue,"* grumbled Armand.

"Okay, Bonnier, it's time to make a run for it." Armand didn't say anything and sat up and ran like hell for the small alley they were near. A staccato of bullets cracked around, and the ground around them exploded in dust as round after round plowed into the ground. They were miraculously unscathed from the enemy firing.

They ran as hard as they could, and when they crossed other alleys and streets, they saw that the rest of the Division was also in full retreat. There was just no helping it. They wouldn't stop the Krauts here, in that no-name town they didn't care one bit about.

The German drive to Paris and the French retreat
The overall picture in early September 1914

What came to be called "The Great Retreat" began in earnest in the last week of August to the 5th of September. Forced to retreat, the Franco-British troops started to move backward from Mons and Charleroi all the way to next door to Paris, near a river called the Marne in northern France, as German forces overran the North. The French leadership fled Paris and moved south to Bordeaux, to make sure the running of the country would continue if the hated enemy stormed the capital. It was not a great time for the Entente.

On the 25th of August, Joseph Joffre issued (reluctantly) his orders for a general withdrawal of the Entente forces to a defensible line (initially set at the Somme) to the Marne River. His reasons for doing so were quite simple: the Germans could not be stopped before that. It was a little late, but the offensive officer had finally caught up to the war he was fighting.

A new French 6th Army was created from everything the French could find by scrapping the bottom of the barrel everywhere across the country and railed to the capital in order to eventually launch a counteroffensive. While the French commander-in-chief dreamed of more offensive, it seemed defeat was in staring the Allies in the face. After Mons and Charleroi and the mega casualties the French incurred in the Battle of the Frontier, it seemed the ghost of the 1870-1871 debacle hung over the French once more. A shroud of discouragement fell on Allied hopes, and only a victory could lift it.

The battered and bruised British Expeditionary Force (BEF), along with the 5th French Army, retreated hard, sometimes ten miles per day, with the German 1st and 2nd Armies right behind them. Once in a while and as needed, the Entente forces turned about and fought quick snap battles like for example, a successful 5th Army counterattack at the town of St. Quentin and a British one at Le Cateau.

But in. They were tired, defeated, demoralized, and worn. In Paris, the situation was chaotic as the more wealthy and capable civilians tried to move out, and civil unrest began to overwhelm the authorities.

Disheartened by his French ally, the British forces on the ground almost opted out of the fight. Fixating his attention on keeping his army alive and trying to avoid it being encircled and destroyed, Field Marshal French decided to withdraw the army as fast as he could to a port where his soldiers could be embarked and shipped back to England. However, things were not seen in that way in London. The British war minister, Lord Herbert Kitchener, put a stop to his intention and ordered him to stay and fight with the French.

By early September, the Entente frontline was finally stiffening again. The French continued to fight like demons in front of Nancy and Verdun, backed up by the string of powerful fortresses protecting these pivotal towns. The 3rd and 4th Armies continued to retreat and lost cities like Reims (5th of September), but slowly but surely, a sort of frontline was taking shape, and as a result, the German forces weren't advancing as much anymore.

The very retreat of the Allies created an opposite situation for both sides. While the Anglo-French were getting nearer and nearer their supply lines, the Germans moved further and further away from them. Furthermore, their troops were exhausted, and there was now a very real danger that the entire offensive would fall apart.

Supplies started to fail across the entire German forces as horse-drawn ammo and food did not make it in time to the frontlines. The German 1st and 2nd Armies, advancing in parallel, started to experience serious difficulties with getting instruction from von Moltke's HQ back in Luxembourg.

The original version of the Schlieffen Plan had dictated that the 1st German Army was to march in a great outflanking move west of Paris, plans were changed because of the developing tactical situation. Von Kluck, the general in command of the army, decided (and got approval from von Moltke) to wheel his force southeast of Paris. This decision, born out of necessity because his troops were worn and mostly without supplies, created a dangerous situation. Kluck's right flank of Kluck's then became exposed to a French counter-offensive. Never in their right mind did the Germans imagine the French capable of mustering yet another army seemingly out of nowhere like they had done in the preceding three weeks; they saw Paris as defended monthly by garrison troops and wanted to destroy the Entente armies southeast of Paris at the Marne River.

Furthermore, Germany had the reserve to face what the Entente Powers were brewing up because of the troops that were never sent east to defend Eastern Prussia (200,000 French soldiers just northwest of the 1st and 2nd Armies). Since Joffre could not ignore the possibility of a counteroffensive to defeat his enemies once and for all, the entire affair took on the disproportionate size that the Battle of the Marne had a few days later.

As the first week of the fall winded down, "the Great Retreat" still happened. The Anglo-French moved on the west bank of the river with Kluck and his soldiers barely a day behind them. While this meant they would soon catch up with the Anglo-French forces, Kluck's decision to turn south instead of going around Paris and his change of direction opened a large area of ground big enough to create a problem (or else an opportunity for the Entente forces), because his troops lost contact with Bulow's 2nd German Army.

While for General Joffre, the moment had yet not become ripe enough for attacking the enemy, his hands were forced by the Army commander in Paris, General Gallieni (6th Army), who decided out of his own accord to attack the exposed enemy flank.

Joffre was still hesitating over the optimum moment to launch his counterblow, but Gallieni, with not only the Paris troops but also the 6th Army under his overall command, forced Joffre's hand. Relieved that his men were again on the attack and accepting Gallieni's initiative on the following day, Joffre informed his armies to launch forward. *"The time for retreat has ended,"* was what he said to each unit commander along with their specific instructions.

And then the Battle of the Marne exploded in all its fury. The moment would define the outcome of the first part of World War One and would shatter one of the two sides' hopes for immediate victory.

CHAPTER 4
The War in the East and the Far East

The Battle of Tannenberg Part 1
The Russians attack, September 1st to September 4th, 1914

General Paul Hindenburg looked at the battlefield with binoculars. He grunted and then dropped the eyepiece to his side to look at his chief of staff, Eric Ludendorff. *"If only we had those planned reinforcements, we could have done the encircling move we talked about."* "Indeed, sir," answered Ludendorff. His commander continued. *"I wonder what those OHL generals are thinking. If we don't pull out a miracle somehow, we could lose Berlin altogether."*

They didn't have enough troops to fight the Russians because the German high command had opted to keep all of its offensive force West to finish the fight with the French first. The OHL commander Helmut von Moltke and the chief of the general staff of the German Army had been overruled a week earlier by the Minister of War (his rival), Eric von Falkenhayn, and the Kaiser himself. Strategically, it sort of made sense, but that little analysis didn't help the two generals in the least. The Germans still had four of five times the number of Russian soldiers bearing down on them.

The Battle of Tannenberg started on August the 26th, 1914, and that was because Hindenburg had found no better way to make this work. Set his forces on the defensive, entrench, and try to wear down the enemy. In doing so, he was playing for time as well. Time the generals in the West (with von Bulow and von Kluck in the lead) needed to finish the Anglo-French. Then and only then would they get the troops to smash the Tsarist forces.

The Russian First Army's five corps were spread over a front of some sixty miles and pushing hard toward the town of Tannenberg. The German XX Corps defending it was hard-pressed, and there wasn't much available to help it weather the storm of steel it was facing.

"We're four or five to one, according to military intelligence and

Zeppelin reconnaissance flights," grunted Hindenburg. "With the 210,000 men of the 8th Army, I don't know what the Kaiser expects us to do except hold the line and retreat," he continued. The General was the newly minted East Prussian commander-in-chief. The Tsarist forces were bearing down on Germany's eastern heartlands with no less than 860,000 men and 1,50 artillery guns against 210,000 German soldiers and 650 guns. Mathematically, there wasn't much that could be done if the Russians were truly aggressive.

Hindenburg turned toward the castle in the distance. The two commanders were close to the Nogat River and could see the fighting, while the castle itself was on the opposite river bank and still seemed peaceful, untouched by battle. The castle was a magnificent and old Teutonic Knights stronghold. But as much as they wanted to protect it from dirty Russian hands, it probably would be overrun soon.

"How long do you think we can last here, sir," asked Ludendorff, being first to break the uneasy silence between the two. They were faced with horrible prospects. The enemy was attacking on a sixty-mile broad front, and they didn't have the men to cover the distance. "As long as we can, Eric. We need to gain time for the western battles to conclude so OHL can finally send us some reinforcements."

A runner came right by them, moving up the small hill overlooking the battle scene a few kilometers away. "Sir, a message from the East," said the young soldier, saluting sharply. Returning the gesture, Ludendorff picked up the folded paper telegram. He made a sour face as he knew the telegram was from the thin veil of troops facing the Russian 2nd Army of General Rennenkampf.

The chief of staff unfolded it, read it for a moment, and then gave it to his commander. Hindenburg's face darkened. "Rennenkampf is on the move, sir." Hindenburg picked up the piece of paper and read it for himself. *"Well, it is as we feared. Eric, make sure Konigsberg is ready for the unavoidable siege it is about to face, and let's start to try and look at how we will disengage from this battle here."* "Yes, sir," answered Ludendorff, saluting and leaving the hill to talk to the staff people. There were only a couple of divisions in the field facing the Russian forces, and he needed to order them to join the Konigsberg garrison. The town was a fortress, and they had made sure, in the last few days, to get the entire area entrenched and ready for an enemy attack. It was the only way to fix the numerically superior Russian Army, while the bulk of his forces would face General Samsonov's 1st Army.

Hindenburg then turned again toward the battle and the rumble of the guns, crossing his arms behind his back. There wasn't much he could do but play for time. He knew that it wouldn't please the Prussian nobles nor his master, the Kaiser, but without the troops he needed, he could not implement any strategy; he could only hold and execute a fighting retreat and get troops into the Konigsberg Fortress and hope it would hold for the duration.

(...) Meanwhile, in Tannenberg, German camp (...)

The heavily entrenched German 20th Corps fired one volley after the other while its machine guns peppered the masses of charging Russian infantry. Behind them (a couple of miles) lay the artillery, also firing continuously at the advancing and attacking Russians. They had plenty of ammo and peppered their enemies, while the Russians had to manage their gun ordinance. Supply was terrible in the Russian Army and as they advanced in East Prussia, it was getting worse. It was one advantage the German Army held over the Tsarist forces. They didn't have the men, but they had the guns firing continuously.

The Germans were hunkering down in a series of long, narrow excavations in the ground like a linear cut dug in the field. The earth from the excavation was shoved out in the front to be used as a shelter from enemy fire or attack. The infantry soldiers were in them, with only their heads and guns protruding out, often protected by sandbag constructions.

Trenches went back pretty far into the history of warfare. Already I ancient times, the Roman Legions encircled their field camps with them to protect from attacks and better guard their troops as they rested for the night. In the 16th and 17th centuries, trenches were again used during siege battles, as they were used to protect the soldiers as they dug closer and closer to the walls of the fortress or castle they were assaulting.

With the American Civil War and the advent of modern rifles and weapons, trenches became a real necessity for soldiers wanting to survive. The trend (humans hiding from artillery, rifle, and machine gun fire) continued through the Boer and the Russo-Japanese War.

While trenches were not a relatively new concept to warfare and had been part of warfare since time immemorial, heavily fortified troops with machine guns and artillery support were a game changer that tilted the advantage to the defensive side. Small numbers of troops with enough machine guns and artillery cannons could hold much bigger forces in check. Frontal assaults were becoming completely futile, a fact that many generals would not master right away in 1914.

(...) Meanwhile, in Tannenberg, Russian camp (...)

General Samsonov, the commander of the Russian 1st Army, had no clue that he was wasting his forces on one futile charge after the other until he got to see the battlefield for himself. As he approached the line of battle on August 27th in his staff car, bumping up and down on the potholed road, he saw that his men had not advanced at all in a full day of heavy fighting. Casualties ran high, and the field of battle before Tannenberg was littered with brown-uniformed Russian soldiers. Beyond them lay the gray-dark lines of the German fortifications. When the car stopped and one of the staff officers opened the door for him, the stench of death hit him like a sledgehammer, and he was appalled at the number of injured soldiers streaming back on the road beside him. It was like a flood of beaten and bloody men. He looked at them with sympathy but soon snapped out of his spell because a couple of Captains came by him, saluted, and told him to follow them to the top of the hill where his corps commander, Lieutenant-General Karensky, was waiting.

General Aleksander Samsonov was an old hand in the Russian Army. His military career went as far back as the Russo-Turkish War and the Siege of Sebastopol (1877-1878). With the declaration of hostilities against the Central Powers, he was given command of the Russian 2nd Army. Along with General Paul von Rennenkampf, commander of the 1st Army, they were entrusted with the invasion of East Prussia.

He walked up the hill, where awaited a shallowly dug-in observation post covered by a canvas tent. Its sides were also covered in sandbags. *"Ah, General,"* said Karensky as he approached. *"We have prepared a secure observation post from which you can see the enemy defenses and the unfolding battle."* From his point of view, things had been going well until they got to this fortified German position, and his men had started dying in droves.

"Lieutenant-General, gentlemen," answered Samsonov with a sharp military salute to all the assembled men, following everyone that saluted him first as was necessary for with military etiquette. He had to speak loudly since the rumble of the guns was drowning out any normal talking.

The observation post was full of officers from the different units in the sector. *"Sir, if you could come here,"* continued Karensky. He moved to the edge of the post to take a large view of the battlefield. In the distance, he could see the German lines. Between them and the observation post was the field of battle, with running Russian soldiers (toward the enemy lines), bursts of fire, towering columns of debris, and numerous tracer fire crisscrossing from one side to the other.

The enemy lines were well-dug in trenches. They had a star-like pattern as they were dug in a way to have interlocking fields of fire and fall back positions. The entire construction looked like a honeycomb. He decided it was a good idea to protect against artillery shrapnel. It also prevented any straight infantry assault from rolling up the entire trench line. Trenches were also dug very narrowly for better protection against artillery shells.

"Do you have binoculars," he asked Kerensky. *"Of course, sir,"* answered the man, gesturing for one of his men to bring a pair to the commander. Samsonov picked them up and looked at the details of the enemy defenses.

The enemy defenses were also protected by rows upon rows of sandbags and other obstacles, including barbed wire and large man-made ditches. He saw many, many Maxim machine gun emplacements. *"How many men have we lost so far, General,"* he asked, still looking at the enemy defenses through the binoculars. *"Over five thousand, sir. It is as I told you. It's like we are sending our troops to the slaughter."*

The ground shook hard as a couple of heavy caliber shells slammed on the side of the hill where they were. A large cloud of billowing smoke rose in the air and blocked Samsonov's view of the battlefield for a moment.

"Very well. If we can't push them from the front, we'll go at the bastards from the side," he said finally, giving the pair of binoculars back to the young man who handed them to him earlier. *"General Karensky, stop the attacks for now. We'll move the two other corps around the enemy position. Tannenberg is a tough nut, but let's see how deep it runs."* *"Very well, sir,"* answered the other man, obviously relieved that he could now put an end to the senseless killing.

"Gentlemen," said Samsonov, saluting everyone as he stepped out of the observation post. On his way back to his staff car, he was a man with a mission. Order the rest of his troops to go around Tannenberg. If his information was correct, the German 8th Army didn't have the men to oppose him on a long front. Since the battle they were fighting was already unfolding on a sixty-mile front, he figured that the Germans didn't have fortified positions like this everywhere.

He sat down heavily in the car, and the driver turned it around and back toward the 1st Army HQ.

Austro-Hungarian Galicia
Russian trench line, September 2nd, 1914

"We are storming Galicia to reclaim it as the land of our ancestors."

Aleksander Brussilov, Russian Invasion commander

Private soldier Dimitri Fedorov had his back to the large farmhouse turned into a fortified position and was busy cleaning his rifle. The thing was dirty as hell, and there came a time in battle when a soldier had to make sure it was cleaned for it to work properly.

The M1891 model was a great weapon and one that equipped many of the Russian soldiers. Fedorov was working on one of its moving parts to clean it properly amidst the distant rumble of battle. It was part of being a soldier. If you wanted to stay alive, weapon maintenance was critical. The sky was grey as it should be in the fall, and a light drizzle was falling from the sky. He wiped the excess gunpowder and other residue on the bolt body and, after a moment, felt it was good enough and thus closed down the weapon.

It was almost time to attack, and he awaited the moment with dread. Even if the Russian armies were victoriously advancing across Galicia and the Austro-Hungarians were reeling back, there was always danger for regular soldiers since the enemy still fired at them with their rifles, their Maxim machine guns, and their artillery cannons.

Dimitri had no clue where he was, and he didn't care. Even if the officers (the only men who knew how to read in the entire unit) did. He knew he was somewhere in an area called Galicia. And had been told by his superiors and NCOs that it was a land of Slavs. That he believed and understood since he'd met a lot of Polish civilians. Some guy had even told him the place had once been part of the Kingdom of Poland, now integrated with the Russian Empire.

He mentally shrugged off the unpleasant thoughts. Dimitri was a simple factory worker from the Moscow area, mobilized like many of his fellow countrymen for the war. He had been part of the reserve, having received his military training in 1912 and 1913. These kinds of problems were for men like 4th Army commander General Anton Jegorowitsch von Saltza.

Fedorov had more pressing needs. He was quite busy surviving and avoiding enemy bullets or shells on a daily basis. He also had to find sufficient food since the bastards at supply kept most of it for themselves to resell and make a profit. The Russian supply system was inefficient and corrupt. What Dimitri didn't know was that it also faced another major problem. The Russian rail gauge was different in width than the rest of Europe. While for men like him, such things were immaterial, it did complicate rail movement since the Russian locomotives could not run on European rail past the border. Thus, the Tsarist Army relied on capturing Austro-Hungarian ones or else modifying the gauge to the Russian standard.

"Is everyone ready," said Sergeant Radetzki. No one answered apart from nervous laughs. They were about to jump over the lip of their shallow trenches and into the maelstrom of fire, the Austrians were sure to unleash on them. Then, one of Dimitri's comrades, one of the more *"intellectually interested ones,"* as he liked to call them, spoke up. *"Sergeant, could you at least tell us where we are?"* Radetzki grunted and then smiled. He figured the poor blokes deserved to know since many of them would not see the sun go down on the horizon that day. *"Soldiers, we are near a town called Rawa, and we need to take the position to smash the Austro-Hungarians back once more."*

And that was that. The next moment, the captains across the entire line blew their whistles, and it was time to jump over and get into the line of fire. The moment Dimitri was standing in the churned-up field, he was aghast at the number of dead soldiers on the ground (from yesterday's attack). Tracers from the enemy machine guns saturated the area, and blasts of fire erupted around them, rocking the ground and catapulting dirt, dead bodies, and smoke all around them. *"Advance!"* yelled one of the pistol-carrying officers near him. He picked up his courage once more and put one foot ahead of the other. Assaulting such a wall of fire was a daunting task.

He ran, sometimes even closing his eyes, thinking he would get hit like several of his comrades ahead, to the sides and behind him, by the enemy bullets. But his good luck kept the course, and he made it to the enemy trench along with others in his unit. He came face to face with a machine gunner trying to unjam his weapon. Dimitri just shot him with a well-placed round to the head. The Austro-Hungarian soldier died instantly, his brain matter exiting from the rear of his skull.

Several other Russian soldiers jumped into the shallow trench, and soon, he was in the middle of a bayonet-firefight battle. Men died all around him, but again, it seemed as if he was touched by God himself.

"Quick! This way!" yelled one of the NCOs. He didn't know him and decided the man must have been from another platoon. The Sergeant was directing them through a gap in the trench which seemed to connect to another one in the back. They'd known from the quick briefings they received prior to the battle that the Austro-Hungarians had a few trenches, one after the other, to erect a defense in depth.

If they'd been given another week or two, they could have made this area into a formidable defensive position. But the Austrians only had a day to prepare since the Russian forces were hot on their heels from the get-go. Ever since the fall of Lemberg, there had been no pause from Alexei Brusilov, the Russian theater commander.

He followed the soldier just ahead of him, and soon, they arrived in the other trench, again full of enemies. The bastards seemed surprised to see the Russians in their trench but nonetheless fought like demons and charged them with what they had. The fight was bloody and intense, but with a continuous stream of Russians getting into the trench and above it (Dimitri saw many of his comrades just jumping over above their heads,) the entire Austro-Hungarian position was overwhelmed in under twenty minutes.

The Battle of Rawa-Ruska
Brussilov shatters the Austrian armies
September 2nd to 4th, 1914.

Franz Conrad von Hotzendorf, the chief of staff of the Austro-Hungarian Army, knew that his troops were in a dire situation and retreating across the board. His force had just been badly beaten in his series of ill-planned and ill-advised offensives against superior forces.

Furthermore, the capital of Galicia, Lemberg, had just fallen, and there seemed to be only one option for the Austro-Hungarians: retreat to the Carpathians and put on a defensive stance to try and save what was left of its eastern forces.

But Conrad was not a man to take such things into account and was living in his own fantasy world. He was completely overestimating the strength and combat capabilities of his forces. The K.U.K. Army was inferior in numbers and equipment and lacked guns to confront the Russians. Nevertheless, he persisted in his idea of a grand offensive to chase the Tsarist forces away and invade Russia itself.

While the Austrian 3rd and 2nd Armies retired west of Lemberg, as they were beaten and could not hold the Russian tide, he decided to try something else to defeat his enemies. His plan for these formations was to retire to a good line on the river Wereszyca, and when the Russians followed, he conjured up that the recently beaten (badly) 4th Army would intervene on the flank to surprise the enemy by marching southeast across Rawa Ruska. Orders for this went out on 1st September, ever hoping to unravel the entire Russian position and march triumphantly back into Lemberg.

Meanwhile, with the capital of Galicia already in Tsarist hands, the Russian 9th Army started to move north to try and intercept the reported Austrian movement toward Rawa Ruska (4th Army), while the Russian 3rd did the same but advanced to the west. The entire affair had the smell of an encirclement, and only Conrad von Hotzendorf didn't seem to see the dangers.

The fight in Rawa-Ruska was pitting nine Russian divisions against nine Austrians. The troops on both sides fought obstinately and desperately, defending every inch of ground or trying to win the same, depending on if they were Russians or Austro-Hungarians. For three full days, the Austro-Hungarian soldiers tried. Indeed, they tried hard and were overwhelmed. Their casualties were horrendous, and the only saving grace was they inflicted twice that on the Russians.

For a moment, the Austro-Hungarian commander-in-chief attack rekindled some hope to stop General Brusilov with a great tactical victory near Lemberg, but it was soon obvious to all that the 4th Austro-Hungarian Army, already defeated badly the week before, could not sustain the tempo of operations, and had not even half the number the Russians had in terms of soldiers and guns.

The battle of Rawa thus ended with the 4th Austro-Hungarian Army reeling back in disarray along with the rest of the K.U.K. forces. This time, there would be no more counter-attack, and the only thought following the defeat in that battle was to retreat and try to find a way to stop the Russians.

The Austrians were thus truly beaten in Galicia, and Russia was victorious. With the added successes happening in Eastern Prussia, Tsarist glory was reaching new heights.

The Empire of the Rising Sun and the German Pacific Empire
Japan vs Germany: War in the Pacific, 1914

(…) The fighter in the red corner: Japan (…)

In 1914, Japan was ready and willing to enter the war on the side of the Entente Powers, thanks in part to their treaty of mutual assistance with Great Britain. The country could have avoided the war altogether but was enticed to fight by the prospect of acquiring new territories from the Germans. The British and the rest of the Allies, eager to hit the Huns wherever they could, promised Tokyo that they would get control of the territories they conquered over the Germans after the war.

Since the coming of age of Emperor Meiji (1869) and the Imperial restoration of power, Japan had been moving toward the establishment of an empire in the Pacific and in mainland Asia. The Japanese worked feverishly to industrialize their nation and to build up a dominant military as a way to avoid the disaster befalling every other nation of the Pacific: European colonization.

It succeeded in staving off and defeating every attempt, although no European nation ever attempted to invade the Japanese Home Islands. By 1914, it was the only country completely free of any type of foreign occupation or influence in the entire Pacific. Once its power base was established at the end of the 19th Century, Japan also started on the path of empire-building.

Following a string of successes with wars against China (1879) and then Russia (1905), the Japanese government and military were emboldened and started to look even further for territorial expansion. The Imperial Navy was still somewhat modest in 1914, but the Japanese leaders felt it could take on what the Kaiserliche Marine had in the Pacific. It sported two dreadnought battleships, 1 dreadnought battlecruiser, five pre-dreadnought battlecruisers, and ten pre-dreadnought battleships, plus a plethora of support ships, including over twenty cruisers and fifty destroyers.

Japanese Imperial Fleet		
BB Setsu	Pre-dreadnought BB HIZEN	Pre-dreadnought BB MIKASA
BB Kawachi	Pre-dreadnought BB IKI	CA X23
BC Kongo	Pre-dreadnought BB IWAMI	CL X6
Pre-dreadnought BC Tsukuma	Pre-dreadnought BB SAGAMI	DD X50
Pre-Dreadnought BC Ikoma	Pre-dreadnought BB SUWO	
Pre-Dreadnought BC Ibuki	Pre-dreadnought BB TANGO	
Pre-Dreadnought BC Kurama	Pre-dreadnought BB FUJI	
Pre-dreadnought BB KASHIMA,	Pre-dreadnought BB ASAHI	
Pre-dreadnought BB KATORI	Pre-dreadnought BB SHIKISHIMA	

The Imperial Japanese Fleet in August 1914

(…) The fighter in the black corner: Germany (…)

Imperial Germany had built up a Pacific Empire since the end of the 19th Century. It compelled China to cede the Liaodong Peninsula (the area surrounding the city of Tsingtao) and bought several island archipelagos (New Guinea, Samoa, and the Carolines Islands) from Spain after Madrid lost the Philippines to the United States.

Japan could plan and drool over all the German territories it wanted; the Kaiser's military in the Pacific had no intention of giving in easily. It had troops, ships, and fortresses all along its properties to protect them, and the task was not forecast to be easy for the Imperial Japanese forces.

Germany, like other European countries (including Great Britain), had expanded its influence in the Far East by meddling in national and local governments. In 1898, Germany arm-wrestled the Chinese into transferring Kioachau Bay in Shandong province to them on a ninety-nine-year lease.

Following the deed, they began to install and impose their influence across the rest of the province by expanding the city and port of Tsingtao. It was located on the tip of the peninsula on a bay on the northeast coast of China; there, they built a railway line, a commercial harbor, and dry docks. It became a fortified naval base, the home of the German Navy's Asiatic Squadron. The German influence and installation in the area meant the province virtually became a German Protectorate.

German Pacific Squadron	
Admival von Graf Spee	
BB Westfalen	CA Sharnhorst
BB Kaiserin	CA Gneisenau
Pre dreadnought BB Pommern	CL Emden
Pre Dreadnought Schleswig-Holstein	CL Nurnberg
	CL Leipzing

The German Pacific Squadron, based in Tsingtao, August 1914

The German Imperial Navy was, of course, involved in the Kaiser's burgeoning Asiatic Empire. The Pacific Squadron, commanded by Vice Admiral Graf von Spee, was a powerful deterrent to anyone who wanted to put their dirty hands on Germanic property in the area. It normally consisted of two heavy (Scharnhorst and Gneisenau), together with three light cruisers (Emden, Nurnberg, and Leipzig), a powerful force numerically comparable to, but technically superior to, British naval forces based in Hong Kong. But the fortuitous presence of a very powerful squadron in the area was due to a stroke of luck (or bad luck, depending on how you saw the situation) for the Germans. Four battleships (two dreadnoughts and two pre-dreadnoughts) had been on a visit of friendship to the Pacific as part of the Kaiser's ever-growing ambitions in the area.

The ships were never intended to stay in Tsingtao to defend it. Still, following the British declaration of war, they couldn't go back to Germany without first going through a lot of enemy ships. In the end, their departure was first postponed as the situation worsened in Europe and then canceled altogether a week before the German declaration of war on France and Belgium. The Westfalen and the Kaiserin were brand new battleships that would give a good run for their money at the two dreadnought battleships the Japanese Imperial Navy had (the Settsu and the Kawachi).

(...) The war itself (...)

Prior to the conflict, both Tokyo and London were alarmed at the potential threat from Germany's colonial expansion in the area. Following the start of the fighting in Europe, the possibility that Germany would attack its convoys in the Pacific led the English to seek Japanese aid. This was despite Britain being worried by the idea of Japan having its influence increased in the region. The Nipponese leadership saw the Germans as a very real problem in the making for the future of their empire. As a consequence, it sought military action to overpower the Germans in Tsingtao and its other Pacific colonies.

On August 15th, Tokyo sent an ultimatum to Berlin demanding the immediate surrender of all German forces and ships in Tsingtao. With no German response, Japan declared war a few days later and the Imperial Navy began preparing an assault against Tsingtao right away. Within days, Japan had planned an attack with 60,000 soldiers on the German city of Tsingtao, flanked by the entirety of the Imperial Navy.

The Battle of the Drina River
Putnik Overplays His Hand, September 6th-7th, 1914.

(...) 21stLAndwher Division, September 6th, 1914 (...)

"Just fire this way," said Helmut, pointing with his fingers to make sure the Slovenian soldier understood what he needed to do. And the damned man still did not understand what he meant, thus just shrugged his shoulders with a question mark on his face. It was, in part, understandable since the two men didn't speak the same language. The scene between Helmut Gottenburg, a German-speaking Austrian, and Radno Karacivs, a Slovene, was playing across the 21st Landwehr Division and in the middle of a battle at that.

Following the heavy losses incurred during the battle of Cer, the entire Austrian 6th Army had been replenished with what was available. And that meant not being overly specific about spoken tongues. Hence, Helmut was privy to the biggest underlying weakness of the Austro-Hungarian Army. The Empire of the Habsburg Monarchy was an assembly of a multitude of nationalities, ranging from Germans to Slavs, Poles, Slovenians, Croats, Serbs, Romanians, Hungarians, and many others, all with different languages.

Helmut lost patience with the clueless man, picked up his rifle, pointed it toward the area the Lieutenant had told them to fire at, and then pulled the trigger. It was a bit of overkill, but the enemy was attacking them; thus, he didn't have time to play games with the new guy. After he fired, Helmut gave the weapon back to the Slovene and the man just nodded his understanding, even adding a wan smile. It was a slog to communicate, and everyone in the unit was getting tired of the futile game.

In an instant, Gothenburg's anger over the matter faded away. He suddenly felt sympathy for the man forced to fight in a German-speaking regiment. The poor bastard didn't ask to come; he had been ordered to. And it wasn't his fault if he didn't speak the language. He should have been in a different unit, but the freaking incompetence of the K.u.k. Army was to blame. He shook his head, put a hand on the man's shoulder to show him he didn't hold any grudge, and picked up his rifle again. The fucking Serbs were attacking them across the Drina River. The entire affair had come as a surprise since the Austro-Hungarians had not expected a counterattack on their own territory.

After his stunning and completely surprising victory over the Austrians, the Serbian Army commander Radomir Putnik ordered his forces to cross the Drina River into Austria-Hungary on September 6th. This was so bold a move that it first froze the Austro-Hungarians into inactivity, but the troops on the ground quickly recovered and fought back.

Helmut aimed at one of the charging Serbs and fired, hitting the man in the rib cage. The round slammed in a spray of blood and sent him somersaulting sideways. *"Dobro streljanje,"* said the Slovenian Radno with a smile. Helmut didn't know what it meant but it looked positive since the man had smiled. In reality, it meant *"good shooting."*

From the looks of it, the enemy attack seemed to be slackening, and he hoped very hard for it to be so since he was dead tired. They had been defending their little patch of ground near the Drina since the beginning of the day when the first Serbian soldiers were spotted crossing the river. And indeed, it was slowing down since he now noticed the regular staccato sounds of the Maxim machine gun firing across their defensive lines were slackening, a sure sign the Serbs were calling it a day. The equation was simple. If the Maxims fired less or stopped doing so altogether, it was because they were running out of targets. It was about time; the sun was starting to get low on the horizon, and both sides were dead tired after a hard day of fighting.

A few minutes after the attack was over, Helmut just dropped where he was and decided it was time for a little bit of sleep. He learned in his first few weeks of fighting that it was important to rest whenever possible. He was about to close his eyes when his Slovene *"friend"* sat just by him. Radno babbled something intelligible to his ears (the language was completely alien to him) and then fished out a small schnapps steel canteen from his backpack. He offered a sip to Helmut. *"I am starting to like you, Radno,"* he answered. The Slovenian soldier just looked at him with a big question-mark face. Helmut then gave him a thumbs-up with a wide smile, indicating he was happy. He quickly followed that by picking up the canteen and taking a long sip. Radno laughed heavily and slammed him on the shoulder, again speaking in his damned Slovene language. He took the canteen from Helmut's hand and then drank a long sip before dropping to his side and closing his eyes. Within half a minute, the man was sound asleep and was snoring. *"That's damn bizarre, man,"* said Helmut laughing softly. *"But I am really starting to take a liking to you."* And he also hit the ground for a quick nap.

(…) 21st Landwehr Division, September 7th, 1914 (…)

Helmut Gottenburg, a Private soldier in the 21st Landwehr Division, cursed out loud as his feet hit the cold water of the Drina River. The drums were beating hard, and the officers urged them on. Bullets slammed into the water all around them as the retreating Serbs tried to kill them. Their fire not being very effective, Helmut felt he was going to survive the crossing since the tracer fire was scattered and inaccurate. He looked to his right, and his newfound Slovene friend Radno was right there beside him. The man smiled, and it was difficult not to start laughing. The scene was so ridiculous that it was laughable. The fucking K.u.k. Army leadership had filled the 8th Regiment with Slovenians and Croats. Hell, the two people didn't even like each other. Just that morning, two of them got into a fistfight over some trivial matter that only people from the Balkans had a reason to bicker over. He shook his head to try and stay concentrated. After all, the Serbs just on the other riverbank were trying to kill him.

Following the Serbian attack, the Austro-Hungarian 6th Army commander, General Potiorek, launched his second invasion of Serbia the following day. Putnik and his troops stopped the advance and started to retreat, surprised by the quick enemy response.

(...) Aftermath (...)

A few days later, the 6th Austro-Hungarian Army was able to push back the 3rd Serbian Army in three different places. Some units from the 2nd Serbian Army were sent by the Serbian commander (General Radomir Putnik) to try and stabilize the line. In the end, and regardless of Putnik's moves, the Austro-Hungarian Fifth Army renewed its attack across the river. The stage was set for continued warfare in Serbia, and it now seemed like the Austrians would be in Serbia for the duration.

Eastern Anatolia
The Ottoman offensive into the Caucasus, September 8th-12th, 1914

If there was one hotly contested border in history, it was the one where the Turks and the Russians faced each other in the Anatolian-Caucasus area. The two powers had fought a long string of twelve wars from the 16th to the 20th century. The rivalry and almost constant state of warfare between the two states was one of the longest in history.

Northeast Anatolia was not a great spot to wage war. Filled with rough terrain, high mountains, bad weather, and hostile tribes, it proved unsuitable for warfare through the centuries. Military movements could only be made through the mountain passes and the few lowlands.

Enver Pasha, supreme commander of the Ottoman armed forces, wanted to push the Russian armies aside and take control of the entire area. After all, the entirety of the Caucasus region had been part of the Ottoman Empire for decades, if not centuries, in the past.

Going against every military logic and every piece of advice from smart and well-meaning military advisors such as German General Liman von Sanders, he launched his offensive regardless in September of 1914. His force numbered 100,000 men and was the cream of the newly trained and equipped Ottoman Army. On the 9th of September, elements of the 3rd Army began advancing on Russian positions across the Allahüekber Mountains.

It was in this terrible setting that Private Soldier Mohamed Mustapha (3rd Ottoman Army) fought amid the bitter cold. He did not understand why it was that cold. After all, it was only September. But they were so high in the mountains that the temperature was cold. In fact, he felt almost frozen, colder than at any time during his life. His skin prickled all around, and he felt itchy. He knew it wasn't a good sign and tried to keep moving by either jumping up and down or walking around when the enemy wasn't firing at him.

The blizzard thundered and howled over him and the rest of the Turkish forces in the trenches. Snow was falling, creating incredibly fuzzy visibility. At least, winter and the rough terrain had stopped the enemy from attacking. The Russian Army attack had fallen on Mohamed and the rest of the Turkish Army like a hammer on a nail. So many of his friends and unit comrades were now dead; it was mind-boggling. Things had started well but soured rapidly. He didn't understand how his leaders could bungle them into such a difficult position. After all, the offensive was only days old, and they were already bogged down facing strong enemy defenses.

The Tsarist forces had attacked on a clear day on the 10th of September. Mohamed and the rest of the 2nd Turkish Division were in the defensive positions their officers had ordered dug in the night before. They were confident and believed in their commanders. They were told that they would repulse the Russians as their ancestors had. The Ottomans of old had conquered the entire region in the 16th and 17th Centuries before losing it all to the damned Russians.

But things had not gone their way from the start. The Russian Army had launched terrible artillery bombardments lasting for half a day, blanketing the area with a maelstrom of fire. Just as they thought they had survived the ordeal with their whole world still buzzing from the blasts and explosions, the Russian hordes had come. Innumerable swarms of screaming soldiers. At first, they had been able to shoot them down, as in the former war, because soldiers were as easy to kill with their machine guns. But then they'd kept coming, and eventually, they were out of ammunition.

After that, he remembered the route. The sheer panic, the running, the dying of his friends. An enemy bullet whizzed overhead, hitting the top of the trench. He was snapped out of his cold daydreaming. *"Private Mustapha,"* yelled one of the sergeants neat him. He picked himself up and snapped his military salute. *"Yes, sir!"* The sergeant grunted. *"Private Haydin has been killed by an enemy sharpshooter up in the cave. Go to the machine gun position and replace him,"* he finished. *"On my way, sir,"* he responded, running toward the machine gun.

The weapon was installed in an elevated position relative to the trench. It had been dug right into a natural cave and reinforced with sandbags. It was built on a rocky bluff that was on the high ground looking over the valley floor they were defending in order to block the enemy from advancing. Mustapha remembered the hard digging in the rocky soil, and he had complained like the rest of his comrades as the Russians lobbed shell after shell at them.

He started to climb the crude ice-carved stairs to the cave, as there was a "hatch" on the floor of the cave while the cave's entrance faced the enemy. But he never got there. The world around him rocked hard while the snow blew in every direction. Another enemy artillery barrage landed amidst the Turkish trenches, and one of the big enemy shells exploded right into the cave entrance, destroying the gun within it and instantly killing all the soldiers. The impact threw Mustapha backward in a flurry of dust, stone shards, and fire. The blast wave pushed him out of the immediate danger zone, and he tumbled back down into the trench, but without a scratch.

For a long moment, he had the wind knocked out of him and struggled for breath as the shells landed everywhere and pandemonium erupted all around him. His ears rang like a broken doorbell, and his body seemed on fire with the pain.

The Russians were again attacking in force, using the cover

of the terrible snowstorm to approach and attack the Turkish defensive positions. All the while, he struggled to dispel his predicament. He was seriously stunned. Intellectually, he knew he needed to get up and help his comrades fight the incoming enemy, but he couldn't move. Then, someone was over him, yelling and gesturing wildly with both arms. He looked at the man, trying to focus, but the smoke and the earth-shaking made it hard. So many enemy shells landed around that it felt like a major earthquake was rocking the land.

He saw the man's mouth move but couldn't hear what he was saying. It dawned on him that he might be deaf from the explosion that had almost killed him. He was slowly returning to his senses and his hearing. *"Mustapha, wake up; the enemy is charging amidst the snow. They are coming. We need to move out!"* He finally heard what the other man was saying, but as if he was talking from far away. And he also recognized him. It was his friend Enver. He stood up with the help of his comrade and started running after him, luckily dodging a major blast and landing almost on top of his former position.

Things were not going well, and the shitstorm was only starting for the Turkish forces. One of the worst defeats in Ottoman history was about to unfold, and poor Mustapha was in the middle of it all: The Battle of Sarikamish had started.

The Battle of Tannenberg Part 2
The Germans fight well but retreat across the board September 1st to 4th, 1914.

The Battle of Tannenberg started well for the German army, but the number of Russians started to tell and gave them an advantage on the battlefield after a few days. The Tsarist armies' frontal attacks floundered on the strong German defenses, but General Samsonov, the commander of the Russian 1st Army, simply used his superior numbers and spilled around the enemy forces.

Hindenburg and Ludendorff reacted well to the outflanking moves and defeated several of the attacks, but in the end, Samsonov just kept pouring more and more troops into the maelstrom.

By September 4th, Hindenburg had no choice but to call for a withdrawal. His armies were not defeated, and he was able to keep casualties to a minimum, but he was forced to move back because the situation called for it.

He might have been able to hold at Tannenberg if he'd poured everything he had within the 8th Germany Army into the battle, but that would have meant leaving Konigsberg defenseless. In addition, some of Samsonov's forces (a couple of light divisions) were attacking further west, and there was a danger of the entire German force being cut off from the country.

In the end, there was no simple answer to the overwhelming numbers of Russians pouring into Eastern Prussia, and thus, Hindenburg did the best he could by preserving his forces and getting them to fight another day.

By the 4th of September, Tannenberg was in Russian hands. For the second time in history, the Slavs had defeated Germanic forces there (1410, 1914). The next day, General Rennenkampf's 1st Russian Army arrived within sight of the powerful

Konigsberg fortress and ordered his troops to lay siege to the city.

The entire German position in the East was threatening to unravel if nothing serious was done. Hindenburg called again for reinforcements, which fell on deaf ears once more. By that time, the Battle of the Marne was in full swing, and all hands were required on deck in the West, for the future outcome of the war in the West depended on it.

The Vistula River Line, envisioned by von Prittwitz, the former commander of the 8th Army, started to make a little more sense now that Hindenburg was in full retreat.

The Tsingtao Fortress defense and the Japanese attack
War in the Pacific, 1914

There was a lot of time for the Germans to prepare for an assault in Tsingtao since they were in control of the area from 1902 onward. Twelve long years, and they used it well.

Two ranges of low hills surrounded the peninsula and the harbor. On two of them (closest to Tsingtao), imperial engineers built three ferroconcrete forts shielded by several naval guns; also, Fort Bismarck, towering above them all in the center of the peninsula, had four 11-inch naval defense cannons. Other forts around Tsingtato had big naval guns as well, making the entire position a formidable defensive spot.

Fort Moltke was constructed in the Ruprecht Hills to the south and had revolving 9.4-inch and 6-inch guns to guard the land approach to the city.

Steel-reinforced concrete redoubts were built along with 10-foot ditches running from one side of the Peninsula to the other. It sported a 7-foot tall wall with a large minefield.

There was yet another line of defenses on the second range of hills north of the town and over the river was the 1,100-feet-high Prinz Heinrich Hill on the eastern side of the peninsula that was ten miles wide at this juncture.

When war was declared between Japan and the German Empire (August 23rd, 1914), the defenders had fifty-seven heavy guns and howitzers, seventy-seven lighter guns, and eighty-seven machine guns ready for battle. The town had a lot of soldiers and sailors defending it as well. The Marine Artillery and the 3rd Marine Battalion numbered a little over 9,000 men, being the backbone of the garrison. These numbers were increased by reservists and volunteers who moved to the fortresses from all over the Pacific region. The Germans were ready for a fight.

With supplies aplenty (stockpiles were numerous enough to

stand over a year of siege) and with hundreds of wells and a distilling plant in the city, there were no worries about losing because the people would go hungry and thirsty. A big load of ammunition was on its way when war was declared, and the three cargo ships transporting them arrived just on time. This enabled von Spee's warfleet, and the fort's guns would have aplenty to fight the battle that was coming toward Tsingtao. The overall commander of the defenses was the military governor of Tsingtao, Alfred Meyer Waldeck.

Toying over the idea of sailing out of Tsingtao until August 14th, 1914, Admiral Maximilian Graf von Spee (the German admiral in command of the Asia Pacific Squadron and now by default of the four battleships that had recently arrived) opted to keep his ships in Tsingtao because he did not have enough coal supplies. He did, however, start to plan for a breakout into the Pacific and sent orders and messages for coal supplies to be accumulated or sent along a route that would bring him to the string of small German colonies in the wide expanse of the Pacific Ocean. He figured that he would be able to make for the high seas sometime in September and hoped the Japanese would take their time.

(…) The Japanese attack (…)

While Imperial Germany had a little over 12,000 soldiers to defend their mighty base, the Imperial Japanese Army and no intention of taking a chance and leaving things to fate. Thus, they brought enough guns, men, and ships to smash their new enemies. The Japanese invasion commander, Lieutenant General Kamio Mitsuomi, had 60,000 soldiers, 11,000 horses, 106 heavy guns or howitzers, and 45 field or mountain guns.

This was no shabby force worthy of a great siege, and there was every reason for the Japanese to think they would need it to master Tsingtao. It was defended by three large fort guns and had a powerful fleet. Admiral von Spee's fleet added its guns to the already powerful defenses and was safely protected by the harbor's naval defenses.

The total Japanese sea blockade (the entirety of the Japanese Imperial Navy showed up in front of Tsingtao due to the strength of the German Pacific Squadron), slowed by heavy storms, could not be put in place until the 27th of August.

Once in position, the Japanese Army felt it was secure enough to land at Laichow Bay, north of the fortress and away from anything the German ships could do about it (out of range). Japan ignored Chinese neutrality by advancing into their territory on to Kioachau. Their progress was painfully slow, with both the advance and consolidation being hampered by truly bad weather and storms transforming the land into a mud quagmire. The weather was not helpful to the defenders since, with so much water their trenches filled with water, with many of the minefields became useless or mired in mud and rendered less efficient; in essence, it was not good for their defensive preparations.

By the 8th of September, Japanese forces had installed their siege around Tsingtao in a concentric ring and entrenched themselves for a long battle. The presence of the German big guns made it necessary for the fleet to clear the way because the land assault was to begin, and so General Kamio signaled to the admiral in charge of the fleet, the legendary Heihachiro Togo, to prepare his naval assault.

Koenigsberg Fortress
The Russian 2nd Army encircles the defensive perimeter and begins the siege.

One powerful position stood between the Russian Imperial Army and their wish to conquer Konigsberg, the capital of Eastern Prussia. It was its impressive fortification systems. For hundreds of years, the city had been one of the most important and glorified cities in Germany. Kings were crowned in Konigsberg; philosopher Immanuel Kant had lived there his entire life, and it was the rampart of Germanic civilization against the hordes of Slavs threatening to flood the fatherland. Conquering the city was, for the Russians, a potentially great strategic victory and a hammer blow to German morale.

General Rennenkampf, recognizing the strength of the defenses, ordered his troops to entrench in a ring around the no less than nine forts in the area. A large tract of land was also protected by interlaying trench positions and minefields. Not all of the forts were modern or could necessarily withstand a true artillery bombardment, but enough could; thus, the Russians were not inclined to send a direct assault as they approached Konigsberg on the 5th of September.

The fortifications of the city included numerous defensive walls, forts, bastions, and other structures built over the centuries preceding the start of the World War. They made up the so-called First and the Second Defensive Belts, built in two phases from 1626 to 1859.

The fortification included twelve powerful forts. All of them bristled with machine guns, artillery, and soldiers ready to kill and destroy any Russians approaching.

In the twenty-five years leading up to 1914, Germany committed a lot of resources to building new forts to meet and adapt to the latest artillery developments, especially after the French developed the high-explosive shells in 1886. Both the French and the Germans began reconstructing and beefing up their old forts by adding concrete and earth to protect them better. These fortifications would soon prove their worth in the battle that was about to start, as defense would prevail for most of the war.

The forts that the Russians would have to master in Konigsberg were the following:

-Astronomic Bastion (erected in 1855-1860 and never modernized)

-Bronsart Fort, constructed in 1875-80 and named after General Paul Bronsart von-Schellendorff, was built with modern standards.

-Dohna Tower was built in 1858. Reinforced with concrete and steel, with several machine guns and field guns.

-Friedrich Wilhelm I Fort, the largest fort of Konigsberg, equipped with the most modern defenses and guns. It would be the toughest nut to crack for the Russians.

-Gneisenau Fort: Named after August von Gneisenau, one of the famous generals of the Napoleonic era. It was also modern, built in 1900.

-Grolman Bastion: Named after General Karl von Grolman.

-Pillau Citadel (built in the 17th century.) It wasn't modernized, but the Germans still garrisoned it, and it was overflowing with machine gun positions and field artillery guns.

-Stein Fort: the large Stein Fort was named after Prussian statesman Baron von Stein. It was finalized in 1893.

-Barnekow Fort: One of the small forts on the periphery, but it was also well garrisoned.

The entire setup was also supplemented with an extensive trench network. Mines were laid by the thousands on and around the area.

Moltke the Elder (the father of the German chief of the general staff in 1914) had wanted the Konigsberg fortress to play the stop-gap role in his grand plan of attacking first in France as the Schlieffen Plan dictated, and thus, the German Army had invested much in building up the city into one hell of a defensive bastion for Eastern Prussia.

This was fortunate that the old and now dead general had the foresight to designate Koenigsberg as such. With the surprising and powerful Russian offensive spilling over all of Eastern Prussia and beyond, it was a good thing the Imperial Army had what it needed to stop the enemy from advancing any further.

Knowing the power of the fortress and not having enough heavy guns to attack it yet, the Russian 2nd Army thus settled in an encircling position, and General Rennenkampf called for more artillery, especially of the heavy types. The siege forecasted to be a long, drawn-out affair of epic proportions.

The Battle of Sarikamish
The Turks are defeated in the Caucasus
September 7th to 12th, 1914.

Sarikamish was an area centered on a town going by the same name in Russia's Kars province adjacent to the Ottoman Empire's border. The area was thought as the entry to Transcaucasia, where the Turks wanted to reclaim the lost provinces of Kars, Ardahan, and Batum.

Enver Pacha, the Ottoman Minister of War, Turkish leader, and for this offensive commander of the forces about to invade, intended to advance on the city of Tiflis, Imperial Russia's administrative center in the Caucasus.n The plan would then follow up with a march deeper inside the area (north) to incite a revolt amongst the local Muslim populations against Tsarist rule.

In order to make this work rapidly once war was declared, Enver had organized the rail movement of the Army as soon as early August, when his country wasn't even at war. Enver had been confident the Empire would join the Central Powers, as he had a direct hand in the decision to send the fleet to bombard the Russian Black Sea Port in the middle of August. A month later, everything was ready for the offensive he had been dreaming about for years.

Russian war planners planned that the Ottomans would not launch an attack across snow-capped mountains and bad weather without the benefit of proper roads and enough time to prepare. Besides, they were contemplating their own attack across the border and wanted to slam the door open and move into Turkish Armenia.

The Ottoman 3rd Army, under the command of General Hasan Izzet (Enver Pacha had overall command of the invasion), was organized into three Corps: 9th, 10th, and 11th Corps, and numbered around 92,000 soldiers. The Russian Caucasus

Army included the 1st Caucasus and the 2nd Turkestan Corps, numbering 64,000 troops. The Imperial Russians also entertained a small reserve of units in Kars, the province's capital of the same name, totaling 14,000 men. General Georgii Bergmann was the overall commander and had no intention of retreating before the hated Turkish enemies.

The overly complicated Ottoman plan intended to smash over the border and attempt to envelop the Russian forces. Success depended on all four Turkish corps reaching their mission objectives on time and in force, which in turn required intricate and complex coordination of troop movements in an area it was almost impossible to do so because of the bad roads and mountains. High mountains, with heavy snowed-out areas, as soon as September, did not give a good prospect for success. The entire affair did not bode well. The plan seemed to have been born out of Enver Pasha's little fantasy world.

Chief of the German Military Mission to Constantinople (the Germans had a large contingent of military officers to help the Turks set themselves up for war in 1914), General Otto Liman von Sanders, gave a stern opinion of the entire project, deeming it pure folly to Enver Pacha himself. He made sure the Turkish leader understood the risk he would expose his men (high mountains, cold, bad supply). Regardless, Enver Pacha decided to go ahead with his plan.

For his part, General Izzet could resist telling Enver that the soldiers about to invade were not trained or ready for a winter or late fall assault in the mountains. They also lacked cold-weather clothing and winter rations. Enver, undaunted and adamant that the attack would go ahead according to his set of plans, forced Izzet to resign and assumed direct command. Since he believed his soldiers weren't advancing fast enough, Enver ordered his soldiers to abandon their heavy winter clothing, their tents, and anything bigger than a haversack. It was an order so stupid that it would have earned a reputation for being a murderer; his men would soon have to face the brunt of the cold Caucasus winter and its high mountains. So many would die because of the weather that it would be remembered as one of the worst blunders of the war.

A few days later, on the 7th of September 1914, Ottoman forces descended from the high mountains, and the Russian troops came under major attack in Sarikamish. A major battle soon blossomed between the two sides that would last five days and conclude with no clear winners.

The Ottoman's 10th Corps, commanded by General Hafız Hakki, managed to skirt around the Russian right flank and took the village of Oltu the following day. Meanwhile, the troops of the Ottoman 9th Corps climbed the high roads and plateaus toward Sarikamish. Encountering a major storm and a bout of extreme cold, thousands died of exposure since they were without tents and firewood.

On 12th September, the Turkish troops began the harrowing march across the Allahüekber Mountains to unite with the Ottoman 9th Corps. One-sixth of the corps died of exposure before they reached the distant approaches to Sarikamish. The battle that was starting would last for several months.

The Battle of Sarikamish
Mohamed fights Russians and weather, September 14th, 1914

Turkish soldier Mohamed manned his little part of a trench somewhere east of Sarikamish, near the Ottoman border. His trench was covered in snow, as his division was somewhere high up in the mountains, where the weather was cold, harsh, and unforgiving.

It had snowed again the night before, and he felt cold. Everyone around him harbored the same worn and discouraged face. Morale was low as the Turkish forces were getting attacked on a daily basis by the Russian forces, trying to dislodge them from their position.

The first few fights had been bad enough, but now, at least, they were getting a break from enemy artillery. The Russians were finding it difficult to move the cumbersome guns into the roadless terrain where they were fighting.

But that didn't mean they weren't finding ways to lob shells at their Turkish enemies. There had been a lull in the fighting for the last few hours, but it now seemed over as a line of brown-uniformed soldiers appeared at the bottom of the slope they were defending. And then, the ignominious whistling sounds of falling artillery started to be heard, and Mohamed started to feel the usual panic coming along with it.

He looked around, but there was nowhere to run. The trench was too shallow, and his other option was to start running backward in the white snow field. This would not be good as the officers would brand him a deserter, and he might be shot by his own side. Stay in place, and if a shell landed nearby, he would die or be horribly wounded like some of his comrades. Those comrades were now frozen stiff from the cold after bleeding to death in the Caucasian mountain wastes.

"Everyone hunker down!" yelled the Captain near him. Not

knowing what else to do, Mohamed dropped to the ground and curled himself into as small a ball as possible. He gathered some of the snow and frozen dirt in the vain hope this would protect him from shrapnel pieces that would soon surely fly around and shred many Turkish soldiers.

Seconds later, it seemed that his world ended. The ground shook, the air shattered, and the very fabric of reality seemed to unravel. Large explosions rocked the ground, the snow, the trenches. And then the screaming started amidst the chaos of the blasting waves of fires and sounds. The Russian artillery attacks plastered the Turkish defensive positions, the ground beneath them lighting up with raging fire and smoke.

Through it all, he prayed to Allah to keep him alive. He also tried to picture an image of his loving mother and the song she used to sing to him when he was afraid as a child.

From above, the Turkish trench line blossomed with balls of fire and catapulting earth in towering columns of debris. Smoke covered the entire view for a moment, and the only thing that could be seen were the bright tracers of the Russian rifle and the Turkish machine gun positions firing into the charging mass of men.

"Fix bayonets!" yelled the Captain through the racket. Mohamed found a way to stir up the courage he needed to unlimber the long knife from the side of his rifle and attach it to the tip of the gun. Through it all, artillery shells fell all around him and his comrades.

He started to hear the weird *"oo-oo-RAAAAAAAAAAAAAAAAAAAAH!"* Russian battle cry through the cacophony of sounds and tried to hurry up, but he fumbled his bayonet on the ground. As he was about to bend down to pick it up, the Russian soldiers were over the trench and jumping inside of it. One of them, yelling madly, tried to fillet him with his own bayonet, but Mohamed rolled to the side, avoiding the piercing motion by a mere couple of inches.

The raving Russian continued to try and kill him while more and more of his countrymen jumped into the Turkish trench. Mohamed saw that many of his comrades were also fighting a desperate hand-to-hand battle. Not finding his bayonet in the mad scramble to try and get away from the enemy's blade, his hand rested on a palm-sized rock. He picked it up and threw it at the bastard, trying to kill him. The jagged rock hit the Russian in the middle of the face, initiating a flurry of blood from the man's forehead, and he fell unconscious on the ground.

Having a couple seconds before the next guy was on him, Mohamed found his blade on the ground and decided to use it as a short sword, picking it up with the hilt. He then narrowly dodged a charging Russian and slammed him with his blade on the neck, making a deep cut. Then, a third man faced him, and he pushed his bayonet-tipped rifle to the side before plunging his blade into his belly. A fourth enemy tried to rush him, and again, he killed the bastard.

This little dance went on for a few minutes before the enemy assault was out of gas, and the Russian soldiers were all killed. He smiled and cheered with his surviving Turkish comrades, but just as they thought they'd won, the ominous sounds of whistling artillery shells started to be heard again.

"Down!" yelled someone, and Mohamed was on the ground while the world around him shook.

The First Naval Battle of Tsingtao
Von Spee vs Togo, September 9th, 1914

If one thing needed to happen before the Japanese made their land attack on Tsingtao, it was a naval battle to destroy the powerful Kaiserliche Marine squadron in the harbor. By their mere presence and the caliber of their guns, they could obliterate any assault on the city or, at the very least, seriously hinder it. With that removed, they could then use the fleet's big guns to smash the three major forts defending the German base. And anyway, such a fight went right into the Japanese military persona of the bushido: Go to your opponent, challenge him, and defeat him.

The Japanese leadership thus decided that the German fleet in the harbor needed to be eliminated, along with the fixed gun defenses protecting it.

But the entire equation had a problem. Admiral Maximilian von Spee, the German commander of the Pacific Squadron, had a powerful fleet. With the added protection and cannons of the harbor defenses, it was a formidable opponent for the yet-still-small Japanese Imperial Navy.

The matter was debated in length in Tokyo; then, it was discussed in the field near Tsingtao and on the ships of the fleet, but on September 6th, things were settled, and it was decided to force the issue by attacking Tsingtao with the full might of the Japanese Imperial Navy. The command of the force was given to legendary admiral Togo Heihachiro, the man who had won Japan's biggest victory in its history in 1905 at the Battle of Tsushima. The man had been made Fleet Admiral in 1913 (honorary overall commander of the Imperial Navy), and while the entire affair had been more or less ceremonial, the size of the task before the Japanese fleet in Tsingtao prompted the Japanese leadership to ask Togo to return to duty. Since the spring of 1914, the Admiral had been entrusted with the education of young Emperor Hirohito but accepted the recall to service with his usual grace and devotion to duty.

Japanese Imperial Fleet		
BB Setsu	Pre-dreadnought BB HIZEN	Pre-dreadnought BB MIKASA
BB Kawachi	Pre-dreadnought BB IKI	CA X23
BC Kongo	Pre-dreadnought BB IWAMI	CL X6
Pre-dreadnought BC Tsukuma	Pre-dreadnought BB SAGAMI	DD X50
Pre-Dreadnought BC Ikoma	Pre-dreadnought BB SUWO	
Pre-Dreadnought BC Ibuki	Pre-dreadnought BB TANGO	
Pre-Dreadnought BC Kurama	Pre-dreadnought BB FUJI	
Pre-dreadnought BB KASHIMA,	Pre-dreadnought BB ASAHI	
Pre-dreadnought BB KATORI	Pre-dreadnought BB SHIKISHIMA	

Togo had a powerful fleet at his disposal, if not the most modern. Most of his battleships were pre-dreadnoughts, but the problem presented by Tsingtao would not prove a disadvantage because the older ships would not have to find the range nor make complicated maneuvers. It would be relatively easy to attack an unmoving target. And besides, the port area and the forts around were so large a target it was impossible to miss after a few shots to find the range.

Maximilian von Spee's problem was quite different. As the defending side, he could not choose when he would fight, nor would he be able to maneuver in case of attack. In short, he was bottled up in port. He positioned his capital ships between the smaller escorts around for them to act as shields. He also figured his battleships would be able to fight even if sunk since the guns and most of the big ship's structure would stay above the shallow harbor waters. His strength was supplemented by the fixed naval guns around the base. These were extensive, and he figured they amounted to several battleships. Furthermore, they could not be sunk, and the Japanese would only destroy them with a direct hit. The Tsingtao Sea Defenses were as follows and promised hell on earth to any fleet crazy enough to approach the German fortress:

Fort Hui-tchien-huk

4 x 24cm/40 naval rifles.

8 x 8.8cm/35 naval rifles

Searchlights in armored cupolas.

A generous ammunition stockpile.

Fort Bismarck

4 x 28.3cm coast defense mortars.

8 x 8.8cm/35 naval rifles

Searchlights in armored cupolas.

A generous ammunition stockpile.

Old Tsingtao Battery.

4 x 21cm/40 naval rifles.

8 x 8.8cm/35 naval rifles

Searchlights in armored cupolas.

A generous ammunition stockpile.

Hsiauniwa Battery.

4 x 21cm/40 naval rifles.

8 x 8.8cm/35 naval rifles

Searchlights in armored cupolas.

A generous ammunition stockpile.

The German admiral also had a very potent fleet, including no less than 2 battleships (two dreadnoughts):

German Pacific Squadron	
Admival von Graf Spee	
BB Westfalen	CA Sharnhorst
BB Kaiserin	CA Gneisenau
Pre dreadnought BB Pommern	CL Emden
Pre Dreadnought Schleswig-Holstein	CL Nurnberg
	CL Leipzing

The Japanese fleet made its approach on September 9th under the guise of darkness. Togo figured that since it would be a slugfest, it was better for his ships to at least have the first few shots.

(...) Dreadnought Battleship Setsu (...)

"Everything is in place, Fleet Admiral," said Togo's chief of staff, Vice Admiral Nomura. Heihachiro didn't answer immediately but merely nodded his understanding. Nomura didn't say

anything else. The mere presence of the great Admiral Togo on the bridge of the battleship Setsu was enough to soothe him into silence. After all, this was Japan's biggest and most famous hero of the 20th Century to date. Togo's slight stature belied his strategic prowess.

Admiral Togo, now in the twilight years of his life, tried to look at the situation for what it was. This was his last call to fame, and he decided he would make it count. His thoughts turned to a time far away, following the Battle of Tsushima, when he visited the defeated Russian admiral in the hospital on 30 June 1905.

"Defeat is common to soldiers from all armies in history. Shame over it is irrelevant. The real question is if we perform our duty to the maximum of our capabilities... For you, especially, who fearlessly performed your great task until you were seriously wounded, I beg to express my sincerest respect . . ."

He pondered at his own words for a moment and turned toward his old battleship, Mikasa. The old lady was still sailing with the ships, but there were talks of retiring her. He would have loved to be on the old battleship again, but alas, it had not been possible; it was better to command the fight from a newer and better-protected ship. And then an old phrase from his own self came back, rushing to the forefront of his mind. *"Vice-Admiral Nomura,"* he started with confidence, feeling every one of the sailors and officers' attention snap up a notch. *"Yes, Fleet Admiral?"* "We will commence firing at exactly one in the morning; get the message to the other ships we are all to fire at the same time." The Vice-Admiral was about to respond when Togo continued. *"And also attach the following phrase to the message: The Empire's fate depends on the result of this battle; let every man do his utmost duty."*

It was ten minutes to one o'clock in the morning during the moonless night of the 8th to 9th of September. Togo's plan was simple, and he sailed the fleet to arrive in range of Tsingtao under the guise of darkness, with all of his ships harboring no lights whatsoever. While the sudden attack would not necessarily win the battle, he'd figured that it was never bad to send a knockout blow right from the start. After all, the combined broadside firepower of over ninety ships was not a bad start to try and kill some Germans.

(...) Dreadnought Battleship Westfalen (...)

Admiral Maximilian von Spee woke up with a yell. He opened his eyes and realized it was the middle of the night, and he was in his Admiral of the Fleet cabin aboard the dreadnought battleship Westfalen. He'd dreamed of the impending naval battle again. He was sweating, and in his dream, he had been fighting on the bridge of the ship, and Tsingtao was in flames all around him. The overbearing feeling of failure still hung with him as he dispelled the last whisps of sleepiness. He looked at his clock and saw it was 1246 in the morning. He decided to go for a stroll to the bridge. His mother had always been good at seeing things that would or might happen, and he had caught some of it, as had his sibling. Over the years, he learned to trust the feeling, especially when it was one of impending doom.

Maximilian von Spee was a career sailor in the Kaiserliche Marine. He had grown in ranks along with the expansion of the Germany Navy and was now one of its top commanders.

Named commander of the East Asiatic Squadron in 1912 and promoted to Admiral. The fact he had four battleships at his disposal was pure luck or bad luck, depending on how you saw the matter. For Tsingtao, it was good, but he wasn't sure his superiors in Wilhelmshaven were stoked to lose so much firepower since they were already at a serious disadvantage with the Royal Navy in the North Sea.

He got to the bridge, and the night watch officer rose sharply from his seat by the helm. *"Admiral on deck,"* he said, and the four night watch sailors stood up at the ready. *"At ease, gentlemen.*

I am just checking up on things," said von Spee, walking by the bridge's viewport.

"What is that, sir," said one of the night watch sailors, pointing at a series of flashes on the horizon. A hell of a lot of flashes. And then von Spee's horrible nightmare feeling came back rushing.

(...) The battle (...)

One moment, there was only the quietness of the night. Then, a multitude of flashes blossomed on the horizon offshore Tsingtao. The next moment, the incredibly powerful salvo combining the full broadsides of over ninety ships ranging from destroyers to dreadnought battleships exploded in all its fury on the high ridges and mountains surrounding the city. The darkness was dispelled in a maelstrom of red fire and blasting rocks.

From a distance, on battleship Setsu, Fleet Admiral Togo and his men only saw a gigantic ball bloom and expand like a fiery and bright bubble. A few of the sailors could not help but gasp in amazement at the awesome showcase of Japanese firepower.

The first Japanese salvo concentrated its fire on the ring of forts because of its naval guns. Togo hoped to smash enough to even the score before the real fight started, and the Germans fought back. Be as it may, several of the Imperial Navy shells overshot and simply blazed above Tsingtao, while others fell into the harbor. There was so much ordinance flying that not one area of the German base was spared.

Battleship Pommern was the first vessel to get hit. To the sleepy sailors and watch officers, it seemed impossible even to count the number of projectiles striking the ship, as many barreled down on it floating in the harbor. They had not only never witnessed such a fire before but had never imagined anything like it. Shells seemed to be plunging upon them in rapid succession. The deck, the armor, and some of the guns were shattered, causing many deaths and casualties. The Pommern shook and groaned under the multiple impacts. All around the battleship, geysers of water towered, as not all the Japanese shells hit home.

Once the thundering aftershock of the Japanese salvo abated, the Germans sailors were running up to their stations. The soldiers up in the high forts above the city also went into action. The gigantic structures got damaged and lost several guns with the first salvo, but enough of them survived to have one hell of a duel with the Japanese.

Fort Hui-tchien-huk, Fort Bismarck, the Old Tsingtao Battery, and Hsiauniwa Battery all opened their powerful searchlights (all had survived because they were protected by armored cupolas) and rapidly zeroed in on the main body of the enemy fleet. Anyway, it wasn't hard to spot since the ships were already starting to send their second salvos at Tsingtao. Hui-tchien-huk gunners were the fastest to react and fired their counter salvo first. Two of their 24 cm/40 and 8.8 cm naval rifles had survived the opening shelling and thus blazed away at the grouping of Japanese in front of them. They didn't aim at any ship in particular since they only saw outlines of vessels, but at least they were pretty certain to hit.

Then Fort Bismarck's three surviving 28.3 cm coast defense mortars added to the German fire, closely followed by the Old Tsingtao Battery sole surviving 21 cm/40 naval rifles and its 5 8.8 cm/35 naval rifles. The Hsiauniwa Battery stayed mostly silent as it had been hit with shells from Kongo and Setsu, and the men inside were quite busy surviving the crumbling state of their fort and the rolling wall of flames racing across its interior. From a distance, the entire structure seemed aflame and was jutting heavy smoke.

The German shells started to slam on the Japanese hulls, and right here and then, ships started to go up in flames. Pre-dreadnought Fuji was hit on the funnel and received a plunging shell from Bismarck's mortar, and the entire vessel was rocked by a powerful explosion moments later. Armored cruiser Mikabishi exploded as it was hit by three shells, while three Japanese destroyers were also destroyed.

Togo's plan was never to stay in front and slug it out in a stationary position, and the Japanese ships continued on in an enfilade style while they sailed northward. Their fire was relentless, and the Tsingtao forts took the brunt of the fire. They fired at the harbor at an angle to try and circumvent the high mountains; thus, their aims were not very precise. It was nonetheless enough to get a shell to slam on both the Westfalen and Kaiserin dreadnoughts, damaging the stern, rudder, and some secondary gun turrets. At that moment (maybe six or seven minutes into the fight), the stricken battleship Pommern exploded in a catastrophic display of destruction. The fire racing inside it had reached its main shell magazine. The blast slammed shrapnel on the German ships in the harbor, and some large parts of the great warship were catapulted into the city, killing several hundred civilians.

Speaking of the city of Tsingtao it was hit by multiple Japanese shells, causing great destruction and starting many fires. Both Kaiserin and Westfalen's guns finally answered the enemy and sent several quick salvoes at the Japanese fleet. Their first two straddled the Jap ships, and then they finally hit home, their powerful shells destroying another cruiser. They also caused serious damage to Kongo's funnels and to Setsu's deck. Three more destroyers died as well. Concentrating their fire on the forts above the city, the Japanese continued to inflict serious damage on them. They were eventually able to silence a second one, the Old Tsingtao Battery. And then ten minutes later, the exchange was over, Togo's fleet sailing away to the open seas.

Fort Hui-tchien-huk

4 x 24cm/40 naval rifles. 3 destroyed, 1 remaining

8 x 8.8cm/35 naval rifles 5 destroyed, 3 remaining

Searchlights in armored cupolas. Destroyed

A generous ammunition stockpile.

Fort Bismarck

4 x 28.3cm coast defense mortars. 2 destroyed, 2 remaining

8 x 8.8cm/35 naval rifles 4 destroyed, 4 remaining

Searchlights in armored cupolas.

A generous ammunition stockpile.

~~Old Tsingtao Battery.~~

~~4 x 21cm/40 naval rifles.~~

~~8 x 8.8cm/35 naval rifles~~

~~Searchlights in armored cupolas.~~

~~A generous ammunition stockpile.~~

~~Hsiauniwa Battery.~~

~~4 x 21cm/40 naval rifles.~~

~~8 x 8.8cm/35 naval rifles~~

~~Searchlights in armored cupolas.~~

~~A generous ammunition stockpile.~~

The final tally was that the naval defenses of Tsingtao were seriously damaged, and the Germans had lost a pre-dreadnought battleship, the Pommern, with damage ranging from light to heavy on the rest of its fleet. The city was on fire, and the entire area was plastered with shell impacts. The Japanese were not unscathed, and the pre-dreadnought battleship Fuji was first crippled and then destroyed by Fort Bismarck's heavy naval mortars. Togo also left two sinking cruisers and six wrecked destroyers in the waters near Tsingtao.

THE WAR IN
THE WEST

We are engaging in a fight with the fate of our country in the balance...Our soldiers can move ahead and attack. They must, at any price, fight to the death, hold on, and attack again when I tell them.
General Joseph Joffre, Order of the Day, 5 September 1914

The moment is decisive. The fate of the Empire will be soon decided. I wish
I could sacrifice my own life to achieve victory for the Reich.
General Helmuth von Moltke, 7 September 1914

The Battle of the Marne Part 1
The great retreat and the leadup to the ultimate battle in the west, up to September 5th, 1914

The so-called "Great Retreat" (French: Grande Retraite) was the name given to the dreadful withdrawal from the Marne River for the forces of the Entente. The Anglo-French, after being soundly defeated in the battle for the frontier and pretty much every battle after that, also lost at the Battle of Charleroi (21st of August) and the Battle of Mons (23rd of August).

What followed was a series of small battles and skirmishes, with the Franco-British executing a fighting retreat westward that spanned over 150 miles in several areas. The Battle of Le Cateau, Le Grand Fayt (of the Battle of Fayt), the Battle of Étreux, the Battle of Cerizy, and a trio of battles (Crepy, Crépy-en-Valois, Villers-Cotterêts) failed to stop or stem the German advance in any significant way.

The Schlieffen Plan was in full swing, and the German 1st, 2nd, and 3rd Armies advanced relentlessly toward Paris. Nothing the Entente put in their wake slowed them down in any significant way.

Without the Germans or the French seeing it, the overall situation was morphing as one or the other army moved forward or backward. The Germans' ever-forward movement made them march further and further away from their supply lines. Cracks were starting to appear in their neatly prepared and executed offensive plan. For the French, it was the opposite. The more westward they went, the better their supply became and the more compressed their troops were, hardening the defense with every mile of the retreat.

Such a massive backward movement went against Joffre's every instinct, and he simply refused to believe he was defeated and that the result was pre-decided and written in the sky. Now, with the bonus of better lines of supply, the ever-offensive Joffre intended to make good use of the newfound opportunity.

The moment for the French to counterattack came when von Kluck and the German OHL decided to change the original design of the Schlieffen plan and to wheel the 1st German Army south-facing Paris instead of going north and around it. His troops had by then far outpaced the supply capability of the German logistical services, and the soldiers were dead-tired. Going around Paris meant that his troops would have to march another batch of miles and it was not the best of options. He thus chose to turn south in front of Paris, presenting his right flank and inadvertently setting the conditions for a big battle near the Marne River.

He was comforted in his decision by the reports giving him an over-optimistic assessment of the state of the BEF fighting capabilities, apparently posing no serious threat to his own right flank. Furthermore, he was quite eager to slam into the French 5th Army's flank.

After some back-and-forth messaging with the OHL HQ located in Luxemburg, the decision was given the go-ahead by von Moltke (as overall commander. The man was also growing concerned about the supply and fatigue situation); hence, he was happy for 1st Army to fix the enemy in position while General Karl von Bülow's 2nd Army, also moved in for the kill to smash the French 5th Army on Joffre's left.

As the *"Great Retreat"* was unfolding, the Anglo-French forces had not just waited for the final disaster and the killing blow to fall. Joffre, the ever-offensive officer, had acted. On the run for more than two weeks, he had begun, like a hunting beast, to smell the scent of a potential kill. He first replaced an impressive number of senior commanders, whom he had decided did not have enough will and *"élan vital"* needed to win.

In all, forty-four of his eighty divisional commanders were replaced, eleven of his twenty-five corps commanders, and two of his nine army commanders (the French had nine field armies in September 1914). Among them was General Lanrezac (commander of the much-bloodied 5th Army), who replaced what Joffre considered a more offensive-minded commander (d'Espérey), who had the offensive dedication the French overall commander sought.

While the French were about to attack in force, for von Moltke, it looked like a major opportunity was presenting itself. 1st Army now turned south and east in a move that could potentially eliminate the entire enemy left flank. The next set of actions would then enable the Germans to roll up the entirety of Allied lines.

Such dreamlike planning, however, did not resist contact with reality; Kluck and the rest of the German high command started dismissing very clear and alarming reports of enemy movements to the west on their now exposed right flank. For two days, German reconnaissance planes and cavalry recon units saw and repotted many instances of numerous troops movement and massing on 1st Army's right flank facing Paris. Kluck dismissed all those reports as alarmist and continued to focus on his own offensive plans.

Using his own experience as a logistical officer (earlier in his career) and in building and moving about with rail lines, the Allied overall commander proved an exceptional logistician once more. His never-ending pool of energy willed two new field armies to existence, the 9th and the 6th. Put under the command of General Ferdinand Foch, the new Army formation would have a pivotal role in the coming battle.

In what seemed like the blink of an eye in terms of time and logistical challenge, the French commander-in-chief had succeeded in creating a powerful counterstroke right on Kluck's flank. He was able to do this by moving troops away from the border with Germany, the very same men and guns that had floundered in the Battle of the Frontiers. These Frenchmen, still proud and eager for a revenge bout against the hated Germans, were motivated and ready to go at it.

All was set for one hell of a battle.

The Generals and their plans
Up to September 5th, 1914

(...) Somewhere south of Paris (...)

French General Joseph Joffre tried to remove the persistent mud off his black boots. It had rained the night before, and the entire land was a quagmire because thousands of men moved about. What had used to be a nice green field was now a brown mush of dirt and mud. He looked in the distance toward the eastern horizon, from where the constant rumble of the guns came. He was near the River Marne, the spot where he'd chosen to make his stand and counterattack the Germans.

Willing a miracle out of what seemed thin air, French commander-inchief Joffre was able to muster France's last reserves and move some of his forces away from the Battle of the Frontier to have the necessary force for the battle that would decide the fate of Paris and of probably the war itself. His forces were poised to launch from the eastern bank of the Marne River, and he was about to give the final go-ahead to launch the counteroffensive he'd sought and prepared for the last two weeks.

Although he'd worked hard and had done everything in his power to make this a victory, he still had his doubts. Looking once more toward the rumble of the guns (he thought he saw a flash reminiscent of an artillery explosion), he turned back toward the assembled group of officers. *"We are a go for the attack, gentlemen."* He was facing all of his army commanders in the area. The generals Gallieni (5th Army), D'Espérey (5th Army), and Foch (9th Army). They all acquiesced with a nod of their heads. Joffre continued. *"Every effort must be made to attack and push the enemy back. A soldier who can no longer advance must guard the territory already held, no matter what the cost. He must be killed where he stands rather than a drawback."* The men facing Joffre all nodded again, this time with grave faces. The time for the survival of France and of Paris was now, and desperate times called for desperate measures.

(...) German 1st Army Command (...)

German General Alexander von Kluck read the report about heavy French troop concentrations on his right toward Paris, and he sighed heavily. It wasn't that he didn't believe them, and the insistence of the air flight reconnaissance about their number did worry him a little. But right in front of him lay the French 5th Army, weakly protected on its left flank by the British Expeditionary Force. Victory was at hand.

The original Schlieffen Pan had called for his Army to stay strong on the right and flank around Paris, just as the originator of the plan, General Alfred von Schlieffen, had advocated. Some parts of Kluck's mind harbored some doubts. Had it not been the great man's last words not to weaken the right?

But then again, Schlieffen was long dead and wasn't here and now. He was, and he had gotten his approval from von Moltke the Younger, the Chief of the General Staff (OHL). And so, they'd changed the plan because they faced an opportunity.

"Sir," said one of his staff officers. They were under a field tent somewhere east of Paris, about a couple of miles behind the frontline. "The lead elements of our forces have started to engage the French 5th Army and the damned British BEF." All of Kluck's doubts faded away like magic. He was now committed to whatever might happen. The battle was joined, and the rest would be decided by fate, skills, and might.

(...) OHL, Luxemburg (...)

Helmut von Moltke, the Chief of the German General staff, felt at peace with his decision. The rest of the men around him were nervous, but he wasn't. His forces had beaten the Entente troops since the beginning of the war, and he didn't see any way the enemy could jeopardize his plan.

As the fight was beginning, he was now grateful for having lost the argument about his wish to send close to 200,000 men into Eastern Prussia. While the situation there was pretty dire, he felt he had the troops where he needed them. The French seemed to want to attack again, and with the beleaguered state of his frontline forces, the two fresh corps coming up behind the 1st and 2nd Armies might make the difference.

The soldiers on both sides
Up to September 5th, 1914

(...) 4th Imperial Division, 2nd German Army (...)

Private Soldier Oskar Dantz felt terrible because his feet were wet and covered in blisters. At least now he had a "new" pair of boots taken from a dead comrade's corpse.

"Sergeant," he said, turning his head toward Sergeant Wilhelm. *"Yes, Private,"* answered the crusty NCO. *"Where are we now?" "We are at a place called the Marne River. I hear from the top brass that this is it, kid. The final battle. The Captain and the Colonel, all the way up to General von Stein, the Division commander, think that the French will be making a stand here and that we can finish this war here and now."*

Oskar looked at the southern horizon, where he could see the glowing balls of fire of their artillery landing amidst French lines. The day was getting late, and darkness was falling over the land. *"Well, Sergeant, I certainly hope so,"* he answered.

The war had been terrible on the Infanterie-Regiment Graf Schwerin. He didn't know the official numbers, and the higher-ups would probably not disclose them anyway, but from his perspective, it seemed half the people he knew were either dead or wounded since the first Battle in Liege a few weeks before.

Bülow's 2nd army, just north of the Marne on the 5th of September, was as worn and depleted as von Kluck's 1st Army to its right flank, having marched 270 miles since leaving Germany and having suffered more than 26,000 casualties and soldiers felled by illnesses. Bülow had begun the war with 260,000 soldiers; in September, he had 154,000. It was fortunate for him that the OHL had decided not to send the two corps and a cavalry division to reinforce Ludendorff and Hindenburg (180,000 men in total). These forces were marching right behind his army and would soon arrive at the most opportune of times.

"Tomorrow, Private, we cross the Marne and its southern tributaries, the Grand and Petit Morin," said Wilhelm. *"Now, get your gun cleaned and try to find some grub to eat; that's an order."*

(...) 14th French Infantry Division, 5th Army (...)

Private Soldier Armand Bonnier and his broad-shouldered giant of a friend Philippe Cren were lying down on the grass by the side of a road the Lieutenant in command of their platoon intended to use as cover for the battle that was sure to happen the next day.

The French 5th Army, which they were both part of, had been retreating for the last ten days, and now it was time to make a stand. Orders had come down from high command for the 5th and the BEF on its left flank to stand and die in place while the French counterattack from Paris and to their right, the French 9th Army (under General Ferdinand Foch) was also going to attack.

The smell of tobacco was heavy all around as several of the men smoked with their tobacco pipes, including Philippe, an avid smoker who did so whenever he had the opportunity.

"You think the Krauts will be coming our way like the officers are saying, Phil," asked Armand, sort of worried about what the next day would bring. Every time they'd faced the Germans so far, they were defeated except for that small skirmish back in Mulhouse in the opening days of the war. Cren took some time to answer, as he seemed to think while taking in a deep tobacco intake from his pipe. The top, where the tobacco was, burned and flashed bright red while he did so. He then exhaled, and the powerful, pungent smell hit Armand's nostrils once more. He had to admit the fragrance wasn't bad, even if he didn't like to smoke. It overwhelmed the stink of unwashed and dirty men for a moment. That was one of the reasons he'd come to like Philippe's smoking, as before the war, he didn't care too much for

the heavy smell.

"You know, Bonnier," he finally said after the billowing smoke from his exhaling dissipated. *"What I think is that it doesn't matter. We fight, and we win or lose; I don't really care as long as I am still alive to see my family again."* Armand grunted in reply. *"Well, I agree with that, Phil."*

The 14th Division was arrayed on a somewhat straight line (following the obstacles, buildings, and roads it could hide behind). It was expected the Germans would soon cross the small river Marne and attack them. In fact, the battle was pretty certain to happen the very next day. Their role (what they'd been told anyway) in the coming battle would be to defend while their comrades attacked from the sides.

But yet another of Joffre's *"offensive opportunities"* would present itself during the battle and they would be part of the units sent to infiltrate the gap between the two German Armies. Fate would have both of the men at the very spot where the battle would soon be decided.

(...) 113th Artillery Battery, south of Grand Breau (...)

"Drop the gun here," said the Lieutenant in charge of their gun and a few others. The man was busy getting the 18-pounders in line for the coming battle.

A bored-looking driver rode the left horse of each pair. The 2-wheeled ammunition limber was attached to the horses, and the tail of the gun was hooked up to the limber. This was to better distribute the total weight of the gun and to have the trail supported on 4 wheels. It was a good thing that it was well-made because the men of the 113th Battery had had to fight the mud and the bad road conditions to get to their position near a small village called Grand-Breau, overlooking what would soon be the Marne battlefield.

Artilleryman Archibald Totenkam was on his own beast, droning along as he was happy to just have the horse walk for him. He was tired, like every one of his comrades. The retreat from Mons and then Le Cateau was gruesome, and not many men in the unit felt confident about the battle soon to explode in fury or its outcome. After all, the Krauts had been beating them at every turn since they arrived in France.

"Everyone," continued the Lieutenant. *"Unlimber and get down from your horses. We're setting up shop here."* Archibald grunted, and William Thorpe, his gunner friend, spoke up. *"Well, we'll have the high ground for a change."* Indeed, Gran Breau was on a sort of elevated plateau above the River Marne, and that meant they would be able to have an advantage over the incoming Germans. *"It's going to be like shooting at a country fair,"* answered Archibald.

The Battle of the Marne Part 2
The French counterattack, September 6th

The battle went to full intensity on the 6th of September 1914, roughly forty miles from Paris, with the newly constituted French 6th Army attacking hard at the German 1st Army's right, starting the critical First Battle of the Marne at the end of the first month of World War One. The road to the Marne was long and winding, and both sides had suffered heavily from the numerous battles fought in Belgium and all across the Franco-German border. It was one hell of an epic battle.

The OHL commanders were surprised by the attack. Helmut von Moltke the Younger, located in Luxembourg, did not expect such a strong push. His imagination had not gone as far as thinking Joffre would attack once again.

General Gallieni's 150,000 infantrymen blazed through the German right flank, and a powerful battle ensued between the two sides. With fresh forces, the French were able to quickly put the enemy in a bad position.

When Kluck received the panicked reports of the BEF attacking from the southern part of his frontline, he was puzzled, and then a little panicked by the very real problem this could cause. He then ordered some more units to the fore, and the fight increased in intensity. Countermanding and confusing orders, linked with deficient coordination between the main commanders, created the conditions for an epic battle where the fate of the war would be decided.

The fighting got so bad, and the miscommunication was obvious that a 30-mile gap opened between Kluck's forces (1st Army) and Bulow's 2nd Army.

This was enough for a man like Joffre, when he was notified by the air reconnaissance of this fact, to act quickly. After all, he was a man obsessed with the offensive and didn't like to stay and defend. The French 5th Army(d'Espérey) and several British infantry units poured aggressively into the widening gap and simultaneously attacked the German 2nd Army.

The soldiers on both sides
September 6th to 8th, 1914

"The French army will accept nothing less than the conduct of offensive operations...
That is the only way to achieve positive results... Battles are only a contest of will,
after all. Defeat is not possible when no one believes in victory. Victory comes to the
side with the most steadfastness, the most boldness, and the most morale."
General Joseph Joffre on offensive spirit, 1914.

(...) French 14th Division (...)

. Soldiers ran, fired their guns, and died. From the East and the West, Armand Bonnier and Philippe Cren, both infantry soldiers in the French 14th Division (5th Army), saw the enemy guns firing because of the smoke hanging an ominous dark cloud over the area. Smoke, fire, and overwhelming noises reigned supreme over the shattering scene of the epic battlefield. As they ran, it was impossible to get an idea of the positions of the enemy on the hill. Their vision bumped up and down as they pounded the earth. A powerful explosion rocked the ground beside them, and they were thrown on the ground like ragdolls by the concussion wave. *"Allez! Allez!"* (*Go! Go!*) yelled one Sergeant as they stumbled back to their feet with their comrades. They had to take a moment on their knees to dispel their stunned minds. The sight that greeted them as they got back on their feet was gruesome.

The attack was going well, and the Germans were on the run. They had poured into a gap apparently thirty miles wide, and for a day, it had felt true for the two men; the enemy had been nowhere to be seen. They were getting awfully tired, however. The marching and the fighting had been non-stop since they started the attack a day and a half before.

In truth, both sides were completely exhausted following the last few weeks of intense battle, marching, and then battling again. However, the French had an advantage in the fact that as they had retreated west, their supply lines got shorter, and it was easier to get the soldiers fed and regularly supplied with ammo and other war materials. Thus, the men of the 14th Division at least had good food and were well supplied with ammo.

The French 5th Army and the BEF (John French), now led by General Louis Franchet d'Espérey, moved up into the 30-mile gap that divided the German First and Second Armies. The Entente troops were thus attacking Bülow's 2nd Army, and both Private Cren and Bonnier were in the middle of it. What began as a desperate move started to look like a great opportunity for an imposing victory in being, and the German situation teetered on the side of disaster.

"Up there!" Several of the men pointed toward a thin line of grey-uniformed soldiers. Then, tracer bullets started to rain down all around them, and French soldiers died in droves. Phil and Armand charged as they yelled, bayonet-tipped rifles in their hands. They just needed to push a little more to win it all.

(...) Infanterie-Regiment Graf Schwerin (...)

"Attack!" yelled the Lieutenant, all dressed in black and wielding his saber high in the sky. The man and his men were conducting an assault as if they were fighting in another age. But there was no choice; the French were assaulting, and there was no cover to hide behind; thus, the best play was to attack and smash the bastards in a storm of bayonets, bullets, and artillery shells.

In war, there is no such thing as complete certainty. The adversary has his own will and may perhaps do something entirely different from what we hope. One can, therefore, only reckon with probabilities and cannot wait for clarification of his intentions. One would otherwise always come too late.
Helmut von Moltke, 1907

Private Soldier Oskar Dantz fought as hard as he could but felt he was hanging on by a thin thread. He was tired and hungry because of the lack of supplies. His legs burned due to the constant marching. Morale was dropping like an anchor in water as he saw the French attack, pushing the Germans hard after they'd thought themselves almost victorious.

And yet, he fought like a demon. He was firing bullet after bullet at the colorful ranks of Frenchmen (he was still amazed to see they continued to be great targets with their red pants), trying to reach the top of the hill. Smoke billowed around everywhere, the ground shook, and tracers crisscrossed in the shattered battle space. Men fell all around him, hit by enemy weapons, with blood and yelling, and injured men everywhere. He decided to try and concentrate on firing his clip and then reloading as fast as he could. About five meters to his left, a Maxim gun team belched a blazing stream of bullets down at the enemy. Looking down the hill again, he decided the French were crazy, suicidal bastards. They continued to come like a wave, regardless of their horrid casualties.

Things were getting desperate. Oskar wasn't stupid and knew that if they didn't receive reinforcements soon, the entire German position was completely doomed.

(...) 113th Artillery Battery, Royal Field Artillery (...)

The 113th Battery's men went through the motions of firing one shell after the other. In the distance, they saw their own comrades in the infantry advancing amidst the smoke, fire, and explosions. They fired just above their comrade's heads to help them break the enemy forces in front of them. Smoke drifted around everywhere, and gunner Archibald Totenkam was happy they were advancing again. It was the middle of the morning on the 8th of September, and they had moved their cannon five times already. And the nice thing about that was that they had moved it forward instead of backward, unlike the last ten days before they finally relaunched their offensive.

The BEF was positioned in a critical spot; it had opened up a wide gap between von Bulow's and von Kluck's armies. Moving along with the French 5th, they were making good progress toward victory.

Archibald remembered the moment when all their despair and feelings of defeat were dispelled. He remembered a couple of days before when the word filtered to them that the Allies were on the offensive again and that victory was at hand. Everyone, including him and even the higher officers in the unit, had been initially skeptical. But then, they had been ordered to move across the river and to take a firing position overlooking the developing battlefield. From their standpoint on a high spot, they could see that the Entente forces were pushing the bastards backward. Within an hour or so, they morphed from demoralized to enthusiastic, winning soldiers.

The British shells exploded in blossoming balls of fire within the German ranks, but the Huns kept the line and continued to fight back. They held the ridgeline and the series of hills they were on with incredible tenacity.

From his safe distance, Archibald shook his head in amazement. The battle was delivering death on an industrial scale that had not been seen before in warfare; he was certain of it. Men on both sides died in the droves. Artillery shattered earth, air, flesh, and buildings. Bullets zipped everywhere, and the landscape was littered with small fires and columns of smoke.

Gunners like Archibald Totenkam contributed their own little piece to the human carnage unfolding before his eyes, and they provided a good part of the casualties. Artillery was fast becoming the dominant force on the battlefield.

The Battle of the Marne Part 3
The brawl, September 7th-8th

By the 7th and the 8th of September, the battle continued to increase several notches in intensity. From Paris, the French continued to push hard, and the Germans buckled under the pressure. Getting creative, they even used taxis to ferry their troops to the frontlines.

With four to five men at a time, the 1,200 Renault Taxis ferried the men, fighting traffic jams, shells, and enemy bullets to get them to the front and to the fight.

As fighting blossomed all along the front, it became apparent to the Germans that Joffre had been able to marshal his forces for a grand counterattack. And it was a serious one that threatened to unravel their entire position.

The largest battle in European memory since the Napoleonic Wars unfolded before Paris, pitting hundreds of thousands of men on each side of the battlefield. Contemplating the prospects of the developing battle, Moltke got nervous from his HQ as his commanders in the field (Kluck and Bulow) tried to frantically save the situation. In his diary, he wrote: *"The decisive moment had presented itself to us...we will either die fighting and lose the war or smash our enemies and take Paris."*

By midday on the 8th of September, the German 2nd Army caved in hard, and the line buckled, then broke on a gap of three miles. French troops, burning for vengeance after all the hardships they'd endured, attacked with abandon. The fighting got worse and worse as the intensity of the battle grew. Two million men busy fighting and killing each other made for a view to behold. From a distance and above the multitude of battlefields in the 160-mile-long frontline, it seemed that the world had gone mad.

The crux of the battle was triggered when, at the end of the afternoon on the 8th of September, the French pushed hard to the northwest, driving the German defenders back in disarray.

The quickly accumulating casualties numbers shocked commanders and leaders alike on both sides. Fighting a war in the industrial age, putting men against machines and accurate bullets and shells changed war forever.

It was a new age, and the fighters on both sides were entering an area with incredibly high death tolls. Technological advances had transformed the fighting into an unbelievable scene of bloodletting on an epic scale.

The heavy German, French, and British guns dropped a storm of steel and might on the poor fighting soldier's heads, mowing the ground and everything in between. The mindboggling power of the artillery made it the supreme ruler of the battlefield, killing men by the hundreds of thousands and rendering many crazy. None of the belligerents had yet noticed because they were too busy killing each other by the tens of thousands, but it was better to burrow the soldiers in holes for them to survive long enough to fight another day.

The obvious option for the losing Germans was to pour them into the widening gap between the two armies, but the German commander-in-chief wanted a man on the ground to help him decide since Kluck continued to call for reinforcement for his attack on the French 6th's left.

Fortunately for the Germans and the Central Powers in general, Hentch arrived first at the 2nd Army HQ (Bulow), and that was where the troops were most needed. After all, no reinforcements were ever sent to the east to battle the Prussians, and that decision would save the German Army.

Extract of von Bülow's account in his book 'Mein Bericht zurr Marneschlacht,' December 1914
On the decision to send the reserve troops into the gap, September 8th-9th, 1914.

(...) On the evening of September 8th, a message was received from Kluck's 1st Army, stating that they were fighting with strong enemy forces on the line Cuvergnon - Cougis. Aerial reconnaissance reports indicated hostile columns were turning north via Rebais and Doue; a third column was advancing northeast from La Haute Maison (the BEF 3rd Division). Furthermore, my Army was well aware that an enemy column detected near Choisy had continued to advance on Thiercelieux.

Under these circumstances, it had to be recognized that there was a high likelihood of strong enemy forces breaking through between the 1st and 2nd Armies and that the reserve troops just to our north were needed right here and right then.

If this did not happen, and since the enemy was across the Marne behind the 1st Army, then there was the danger, with the French threat from the west, of the 1st Army becoming completely surrounded. Without any reserves, we would have been forced to order a retreat as early as the 9th of September, but as it happened, fate intervened on the side of the German Empire, and the troops slated for reinforcements to the East were never sent there.

I, therefore, stressed in no uncertain terms to the visiting OHL representative, Lieutenant-Colonel Hentsch, that I was convinced the reserves corps and the cavalry division should be poured directly toward my right flank to support my forces north the Marne, re-establishing contact for 1st Army's left wing around Fismes. This decision, which was not easy because the 1st Army was victorious everywhere, made it clear that the plan of the French army command was to continue their obviously successful forward offensive at the center of our position and between our two armies. Only with a quick action with strong forces could the situation *be salvaged. The Lieutenant-Colonel agreed with me that this was indeed the correct play and sent his recommendation to Moltke back in Luxemburg.*

On the morning of the 9th of September, the OHL sent its reply to Hentsch's suggestion to pour the reinforcement directly on my right wing. (...)

The message was as follows: (...) *In accordance with Hentsch (OHL's representative), the situation is summarized as follows: 1st Army is in danger of being encircled by the gap between it and 2nd Army. Also, being attacked from Paris and in danger of being outflanked on its right wing, the 1st Army is in a dire situation. The recommendation was accepted; orders were sent to the two reserve corps and the cavalry division to march down toward the 2nd Army's right flank as soon as possible. Hentsch to go to 1st Army HQ and convey to Kluck to defend and fight back while we re-establish the situation in the gap between our forces (...)*

All was thus set for the counterattack that would win us the battle and the French capital.

The soldiers on both sides
The wave breaks, September 9th, 1914

"Where are those reinforcements," yelled Sergeant Wilhelm. Private soldier Oskar Dantz of the 4th Imperial Division stopped firing for a moment, looking at his superior. He was startled by his NCO's sudden and desperate plea but not surprised. *"I don't know, Sergeant,"* he answered in between two shots.

The entire German line was buckling inward, and things were looking like a rout was in the works. The platoon was down to three men, including Wilhelm, Oskar, and a tough guy from Kelheim, a fellow named Florian Storch. He suspected the other units weren't faring much better. The stench of fear and defeat was palpable, and he knew that the officers would soon order the retreat.

They were hiding behind a crumbled-down stone wall that must have been a building foundation at one point in the past. Enemy bullets slammed into it, sending chunks of rocks flying everywhere. *"They are close, Sergeant,"* added Storch, and Oskar agreed since he heard the multitude of footsteps like a ground tremor. The three men were crouching between shots, and things were getting truly dire. The rest of the now very thin German line of defenses barely held against a sea of Frenchmen charging them.

Losses were humongous. Almost all the senior officers were either killed or seriously wounded. Despite this, the regiment tried to keep its ground, as they had been told troops were coming. But the enemy, advancing relentlessly and without regard for casualties, forced them to ground every time with horrific machine gun fire. It was a miracle the three were still alive.

There seemed to be an endless river of red and blue French soldiers coming at them and the rest of the 4th Division. The ground shook hard, and he thought for a moment that even more of the bastards were coming at them. As he rose up to fire once more, Oskar started to get the feeling that something was amiss. Some of the pounding sounds seemed like they came from behind. And then, Frenchmen were getting hit by the dozens with sprays of blood, with some having stopped running and some even falling back. They were receiving a lot more hits than the number of men they had left. Then, artillery shells started to fall on the enemy, and that was the moment when his mind registered that they were saved. Storch slapped him hard on the shoulder. *"Look, Dantz!"* And he turned to see a wave of grey-uniformed soldiers. The reinforcements had arrived, and the day was saved.

(...) French 14th Division (...)

Private soldiers Philippe Cren and Armand Bonnier were about to reach the top of the small hills they had been attacking for the last few hours when all hell broke loose. The enemy fire started to increase in intensity, and a powerful, guttural yell was heard from the top of the hill. Then, suddenly, they saw them. Ragged but numerous lines of grey-uniformed Germans ran down and at them. At first, Armand blinked, not believing what he was seeing. His mind took some time to register that they were rapidly morphing from victory to defeat.

But when his comrades started to die in droves beside him, he registered that it was time to take a step back and stop running uphill. Most of his comrades stopped almost at the same time, mouth agape. And then the orders to fall back were issued, and they turned tail and ran in the other direction, only stopping to fire and hope that checked the German attack.

A few hours more, and the Germans rolled over the hard-won gains of the last few days while they reeled back in disarray.

(...) 113th Battery, Royal Field Artillery (...)

Archibald Totenkam and his comrades started to see it before the infantry on the ground because they fired on the Germans from an elevated position. The long lines of field-gray soldiers appeared over the horizon and then charged toward the attacking French and British infantry units. *"Those are fresh German troops,"* said Lance-Bombardier Stimms, their officer. The man seemed stunned. *"Quick, we need to adjust our fire and smash the bastards,"* he continued, signaling for the cannon handler to traverse the weapon to the proper angle.

A few minutes later, and into their 10th shot, it was obvious it was something very serious. *"Looks like it's at least a corps-sized unit out there,"* said Stimms with his binoculars in his eyes.

A few minutes more, and the sky dropped hard on them. Loud, very loud whistling sounds started to whine above the battlefield and right for the 113th Battery and the rest of the British gun line on the ridge. *"German counter-battery fire,"* yelled the Lance-Bombardier, and they went through the now normal motion of dropping into their trenches.

Archibald plunged into his own hole as the first enemy shell slammed on the ground, rocking their world. Then another, then multiple others. Then truly powerful ones. The intensity grew and grew until there was nothing but the hellish fire, ground shaking, and blasting sounds of the enemy ordinance exploding everywhere around him.

The 113th Battery had not yet realized it, but they had been taken under fire by the Big Berta guns and the 305 mm Austro-Hungarian mortars, which arrived directly from Liege the night before for the planned counterattack. The enemy shelling went on for over twenty minutes, and by then, nothing was alive on the crest where Archibald Totenkam had been. The 113th Battery was shattered, all of its remaining guns destroyed, and its men dead.

The Battle of the Marne Part 4
The Fall of Paris, September 9th-12th, 1914

The German reinforcements, namely the Guard Reserve Corps from Bulow's 2nd Army and the 11th Corps (plus a Saxon Cavalry Division) from Hausen's 3rd Army, did the trick for the Germans at the very moment when the battle was about to be decided.

The Entente powers, thinking themselves on the right foot and advancing through the large 30-mile gap between the 1st and 2nd German armies, might well have won the day if not for those timely new troops. The Battle of the Marne was at that moment when defeat and victory hung in the balance.

But a fact remained: both armies were exhausted, and the Franco-British were making their last stand before Paris. Joffre put everything in a throw of the dice with one last-ditch offensive to win it all, but it ultimately failed. The Kaiser's troops were also at the very end of their tether, but the new troops clinched the deal for them and ultimately won them the day.

The German troops that intervened on that day broke the back of the French 5th Army and the BEF attacking between the two German armies, while the German 3rd Army, under General Max Von Haussen, actually defeated the French 9th Army in a bold attack intended to support his beleaguered colleagues before Paris.

After another day of fighting, the entire Allied line of battle broke down, and whole divisions started either to fall back in disarray or else get captured or encircled.

Germans pursued, but not as vigorously as they could have, as they were worn, tired, and almost without supplies. From one instant to the other, the frontline went from complete pandemonium to quietness as the Allies retired southward and the Germans got busy getting into Paris and seizing their war prize.

EPILOGUE

Aftermath

By the morning of the 11th, Paris was declared an open city by Joffre, and the general retreat southward was ordered. The French fortifications along the border were kept in place with Verdun as its northernmost pivot, and the Allied troops started to entrench themselves where they were when the German pressure wasn't too great. For the troops that fought at the Marne, they retreated south of Paris and started to look to build a defensive line.

As the lead elements of the German 1st army made their way into the Paris suburbs, the French Government sacked General Joffre from overall command, replacing him with a dynamic and *"more "level-headed"* commander, General Ferdinand Foch (the commander of the defeated 9th Army). His first order of business was to order the troops to entrench and fight where they were.

The French dug in along a frontline from the south of Paris to Verdun and running northwest of Paris to the Channel. The German Army, too exhausted to do anything about it, just stopped marching and consolidated.

Many called for peace in France and Germany, but the people who wanted war to continue prevailed. First and foremost, the Germans and the Austrians were engaged in a life-and-death struggle against Russia, while the French decided they had no intention of caving into anything the enemy proposed in terms of a peace offer. Anyway, the Kaiser had no intention of calling it quits and wanted to teach the French a lesson, while the French wanted all of France back (including Alsace-Lorraine) and were not inclined to any discussion.

The beaten British Expeditionary force retreated at the same time as its allies and dug in alongside them since there was no immediate way to evacuate them anyway.

The fall of Paris meant many things in strategic terms. First and foremost, it diminished the French capability to wage war. But other important considerations would soon surface. The control of Northern France and the many harbors would open a world of possibility for the Kaiserliche Marine and for Germany as a whole to enable it to wage total war on Great Britain. Suddenly, it was an entirely different war, and any blockade against Germany would now be very difficult to enforce for the Royal Navy.

It also meant reinforcements to the East to bolster the by-now beleaguered 8th Army, barely holding the line behind the Vistula and the fortress of Konigsberg. The Austro-Hungarians were about to get some German help as well to fight the Russian hordes pouring all over Galicia and threatening Hungary. In short, the Central Powers would now be able to send a great army to the East.

The diplomatic implications of the defeat of the Marne and the subsequent fall of Paris were immense. Many countries in the Balkans started to rethink their stance and wondered if it was not better to lean toward the Central Powers (Romania and Greece), while the Bulgarians became a lot more eager to join in.

Most importantly, the Italians, members of the Triple Alliance (alliance with Germany and Austria-Hungary), who had decided to stay neutral at the start of the conflict, began to look at Germany and Austria as a potentially better option than the Entente Powers. After all, nobody in Rome wanted to be on the losing side.

As the German Army paraded under the Arc de Triomphe in Paris and as the Kaiser prepared a visit to the French capital, the rest of Europe watched and awaited what would happen next. The war was not over, but the Central Powers had the advantage now that the Entente Armies were defeated.

Author's note: Well, now that we've got our story established,

imagine the rest. Coming up this summer or fall to an Amazon near you.

THE STORY WILL CONTINUE IN BOOK 2
OF THE WW1 ALTERNATE SERIES:

GREAT WAR ALTERNATE

Thank you very much for reading my work.

I HAVE A NEW FACEBOOK PAGE!
PLEASE GO AND VISIT:
**https://www.facebook.com/profile.php?
id=61558770082344**

*** Please review my book(s) on Amazon and Goodreads.com and try not to be a troll.

.

*** Send me an email at **souvorov@hotmail.com** if you feel like chatting with me. **I respond to every email.**

www.maxlamirande.com

THE GREAT WAR ALTERNATE SERIES
BY MAX LAMIRANDE

Book 1: *Schlieffen Alternate*
Book 2: *Great War Alternate (Summer-Fall 2024)*
Book 3: *Falling Empires*
Book 4:
Book 5:
Book 6:

THE BLITZKRIEG ALTERNATE SERIES
BY MAX LAMIRANDE

Book 1: Blitzkrieg Europa
Book 2: Battle Europa
Book 3: Struggle Europa
Book 4: Fortress Europa
Book 5: Stalemate Europa
Book 6: Staggering Europa
Book 7: Faltering Europa
Book 8: Crumbling Europa
Book 9: Falling Europa
Book 10: Soviet Europa
Book 11: Red Europa
Book 12: Climax Europa
Book 13: The Walder Chronicles Part 1
Book 14: The Walder Chronicles Part 2
Book 15: The Walder Chronicles Part 3

THE PACIFIC ALTERNATE SERIES
BY MAX LAMIRANDE

Book 1: Blitzkrieg Pacific
Book 2: Battle Pacific
Book 3: Struggle Pacific
Book 4: Staggering Pacific
Book 5: Burning Pacific
Book 6: Sallying Pacific
Book 7: Siege Pacific
Book 8: Faltering Pacific
Book 9 Crumbling Pacific
Book 10: Collapsing Pacific (June-July 2024)

THE NAPOLEONIC ALTERNATE SERIES

BY MAX LAMIRANDE

Book 1: *Austerlitz Alternate*
Book 2: *Friedland Alternate*
Book 3: *1809 Alternate Summer-Fall 2024*

THE AXIS ALTERNATE SERIES

BY MAX LAMIRANDE

Book 1: *The Bear and the Swastika*
Book 2: *World War*
Book 3: *Axis Triumphant*
Book 4: *Axis Victorious*
Book 5: *Axis overwhelming*
Book 6: *Stalemate*
Book 7: *Axis resurging (summer 2024)*

Also, from the same author:
BLITZKRIEG PACIFIC

The year is 1942.

The world is at war. Almost every major nation has declared support for the Allies or the Axis. The Third Reich occupies Europe, and the British Islands have been invaded and conquered by the Germans. Metropolitan France has fallen, along with its North African colonies. Spain and Turkey have joined the Axis. The Middle East is Axis. The USA and Soviet Russia are also at war with the Third Reich.

Only one major power is still on the sideline. Imperial Japan, already busy in its war of conquest in China, dawns on the idea of conquering the Pacific and Southeast Asia following German successes in Europe and the subsequent weakening of the resource-rich Franco-British and Dutch colonies.

The United States, following Japan's occupation of the French colony of French Indochina in 1940, froze all of Tokyo's assets, stopped scrap metal deliveries, and was just about to stop delivering oil to the hungry Japanese military machine, a move that is certain to trigger a reaction from the warmongers in Tokyo.

President Roosevelt's decision to do so is about to have dire consequences for America. The Imperial Navy has set its sights on the main US base in the Pacific, Pearl Harbor. And all across the Japanese-held islands of the Pacific, the forces of the Rising Sun prepare for a full-scale invasion that they hope will give them control over the resources the country needs to continue on its expansion.

This is the story of the War in the Pacific.

Also, from the same author:
THE BEAR AND THE SWASTIKA

The year is 1939.

The world rocks with the news of the signing of the Germano-Soviet pact. A dark veil soon falls on Europe as Poland is invaded and destroyed by the overwhelming forces of the Wehrmacht and the Red Army.

France and the United Kingdom can only sit by and watch the two military juggernauts obliterate the Polish state. No one believes the two totalitarian regimes can agree in the long term as their ideologies completely contradict each other.

Russia wants influence in the Balkans, has eyes on Finland, and wants an opening to the Mediterranean. Germany needs Romanian oil to keep its war machine operational, and Hitler is adamant about not letting the Bolsheviks gain another inch of ground in Europe. At least not more than he has already given out in the treaty of non-aggression signed before the Polish campaign.

The year is 1940.

The French campaign then unfolds with a disaster for the Allies, and the Germans win an incredible victory over the combined forces of the United Kingdom and France. British forces narrowly escape to their island with the remnants of their armies, and France surrenders. Half of the country is occupied by the Germans. It seems that the swastika will conquer the world, especially with the Russian bear watching its back.

Germano-Soviet Axis talks were organized in October 1940 concerning the Soviet Union's potential entry as a fourth Axis Power during World War II. The negotiations include a two-day conference in Berlin between Soviet Foreign Minister Vyacheslav Molotov, Adolf Hitler, and German Foreign Minister

Joachim von Ribbentrop. The two powers will try to agree on a formal alliance to divide the world.

The fate of liberty hangs in the balance.

Also, from the same author:
BLITZKRIEG EUROPA

September 1st, 1939.

Germany invades Poland, igniting a major European war. A few months later the French are also invaded, and the allied armies are utterly defeated. Then the Dunkirk disaster happens, and the United Kingdom loses most of its land army.

Soon, the British Isles are also attacked, and the British are hard-pressed with a serious German invasion. The French struggle to resist the Axis forces bent on conquering all of their mainland home country and the Western African Colonies.

America, watching from its safe shores, cannot stay still while Western Europe and all of the Mediterranean fall to the forces of the Axis. And when the Afrika Korps plunges over the Suez and invades the Middle East, the Soviet Union finally decides to join in.

This is the story of the Second World War.

Also, from the same author:

The Empire built by Haakon the Great is no more. It's 4124, and the Human race has spread to the stars in four different star clusters by achieving the speed of light and wormholes. A civil war has broken out between the different human enclaves to see who the next emperor of humanity will be.

The Ptolemy and Hadesian Star Nations are invading Elysium, allied with New America from the Alpha Perseis Cluster. Large battles are being fought in star systems between former comrades of the Imperial Fleet. In space, battleships unload their powerful weapons at each other while giant battle mechas fight for control of the ground.

The opportunity is too great for the evil Cybernetic forces in the Caldwell 14 Star Cluster. Having fought – and lost – a terrible war against the Empire two hundred years ago, they are gathering for a return engagement against humanity.

A thousand years ago, Haakon dreamed and foresaw a terrible time for humanity. The Black Death is coming to consume all, and his Empire will not be there to fight it.

Also from the same author:
AUSTERLITZ ALTERNATE

DECEMBER 2ND, 1805

The War of the Third Coalition rages in Europe. Battles have been fought, and Napoleon Bonaparte's Grande Armée sweeps everything before it. After a big victory over an Austrian Army in Ulm, the French occupied Vienna, the capital of the Austrian Empire.

The Russians entered Austria to come to the help of their Allies and under pressure from the British. The Austro-Russians and the French are about to clash in a small, unknown town called Austerlitz.

And then everything changes. The French stop trying to retake the Pratzen Heights, and the day's battle ends in a stalemate for both armies. Kutusov, the allied army's leader in the absence of young Tsar Alexander (who fell ill and is still somewhere in Galicia), decides to retire the army northward with the Austrian Emperor's approval.

The news galvanizes the Revolution's enemies and of the Empire, jealous of Napoleon's success and wanting him gone. The Prussians decide to join the war and move their troops into Austria to link their forces with the two other powers. The German states and other countries like Naples rethink their stances in the conflict. And the French Emperor's internal enemies, ever wishing the old regime's return, start plotting to overthrow the government in Paris.

All the while, the Ottoman Empire, convinced by the French several months earlier to enter the war, has decided to intervene in favor of Bonaparte and invade southern Hungary with an Army. Austria is on the brink of annihilation, but Napoleon's Grande Armée also has a big challenge ahead since it now needs to defeat three major powers simultaneously.

Everything will come down to either Napoleon's genius to overcome the odds and win regardless of the troops arrayed against him, or his defeat and the end of the French Empire.

This is the story of the Napoleonic Wars.

Made in United States
Troutdale, OR
04/21/2025

30784940R00146